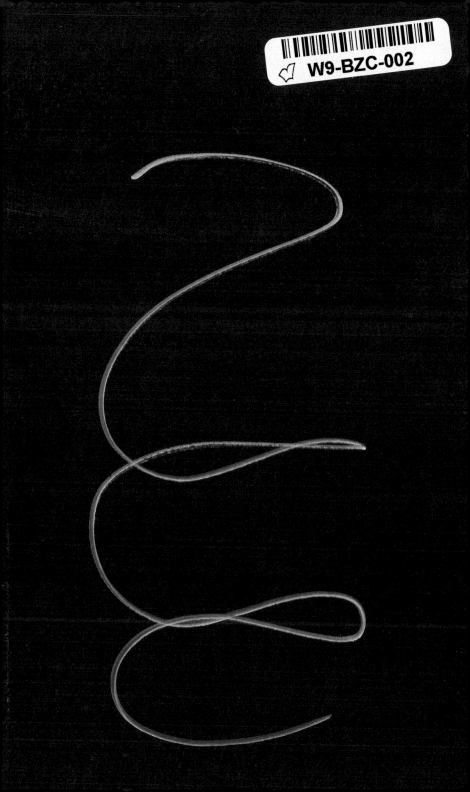

ASYLUM

MADELEINE ROUX

HARPER

An Imprint of HarperCollinsPublishers

Asylum

Copyright © 2013 by HarperCollins Publishers

www.epicreads.com

Library of Congress Cataloging-in-Publication Data
Roux, Madeleine.
  Asylum / Madeleine Roux. — First edition.
    pages cm
  Summary: "Three teens at a summer program for gifted students uncover
shocking secrets in the sanatorium-turned-dorm where they're staying—
secrets that link them all to the asylum's dark past"— Provided by publisher.
  ISBN 978-0-06-222096-7 (hardback)
  [1. Supernatural—Fiction. 2. Colleges and universities—Fiction. 3. Mental
illness—Fiction. 4. Haunted places—Fiction. 5. Psychiatric hospitals—
Fiction. 6. Ability—Fiction. 7. Mystery and detective stories.] I. Title.
PZ7.R772Asy 2013   2013007302
[Fic]—dc23   CIP
                                                              AC

Typography by Faceout Studio

13 14 15 16 17   CG/RRDC   10 9 8 7 6

❖

First Edition

Deep into that darkness peering, long I stood there,
Wondering, fearing, doubting, dreaming dreams
No mortal ever dreamed before.

—EDGAR ALLAN POE

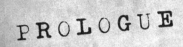

PROLOGUE

They built it out of stone—dark gray stone, pried loose from the unforgiving mountains. It was a house for those who could not take care of themselves, for those who heard voices, who had strange thoughts and did strange things. The house was meant to keep them in. Once they came, they never left.

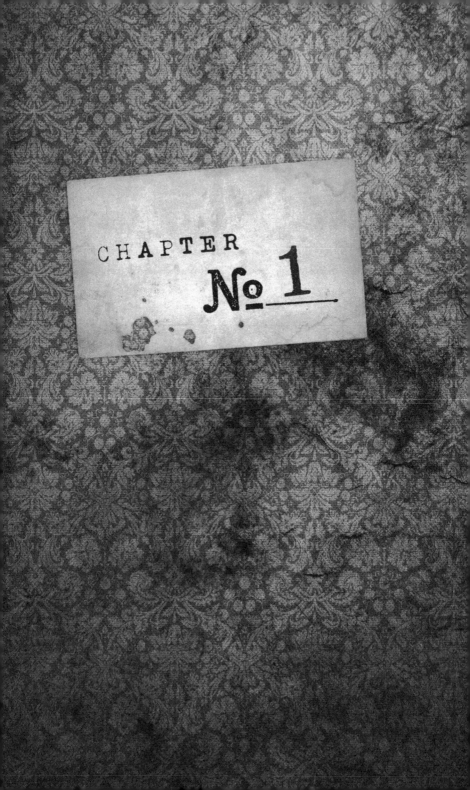

CHAPTER

№ 1

*D*an felt like he was going to be sick.

The narrow, gravelly road had been jostling his cab for at least five miles now, and that was on top of his first-day jitters. His driver kept cursing about dents and flat tires. Dan just hoped he wouldn't be expected to pay for any damage—the trip from the airport was already expensive enough.

Although it was early afternoon, the light outside was dim thanks to the dense forest on either side of the road. *It would be easy to get lost in those woods*, Dan thought.

"Still alive back there?"

"What? Yeah, I'm fine," Dan said, realizing he hadn't spoken since he'd gotten in the car. "Just ready for some even ground is all."

Finally, the cab came to a break in the trees and everything turned dappled and silvery green in the summer sunshine.

There it was: New Hampshire College. The place Dan would be spending the next five weeks.

This summer school—Dan's lifeline—had been the proverbial light at the end of the tunnel all school year long. He'd be hanging out with kids who wanted to learn, who actually did their homework beforehand and not up against their lockers in a messy dash before the bell. He couldn't wait to be there already.

Out the window, Dan saw buildings that he recognized from the college's website. They were charming brick colonials placed around a quad with emerald-green grass, perfectly cut and trimmed. These were the academic buildings, Dan knew, where he would be taking classes. Already a few early birds were out on the lawn tossing a Frisbee back and forth. How had those guys made friends so fast? Maybe it really would be that easy here.

The driver hesitated at a four-way stop; diagonally to the right stood a pretty, down-home church with a tall white steeple, then a row of houses stretching beyond. Craning forward out of his seat, Dan saw the cabbie flick on his right turn signal.

"It's left, actually," Dan blurted, sinking back down in his seat.

The driver shrugged. "If you say so. Damn machine can't seem to make up its mind." As if to illustrate, the cabbie banged his fist on the GPS display bolted to the center of the dash. It looked like the path it had mapped out for them ended here.

"It's left," Dan repeated, less confident this time. He wasn't actually sure how he knew the way—he hadn't looked up directions ahead of time—but there was something about that pristine little church that stirred a memory, and if not a memory, a gut instinct.

Dan drummed his fingers on the seat, impatient to see where he would be living. The regular dorms were being renovated over the summer, so all the College Prep students were being housed in an older building called Brookline, which his admissions packet had called a "retired mental health facility and historical site." In other words, an *asylum*.

At the time, Dan had been surprised to find there were no pictures of Brookline up on the website. But he understood why when the cab rounded a corner and there it was.

It didn't matter that the college had slapped a fresh coat of paint on the outer walls, or that some enterprising gardener had gone a little overboard planting cheerful hydrangea bushes along the path—Brookline loomed at the far end of the road like a warning. Dan had never imagined that a building could look *threatening*, but Brookline managed that feat and then some. It actually seemed to be watching him.

Turn around now, whispered the voice in his head.

Dan shivered, unable to stop himself from imagining how patients in the old days felt when they were checked into the asylum. Did they know? Did some of them have this same weird feeling of panic, or were they too far gone to understand?

Then he shook his head. These were ridiculous thoughts. . . . He was a student, not a patient. And as he'd assured Paul and Sandy, Brookline was no longer an asylum; it had closed its doors in 1972 when the college purchased it to make a functional dorm with co-ed floors and communal bathrooms.

"Okay, this is it," said the cab driver, although Dan noticed he'd stopped about thirty feet shy of the curb. Maybe Dan wasn't the only one who got weird vibes from this place. Still, he reached into his wallet and forked over three of the twenties his parents had given him.

"Keep the change," he said, climbing out.

Something about rolling up his sleeves and grabbing his stuff from the trunk finally made the day feel real in Dan's mind. A guy in a blue baseball cap wandered by, a stack of worn comic books in his arms. That made Dan smile. *My people*, he thought. He walked into the dorm. For the next five weeks, this was home.

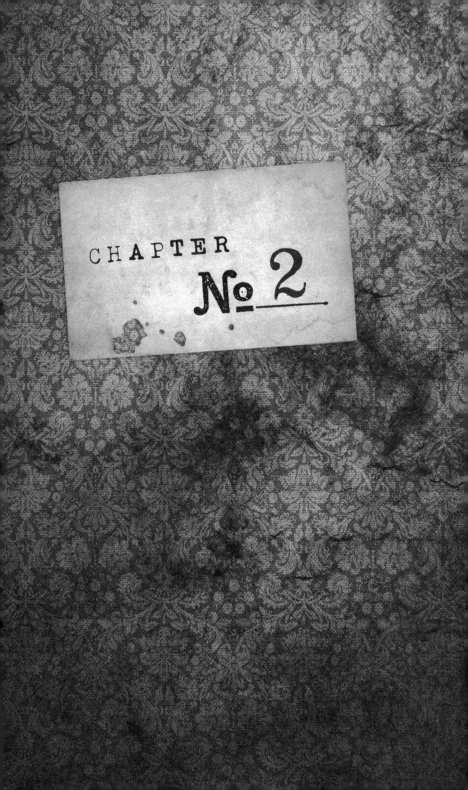

CHAPTER
№ 2

If a new BMW in the school parking lot gave you clout at Dan's high school, then Apple products and sheer volume of books seemed to grant the cool factor at NHCP.

That's what they were supposed to call the program, as Dan quickly learned. The college student volunteers who were there to hand out room keys and help kids move in kept saying, "Welcome to *NHCP!*" and the one time Dan actually called it "New Hampshire College Prep," they gave him a look like he was sweet but simple.

Dan walked up the front steps and found himself in a large entrance hall. The enormous chandelier couldn't overcome the darkness caused by all the wood paneling and overstuffed furniture. Through a grand archway across from the entrance, Dan spotted a wide staircase, and halls leading in on either side. Even the students bustling in and out did nothing to dispel the feeling of heaviness.

Dan started up the stairs with his suitcases. Three long flights later, he arrived at his room, number 3808. Dan put down his bags and opened the door, only to discover that his assigned roommate had already moved in. Or maybe *filed* in would be more accurate. Books, manga magazines, almanacs of all shapes and sizes (most tending toward biology) lay in neat, color-coordinated order on the provided bookshelves. His roommate had taken up exactly half of the space in the room, with his suitcases zipped up and tucked neatly under the closer bed. Half of the closet was already filled with shirts, slacks, and coats on hangers—white hangers for shirts and jackets, blue for pants.

It looked like the guy had been living here for weeks.

Dan hauled his suitcases onto the unclaimed bed, then checked over the furniture that was his for the summer. The bed, bedside table, and desk all seemed to be in good condition. He opened the top desk drawer out of idle curiosity, wondering if he would find a Gideons Bible or maybe a welcome letter. Instead, he discovered a small slip of what looked like film paper. It was old, faded to the point of being almost completely bleached out. Faintly, he could see a man staring up at him, an older, bespectacled gentleman in a doctor's coat and dark shirt. Nothing about the photo was all that remarkable, except for the eyes—or to be more accurate, where the eyes had been. Messily—or perhaps angrily—someone had scratched them out.

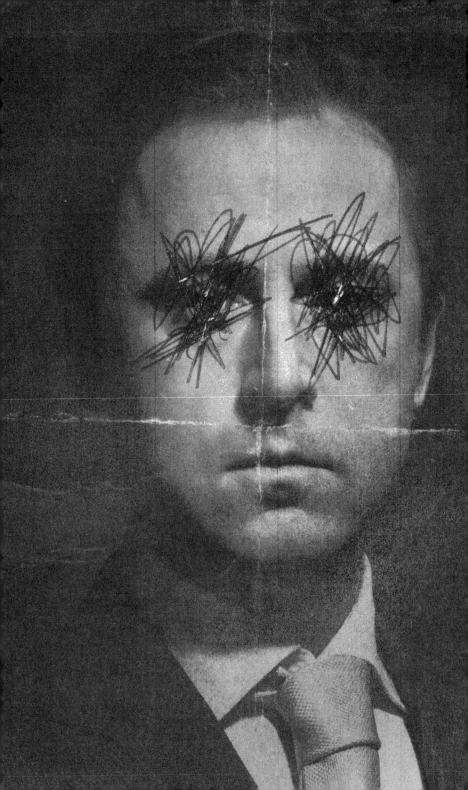

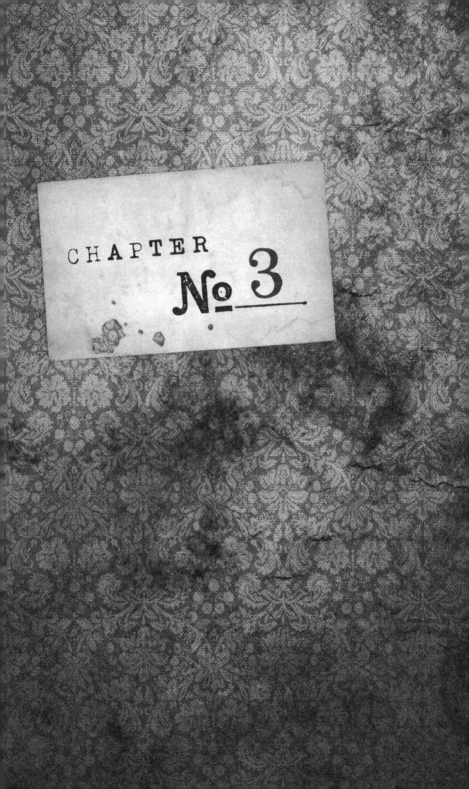

CHAPTER
№ 3

"*D*aniel Crawford?"

Dan spun around with the photo still in hand. A lanky teenager stood just inside the doorway, dressed like a door-to-door missionary in a starched white shirt, dark tie, and pleated trousers.

"Hey," Dan greeted him, waving a little. "You my roommate?"

"It looks that way, yes." The sentence came out more earnest than sarcastic. "Felix Sheridan," the boy added. "Did I startle you?"

"No, no, I just—I found this photo. . . . At least I think it's a photo, could be a postcard or something, I guess. Anyway, someone went to town on it. It's pretty freaky." Dan held up the picture and shrugged. It didn't seem like an ideal icebreaker, but then he never was very good at first impressions. "Did you get one of these? Maybe it's part of a scavenger hunt or something."

"Nothing like that, no." Felix blinked his milky-blue eyes. "I got my new student pamphlet, dorm safety information, and the course catalog. But that all came in the mail a few weeks ago."

"Yeah, I got all that, too." Dan shrugged again awkwardly. "Just wondering. No big deal."

Dan put the photograph back in the drawer and shut it. Surely he could get by this summer without ever opening it again.

"I could scan the picture and research it for you. Easy enough, really, just a reverse image search. Although actually, now that I think about it, it sort of reminds me of—"

"Thanks, but never mind," Dan interrupted, wishing he hadn't brought it up in the first place. "Hey, isn't there some welcome party or something we're supposed to be going to?"

"If you'd allow me to finish . . . ," Felix said calmly, then waited an extra-uncomfortable beat. "I was going to say that it reminds me of some photos I found downstairs."

"Wait, seriously? What do you mean?" Dan couldn't help it; his curiosity was piqued.

"There's this abandoned office on the first floor," Felix explained. "I think it belonged to the old asylum's warden or something. There were papers and pictures and things just sitting out for anyone to see. The sign down there said it's supposed to be off-limits, but the lock on the door was busted."

"You actually went inside?" Dan wasn't a rule breaker, but then, based on the little he knew about his roommate so far, he wouldn't have guessed that Felix was either.

Felix nodded. "I was just there, in fact. And I didn't look too closely, but I'm pretty sure there were some photographs like yours."

Not mine, Dan thought with a shudder. *I'm just the unlucky guy who found it.*

"Maybe you should check it out for yourself, but I have to warn you, the place was pretty unsettling, to put it mildly."

Felix didn't seem unsettled, though. If anything, standing there blocking the doorway, he looked like he was offering Dan a challenge. But Dan had other things on his mind.

"So, about that party?" he said.

Felix stepped inside and went over to the closet, his hand going right to a navy blue blazer. "Indeed." He joined Dan at the door. "Have you run into many girls yet? Our floor only seems to have a handful. But I'm betting there will be more at this party, eh, Daniel?"

Dan stared at his roommate, trying to add up all the things he'd just learned about him into one coherent person. He wondered if everyone at this program would be so full of contradictions. In theory it would make for a refreshing change of pace from high school, where everyone Dan knew was so predictable. *In theory.*

"I'm sure there will be girls, yeah, but . . ."

Felix watched him expectantly.

"Listen, I'm not much of a wingman. You might have better luck chasing girls on your own." It made him feel a little jerky, brushing Felix off like this when he was just trying to be friendly, but Dan found himself wanting to keep his roommate at arm's length. *Especially* when it came to girls.

"Fair enough. Probably better if we're not fighting over the same ones anyway, am I right?"

Dan let out a tiny sigh, nodding.

The hallways were jam-packed with kids still moving their stuff in. Many were milling around in groups, talking. Why couldn't Dan have ended up with one of *them* for a roommate?

"Look, Daniel Crawford," Felix commanded, pulling him to a stop when they reached the main entrance hall. He pointed out the front door to where students were heading across the lawn. "*Girls.* Enough for both of us."

Gently disengaging his arm from Felix's clammy grip, Dan went through the door. The day would improve. It had to.

✗ ✗ ✗ ✗ ✗

"Well, I feel like a grown-up, how about you?" Dan took another bite of mint-chocolate-chip ice cream.

Felix stared blankly. "I'm not sure I know what you mean."

"I mean this." Dan held up the little paper dish of ice cream and danced it side to side. "This whole ice cream social thing. Feels like . . . I don't know, like we're little kids again at a birthday party." He eyed the tiny wooden shovel that had come with the cup. It only made him feel sillier.

They were in Wilfurd Commons, a huge cafeteria-cum-ballroom located in one of the buildings off the quad. Above them a domed skylight let in the last traces of sunlight. The coming dusk gave the room a violet tint, while outside a fog was settling low to the ground.

"I don't connect ice cream to my childhood," Felix said.

That's probably because you never went to any birthday parties. Dan immediately chided himself. He really had to be nicer, but conversation had so far been hopeless.

"Personally, I was hoping I'd have a chance to get some advice on which biology classes to take, but I don't see any of the professors associated with— Wait! I think that may be Professor Soams now. I read his dissertation on the evolution of microbial pathogens. . . ."

Dan missed the rest of what Felix was saying, all too happy to see him wading through the crowd toward an elderly man in the opposite corner. Still, relieved though he was for the break from Felix, he was now painfully aware of being alone in a crowd.

Hoping that he didn't look as awkward as he felt, Dan put another spoonful of the melting ice cream into his mouth. It tasted chalky, like medicine. The unpleasant smell of a burning cigarette wafted in from the open doors leading outside, and Dan felt himself clamming up.

Calm down, Dan, you're fine, you're fine.

A cold, prickly sweat gathered at the base of his neck. He felt dizzy, and the skylight spun. The whole room spun. He tried to grab the table behind him but missed and stumbled backward. Any second he'd hit the floor.

A strong hand caught him by the arm and pulled him upright. "Whoa! Careful, slick, or you'll be wearing that ice cream." Dan blinked and the world came back into focus. In front of him, still holding his arm, was a girl, petite, with large brown eyes and creamy olive skin. She was wearing a big button-down shirt that had splatters of paint on it over a tank top. Her jeans were ripped, and she had on a pair of heavy black boots.

"Thanks," said Dan, checking his own shirt to make sure he hadn't spilled anything. "I guess it's just a little too hot in here."

She smiled.

"I'm Dan Crawford, by the way."

"Abby, Abby Valdez," the girl said. They shook hands. Her grip was strong and warm.

"Anyway, you said it." Abby snorted and tossed her wavy hair. It fell like a black curtain over one shoulder, purple and green feathers threaded into the curls. "They could at least turn on a fan."

"Right? So, um, what do you think of this place so far?" Dan said. It seemed like a good, normal question to ask, especially after his decidedly *not* normal fainting spell. Dr. Oberst always told him that if he felt anxious in conversation, he should just ask the other person questions and let them do the talking for a minute.

"I could live without staying in an old loony bin, but otherwise it's cool. What are you here for? Classwise, I mean."

"I'm going to study history, mostly, and maybe some psychology. What about you?"

"I'll give you one guess," Abby replied with a laugh. "And it's not astrophysics."

Dan looked at the paint splatters on her shirt and the dark smudges on her hands, traces of pencil rubbed into the creases of her knuckles and palms.

"Um, art?"

"Got it in one!" Abby punched him lightly on the arm. "Yeah, the studio classes here are supposed to be great, so I felt like it was a good chance to work on my technique before portfolios are due for college apps. But who knows, right? There's so much to choose from." She spoke quickly, energetically, flitting from thought to thought with hardly a breath in between. Dan nodded and said "Uh-huh" at what he thought were the right moments.

Without discussing it, they drifted toward the open door.

"You feeling all right now?" Abby was saying.

"How do you mean?" Dan paused at the doorway. Outside, a glow-in-the-dark disk flew by. A dozen or so students were congregated on the lawn, playing another impromptu game of Frisbee.

"Before? When it looked like you were about to pass out?"

"Oh, that. Yeah, I'm fine. I think it was just the heat, and I haven't eaten much today." It was as good an excuse as any, considering he never knew for sure what triggered the episodes. Honestly, though, he was kind of glad it had happened this time—he wouldn't have met Abby otherwise.

Dan pointed to the students running around on the grass. "You into sports much?"

"Me?" Abby laughed, playing with one of the feathers in her hair. "Not really. At our school games I'm usually in the stands. I play the piccolo in the marching band. It's not my favorite thing, but Pops says it'll make me look 'well-rounded' to colleges."

"I've never been one for sports either." They lingered at the top of the steps, watching the game. "My dad's a little disappointed. . . . He was big into baseball as a kid."

That was an understatement. His adoptive father, Paul, had gone to college on a baseball scholarship, and he'd pressured Dan into T-ball and then junior leagues before Dan finally broke down and told him he'd rather go to science camp.

"Well, if you're here, then he can't be *that* disappointed. You've got to have brain power just to make it in—" She broke off and started waving vigorously at a guy who was walking toward them. The guy strolled blithely through the Frisbee game, ignoring the players' shouts for him to get out of the way. Dan looked between Abby and her friend, feeling his stomach sink. Not that he had any claim on her—he'd known her for all of ten minutes—but he had to admit he'd been pretty psyched thinking he'd met another person who'd come here alone, like him. Now he couldn't help looking at stranger boy, with his broody hair and broody face and cool, broody clothes, and thinking, *Well, I can't compete with that.*

"What's up, nerds?"

"Jordan, be nice," Abby said, rolling her eyes. "This is Dan. Dan, this is Jordan, and I promise he's not a jerk."

"Nope," Jordan said. "Just an asshole. So how's it going, Dan? Settling into geek camp all right?" He wore slim, trendy glasses and a shredded green scarf looped loosely around his neck. Dan envied the kid's perfect five o'clock shadow, something Dan could never emulate given the way his facial hair grew in patches.

"Seriously, Jordan. Who are you trying to impress? I'm sorry, Dan, he's just showing off. I met him totally by chance on the bus coming here, and he's really a nice person once you get to know him." Abby squeaked as Jordan pulled her into a one-armed side hug. Dan felt a strong urge to look away. He didn't need their canoodling rubbed in his face.

"Fine, fine, wipe the slate." Jordan stepped back, swept his palms together, and then adjusted his glasses. "I'm Jordan, pleased to meet you. Now stop glaring at me. Abby's really not my type, all right?"

"God, Jordan, that was *not* an improvement!" Huffing, Abby hugged herself, turning to hide the flush sweeping up to her cheeks.

"I'm sorry, Abbadabadoo, you're just too easy to tease."

Dan must have missed something, because then the two of them were laughing hysterically and somehow he'd been knocked sixty miles out of the loop. His confusion must have shown on his face because Abby raised her eyebrows at Jordan, and Jordan, rolling his eyes, explained in a patient voice that made Dan feel like he was about five years old, "I'm gay. That's why Abby's not my type."

"Oh. Right. Yeah."

Dan didn't care that Jordan was gay, but he knew anything he might try to say in his defense now would only make him sound like more of a dork. Already Abby and Jordan had moved on to happy, relaxed banter, and just like that, Dan was an outsider looking in. If they could become such close friends over a single bus ride, surely they'd have no problem making other new friends. Friends who weren't as stiff and clueless as Dan.

"So there's a creepy old office on the first floor of our dorm," Dan blurted. His cheeks were glowing, he just knew it. Tiny pinpricks of heat spread across his face as Jordan and Abby quit talking abruptly. They turned to face him in unison.

"Come again?" Jordan prompted, frowning.

"In Brookline? Near the lobby?" He didn't want to look too eager, but Abby at least seemed interested, tilting her head to the side and chewing her lip thoughtfully.

"I think I walked by that. It looked locked up though. Quarantined or something," she said.

"My roommate, Felix, managed to get inside. He said it was totally open. It sounded like something cool to check out, you know, maybe after hours." It wasn't until that last bit came out of his mouth that he realized how strange the proposition sounded. Inviting them to creep around after dark when he hardly knew them . . .

Jordan seemed to read his mind, shaking his head and playing idly with the fringy end of his scarf. The bravado he'd shown just moments ago was gone. "Sounds against the rules. I don't mean to be lame, but I'm not looking to get kicked out, not on the first day. Well, not *ever*, but definitely not on the first day."

"He said it was unlocked, Jordan. That hardly sounds off-limits," Abby put in. She offered Dan a bright smile. "I think it sounds interesting . . . and I'm always looking for inspiration. I bet there are all sorts of vintage goodies hidden in there."

"There are photographs," Dan said, before Jordan could rain on the parade again. "Felix said there were lots of photographs."

"Photos! Even better. I love old black and whites." She was elbowing Jordan, who still didn't look keen to give in just yet.

"It was just *open*? Are you sure?" he asked.

Dan nodded. "According to my roomie, anyway, and he doesn't strike me as the exaggerating type. He said there was a lock but it was broken."

"Talk about lax," Abby said.

"And weird," Jordan added, rubbing at his elbows as if suddenly cold. "I'm not sure, Abby, this sounds more up your alley. I'm not into all that macabre crap."

"You're not sitting this one out," she told him firmly. "Right, Dan?" Abby's eyes sparkled.

"Of . . . of course not! You've got to come along." For a minute there, he'd hoped he and Abby would end up checking out the office alone.

"I don't know . . ." Jordan kicked at an invisible speck on the ground. "Just seems risky."

He *did* have a point. No matter what Dan said about the broken lock, he was pretty sure the room was supposed to be off-limits. And if they did get caught and kicked out as Jordan feared, Dan would never forgive himself. Worse than having his own summer ruined, he'd be responsible for ruining their summers, too. Wouldn't *that* make a good first impression.

But he felt like he'd opened a Pandora's box—that the possibilities unlocked by a trip to the old wing had already grown and gotten away from him. Plus, if he was being honest, Dan really did want to know if there were more photos like the one he had found in his room.

"Come on," Dan needled, pointing out Felix's lanky frame weaving through the crowd still inside. "*He* went in there. How bad could it be?"

Jordan took a discreet look, then snorted. "What are they always saying about peer pressure? If your friends jump off a bridge, something something?"

"Well, Dan and I are going with or without you, aren't we, Dan?" Abby said with a confidence that Dan admired.

"All right already!" Laughing, Jordan nudged Abby's side. "You two win—let's go jump off that bridge."

CHAPTER
№ 4

$\mathcal{D}$an found them waiting at the bottom of the stairs. A phone call from his parents had almost made him late, but when he assured Paul and Sandy that he'd arrived just fine, and that his friends Jordan and *Abby* were waiting for him downstairs, his mother had let him go with a happy little chirp.

Behind Jordan and Abby, a few lights flickered in the entrance hall. Jordan leaned against one of the tall white columns that supported the archway. He waved at Dan's approach, swinging a flashlight in his other hand.

Abby had changed into a turquoise sweatshirt and pulled her hair up into a loose ponytail.

"Hey," she whispered, glancing around. "We saw a hall monitor go by a few minutes ago, but nothing since. You ready?"

Dan nodded and joined them under the arch. Jordan tested the flashlight, shining a beam of light at each of them in turn.

"Last chance to go back and do something sensible," Jordan offered, "like drink in my room and watch *Thundercats*."

Abby's nose wrinkled as she leveled a soft punch at his shoulder. "You are not chickening out now. Besides, we can do that after."

"I'm going to hold you to that," Jordan murmured, following them into the dim, silent hall. "Because I'll definitely need a drink after this."

Dan knew what he meant. Now that he was here, he was so beyond nervous it was like he was giddy. It wasn't a pleasant feeling exactly, but it was markedly better than the kind of anxiety he was used to.

Softly, they crept across the empty hall, passing the notices and activities corkboard, the vending machines, and a rickety elevator that was out of service. Fewer lights shined overhead the deeper into the hall they went, and when they reached the old office door they found themselves in almost total darkness. Jordan lifted his flashlight from their feet to the door, and Dan's heart sank: it was clearly locked. And the sign Felix had mentioned turned out to be a poster board that said KEEP OUT in rather serious red letters.

"I thought this was an unfettered access situation," Jordan whispered.

"I swear . . ." Had Felix lied to him? What would the point even be in that? "They must have figured out students were going in and locked it up. Damn it. I'm sorry for dragging you guys here."

"All right, all right, don't look so sad." From his pocket, Jordan produced a paper clip, which he proceeded to straighten. When he'd finished, he put one end into the padlock and started to wiggle it around gently. "Just know that you owe me a lot more than *Thundercats* for this."

"Pretty impressive," Dan whispered. He had seen lock picking on TV, but it didn't compare to the sneaky thrill of watching someone do it in real life.

Jordan smiled, pausing for a moment. "I can do it with a hairpin, too."

"Would you two keep it down?" Abby looked over her shoulder.

"You're breathing louder than we're talking." Jordan bit down on his lower lip with an impatient sigh, the padlock shaking in his grasp.

"Maybe hurry it up just a little," Dan murmured.

"I'm going as fast as I can. This is an art. You can't rush *art*." A light sheen of perspiration broke out over Jordan's forehead, soaking the ends of his bangs. "Just . . . almost . . ." Dan heard the softest of clicks. *"Gotcha."* Jordan pocketed the paper clip in his hoodie and looped the open padlock through the ring on the door frame. He pushed the door. It didn't budge.

"Damn, it's stuck," he said. "Give me a hand. . . ."

Dan and Abby put their hands on the heavy door and pushed. The door felt like it was pushing back at first, but then it started to give.

After one final push, the door shuddered open. A cloud of dust swirled up and blew out to meet them like a relieved sigh, as if some pent-up force had finally been released. As quickly as the dust came it dissipated, presumably less potent after Felix's trip inside.

"Ugh, that is *foul*." Coughing, Abby reeled back, covering her mouth to keep the dust out.

"It smells like my grandpa's house," Jordan said, his voice muffled through the fingers clamped over his mouth.

"They probably don't clean in here anymore." Dan squinted into the dark behind the door. Beside him, Jordan flicked his flashlight around, illuminating a wide reception-type room.

"When do you think was the last time someone worked here?"

"The Stone Age, maybe?" Abby joked. She and Dan turned on their phone lights as all three of them moved into the darkened room. Their lights made little pools of blue and white, but were hardly bright enough to fight the darkness.

They moved farther in. Slowly, details appeared—a low counter to the left where the secretary might have sat, a cushioned bench fixed into the wall on the right, austere overhead lights long bare of working bulbs. Across from them, along the far wall, was a slim door with a frosted glass window.

"This is crazy," Jordan whispered, huddling closer to them. "It's like . . . it's like it's all just frozen in time. Like they just got up and left one day." He passed Abby and Dan, going to the counter and peering over it. "Phones, typewriters, *everything*."

"It must have closed suddenly," Abby said. Together, she and Dan walked ahead of Jordan and approached the inner office door. The flashlight beam shined over Dan's shoulder, giving them all a better view of the letters that had flecked away on the door's glass.

W   D N RA F   D

"What do you think?" Dan leaned closer, studying the letters and trying to mentally fill in the blanks. "Is this the warden's office?"

"Most likely," Abby agreed. "Think it's open?"

"Only one way to find out . . ." Holding his breath, Dan reached for the knob, noticing that it showed visible fingerprints in the dust that disappeared under his palm. Traces of Felix, probably, who must have gone farther in since Dan hadn't spotted any pictures so far.

The door gave with a quiet squeak, swinging inward on tight hinges.

"Whoa," he heard Abby breathe.

"My thoughts exactly," Dan whispered.

Wiping his hands to get rid of the clinging dust, he went first, shoved a little by Jordan at his back. It was only fair, given that

this whole trip into the unknown was technically his idea. They stepped into an office that might have been spacious if not for all the bookcases and filing cabinets crowding around, not to mention the piles and piles of loose papers. Dan tripped over a fallen lamp stand, catching his balance by grabbing the edge of a large desk.

On the desk, Dan noticed an old rotary telephone next to a stack of worn journals and notepads. Then he realized that what looked like an in-box of papers was actually a pile of faded photographs, less dusty than everything around it.

"I think I found the photos Felix was talking about," Dan said.

He shined his phone on the top one—a tall man in a long, white coat, with glasses Dan recognized. He squinted to make out the other details of the image. It was the same man from the photo in his desk drawer. He quickly flipped to the next picture and let out a yelp.

"What is it? What's wrong?" Abby said.

"Nothing," Dan replied. If he admitted the connection he'd just made in his head, he could no longer pretend that he was imagining it.

The next photo in the stack showed a group of physicians standing around a gurney. Lying on the bed, oddly placid, was a young man in a hospital gown. One of the doctors was cradling his head in his hands, while another was buckling a heavy leather strap across his forehead. Nearby, a nurse was holding a syringe.

Abby sidled up next to him to stare at the picture, both of them trying to make sense of the image.

"It must be a treatment of some kind," Dan said finally. "He must have been a patient here."

"He's so young," Abby said. "He could be our age."

He could be me. Dan shook the thought from his mind, peeling off the photo and aiming his cell phone at the next one.

This picture showed a woman restrained on a table. Fitted over her head was a helmet with wires coming out of it. A wooden bit was wedged between her teeth. Between the helmet and the bit, she looked like she was being tortured, like some kind of martyr.

The photographs were horrible, but Dan couldn't stop flipping to the next one, and the next. Each picture showed a patient enduring some kind of treatment, from painful-looking shots to solitary confinement. A photograph depicting hydrotherapy turned Dan's stomach. Orderlies were aiming hoses of water at a patient, who was huddled and shivering in the corner of the room, completely naked. A doctor stood to the side, arms crossed, indifferent.

Dan had read about this kind of outdated treatment before—he had a morbid fascination for the subject, really. Growing up in the foster system had given him an interest in social machines, systems that made decisions *for* people instead of with them. Not that he was comparing his life to the plight of these poor people—if anything, the system had made a *good* decision for him, all things considered. He wouldn't trade his family for anything.

"Wait, you guys, come take a look at this. . . ." Jordan said, and the catch in his voice got their attention.

He was standing on the far side of the desk, his flashlight pointed at the wall, where there were even more photos, hanging in frames.

"How awful," Dan said.

"*Quiet.*" Abby spoke in barely a whisper.

She moved closer to one of the pictures, gently wiping the dust off the glass frame with her sleeve. It was a photograph of a little girl, no older than nine or ten, with light-colored hair down to her shoulders. She was standing up, her hand resting on what looked like the armrest of a chair, like she was posing for a formal portrait. She had on a patterned dress and was wearing fine jewelry. But a jagged scar slashed across her forehead and there was something wrong with her eyes.

"She looks so sad," Abby said.

Sad was one way to put it. Empty was another.

Abby stood still, staring so deeply into the photograph that it looked like she was in a trance. Dan didn't have the heart to tell her that given the scar on the little girl's forehead and the emptiness in her eyes, it was likely that she'd been given a lobotomy. What kind of monsters would perform a lobotomy on a little girl?

The picture hanging next to it shocked him from his thoughts. It showed a patient struggling, pinned by two orderlies in white aprons and restrained by a muzzle on his face. One of the orderlies holding him looked positively evil. Dan was mesmerized by the photograph. Who had taken it, or any of these pictures for that matter, and who had hung them up on the wall?

"It's hard to remember they were here to get help," Jordan said.

"He was ill," Dan replied automatically.

"So? Does that look humane to you? Those doctors wouldn't know the Hippocratic oath if it kneed them in the balls."

"You have no idea what was going on," Dan shot back. Then he stopped himself. Why did he feel the need to defend the very doctors who had probably performed a lobotomy on a child? Or

who were getting ready to torture a man? When he looked down at his crossed arms, a bolt of fear shot through his body, and he rushed to fill the awkward silence. "I guess we're just lucky the field has come a long way since then."

"Why leave these here?" Abby cried suddenly, gesturing at the photographs. Her chin was quivering. "They're . . . horrible."

"Well, at least it's honest," Jordan replied, putting an arm around her. Abby shrugged him off. "I hate when people skirt around the truth. And lest we forget, this *was* locked."

"I don't care if they locked it up." She wouldn't stop looking at the photograph of the girl. Dan had an urge to grab Abby away before the hollow girl in the frame could reach out and pull her in. But of course that was ridiculous. "She shouldn't be here. She should be put somewhere safe."

Slowly, Abby raised both her hands and pulled the frame off its hook. A light patch showed on the wall where the picture had been. Abby hugged the photograph to her chest, her arms wrapping protectively around it.

"What are you doing?" Dan said, unable to stop himself.

"I'm going to take her back to my room. She'll be safe there."

"You can't take it, Abby," said Dan, trying to keep the desperation out of his voice. "It's *supposed* to be down here. You need to leave it alone."

Abby was about to say something else when Jordan spoke up. "Hey, relax, both of you. It's not like you know her, Abs. You should put it back. Someone might notice it's missing."

"Who?" she demanded with a soft little scoff.

"Someone," Jordan replied testily. "I don't know. . . . Maybe there's a catalog of all the crap in here somewhere."

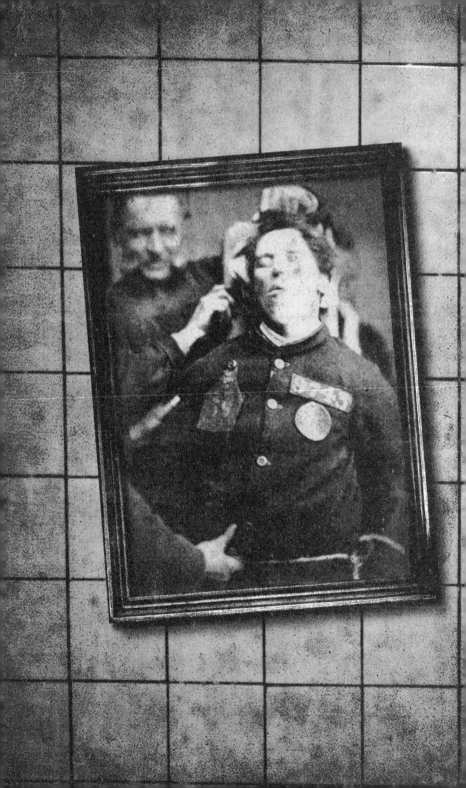

Abby didn't seem to hear what Jordan had said. She stood silently, like a statue, gripping the picture to her chest.

"Please, Abby, leave her where she is. She belongs with the others," Dan insisted. *"Please."* He couldn't believe he was arguing with one of the hottest girls he'd ever met.

Just let her have it, Dan. You want her to like you.

But the need to speak was more compelling.

Abby's eyes seemed almost as vacant as those of the girl in the photograph. Then a shiver came over her and she blinked. Gently, almost *affectionately*, she put the picture back on the wall. She touched it one last time and said, "Poor little bird. I wonder if she ever escaped her cage."

With the picture in place, Dan felt a sense of relief. He couldn't exactly say why.

"Come on," Abby said. "Let's go back. I've had enough."

That was all they needed. They scrambled out of the old office like it was a race, and Dan was only too glad to shut the door behind them.

"Hey, the lock," Jordan said, just as they reached the vending machines.

"Don't worry, I already took care of it," Dan said, ready to be far, far away.

"You sure?"

Without waiting for an answer, Jordan turned back to double-check. The lock was still hanging on the door where he'd left it.

"My bad," said Dan, laughing nervously. He really could have sworn he'd locked it. But then, his memory had been known to play tricks on him.

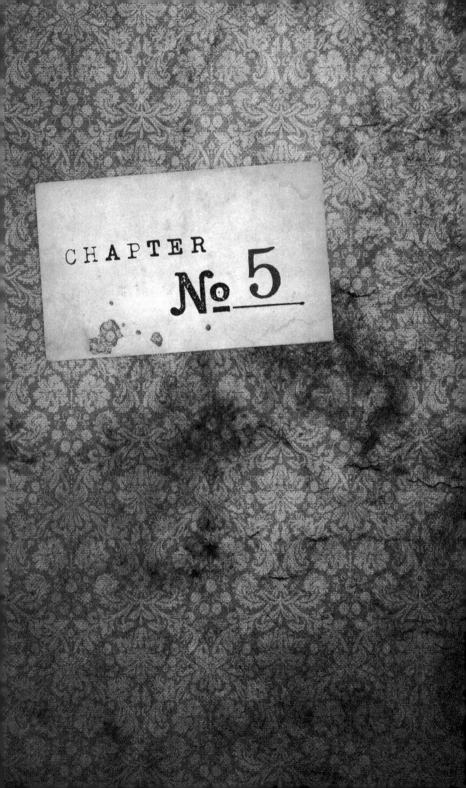

CHAPTER № 5

$\mathcal{D}$an was dusty and exhausted by the time he got back to his room. Opening the door carefully, so as not to wake Felix, he took a step in and was gripped by cold.

This isn't my room. Dan blinked, disoriented. It looked like a cell of some sort, with floors and walls made of heavy gray stone. An operating table covered with a thin, white sheet stood in the middle of the room. In the corner nearest him was a drain—why, Dan could only guess. A small window cut into the top of the far wall was covered by crisscrossing metal bars. But the most unnerving thing about the room was the pair of shackles that were bolted to the wall on the left. At first, Dan had thought they were rusty, but now that he really looked at them, he could see that the dark red stains were far too wet to be rust.

Why do I know this room?

Dan quickly closed the door and started rubbing his arms with his hands to get rid of the chill. He tried to rationalize what had just happened. Had he opened the wrong door by mistake? That would explain it. He was extremely tired and had just taken a wrong turn and ended up at the wrong room. A nightmare room that hadn't been used in decades.

Yeah, right.

He checked the door number. 3808.

That *was* his number. *What was going on?*

After rubbing his eyes with trembling hands, Dan opened the door again. And there was his room, two desks, two chairs, and two beds, with the sleeping lump of Felix on the nearer one.

Dan stepped in and closed the door. Leaning against it, he tried to catch his breath, coughing from the dust still lodged in his nose and throat. His mind had wandered, that was all. It had wandered far, but now he had it back.

ɣ ✕ ✕ ɣ ✕ ✕

Unsurprisingly, Dan couldn't sleep. Tossing and turning, he'd banish the photographs from his head only to be overcome by the weird hallucination he'd had. Intermittent snores from Felix didn't help. Around two thirty, when he finally gave up trying, he grabbed his laptop from the desk and crawled back into bed with it. Maybe he could find out more about Brookline, something that might explain those horrid photographs.

He typed in "Brookline and History," and that brought up a list of various towns called Brookline. Adding in "New Hampshire" turned up a vague summary of the sanatorium's history which contained nothing Dan didn't already know—that it had housed the mentally ill, both men and women, and had been bought by the college after it closed. He decided to try an image search. Instantly, a results page full of vintage photographs of Brookline's exterior showed up. In black and white, the building looked even more menacing.

Narrowing the parameters further, Dan typed in "Brookline AND history AND asylum." And there, finally, was a link that looked promising. Judging by the garish purple background and abundance of animated gifs on the page, it was a "homemade" website, to put it nicely. The title was what caught his interest, though: "Brookline—Curing the Insane or Creating Them?"

Pretty sensationalistic, Dan thought. But it only went more over the top from there. The page was long and gave off some serious conspiracy-theory paranoia vibes. Sal Weathers, investigator, hobbyist, and—*oh, boy*—ghost hunter, had painstakingly compiled what must have been every bit of news Brookline had ever made in local or national papers into one long text block. Statistics about how many patients had been at the asylum at its peak, stories about how when it closed in 1972 patients had been relocated to other hospitals or released . . . Repeatedly, Dan came across references to the difficulties Brookline had had in keeping a warden. The turnover sounded worse than McDonald's.

Finally, about three-fourths of the way through Sal's winding write-up, Dan found something—a line, a throwaway maybe, but he read it to himself several times:

> *It wasn't until 1960 that Brookline found the man who would redefine and refocus its entire purpose.*

And his name was? And what was the new purpose? But the article didn't say.

"It's called narrative focus, Sal—look it up," Dan said aloud. Then he remembered he had a roommate. Luckily, Felix seemed to be a deep sleeper.

Dan scanned down the page. The reason behind Sal's literary ADD quickly became obvious. Why fixate on garbage like the rate of warden employment when there were *serial kill-ers* to discuss?

By far the most controversial of Brookline's patients was the serial killer Dennis Heimline, known more commonly as the Sculptor. Between 1960 and 1965, he terrorized a small rural community in Vermont. Police estimate that he killed more than a dozen people, earning his name from the grisly way he left his victims posed like statues. One report described the "cold, terrible beauty" of a young woman found "dancing" in the wilds of the White Moun-tains, her mutilated arms tied to tree limbs high above. The most horrifying crime he committed occurred at a local pub. The victims were posed in various places throughout the bar—some standing, some sitting, and some engaged in a kind of revelry on the dance floor. All held in place by ropes and wires.

Perhaps more disturbing than the Sculptor himself was the fact that when Brookline closed, no trace of the Sculptor could be found. . . .

Dan was riveted. A serial killer had been a patient here, in *this* building. Where had they kept him? What kind of treatment had he received? And where had he *gone*?

Dan closed his laptop and lay back on his bed. Just as he was drifting off he remembered the photo of the struggling patient and wondered if that could have been Dennis Heimline. Maybe his parents had been right to worry about him coming here. Having a speckled past was one thing, but a serial killer? Treat-ment photos? Well, he wouldn't be sharing these discoveries with Paul and Sandy, that was for sure.

CHAPTER
№ 6

"No offense, Dan, but you look like crap. Did you have trouble sleeping or something?"

Abby's voice sounded like it was coming from the bottom of a pool. Realizing he'd begun to nod off, Dan roused himself enough to lift his head and shove a bite of cereal into his mouth. He wondered if the halo of fuzzy light that looked so at home around her head was from the morning sun through the skylight or from his almost total lack of sleep.

He decided against telling Abby about what he'd found online, because he was worried it would sound too weird—that it would make *him* sound too weird. He was only just getting to know her; he didn't want to blow it in the first twenty-four hours.

"Felix snores. Like he swallowed a frog. Or a lion."

"That bad?"

"Yeah, and then he was up at the crack of dawn to go work out, of all things. Needless to say, I don't think I'll be getting much sleep this summer."

"You sure you're not just worn out from our little ordeal last night?" She didn't beat around the bush. He liked that.

"I guess it was pretty intense," he said. She had certainly seemed enamored of that one photo. They'd almost had a fight over it. Dan frowned; he couldn't even remember now why he'd been so adamant about her leaving it there.

A stab of pain in his head made his eye twitch. "Damn it. I did not want to feel like this on the first full day."

Abby pushed a cup of coffee across the table. "Try that. It's strong enough to fuel a jet."

He turned the cup, careful to avoid the little smudge of pink she'd left on the rim. He took a sip and tasted something between lighter fluid and maple syrup and rushed to swallow before the sweet sludge could make its way back out. "Wow! How do you *drink* that?"

"I actually hate the taste of coffee, but the sugar helps cover it up," she admitted. "And you can't be an artist and not drink coffee. It's just . . . not done. Every installation I've ever gone to has either coffee or wine, so you've got to suck it up and deal."

Dan laughed. Abby didn't seem like she cared if she fit in or not, but maybe everyone made a few concessions here and there. Just last year he'd broken down and bought a tan corduroy blazer to wear to a community college lecture on Jung's last years. He'd sat in a sea of tan and navy sports jackets, wondering what his favorite psychoanalyst would say about so many people trying so desperately not to stand out.

"Hey," Dan said, forcing a smile as he sat up straighter. He remembered something Abby had said yesterday. "So you took a bus here?" Dan had flown from Pittsburgh, and then taken a taxi from the tiny airport that looked like it had just one runway.

"A couple buses, actually. Pops couldn't take the time off, but it's no trouble. Bus, train, subway . . . It's all second nature when you're from New York."

"And that's where Jordan's from, too?"

"No, Jordan was coming from Virginia. We shared the last leg of the trip."

"That's an awfully long ride. Why didn't he fly?"

"Oh, his parents got him plane tickets all right," Abby said, "but they were to California, not New Hampshire."

Dan raised his eyebrows.

"Apparently, they think he's at some pray-the-gay-away camp or something right now. His uncle is paying for this program, and he used the cash from his part-time job to buy the bus ticket." Abby drained the remaining coffee and finished the last of her oatmeal.

"But what if his parents find out? What happens then?"

Abby frowned. "Beats me. World War Three?"

No wonder Jordan was so afraid of getting kicked out.

Dan felt grateful for his open-minded and easygoing parents, strict as they could be sometimes. He always felt like he'd lucked out with Paul and Sandy, even before they'd officially adopted him. Lots of kids weren't so fortunate. "It's nice he has you here to talk to about it," he said. Abby was so easy to be with. It was no surprise that Jordan confided in her.

"We just get each other. We're connected." Abby gathered her things. The buzz of voices in the cafeteria died down as the students ambled outside, all of them headed to registration. "It was a long bus ride, not much to do but play hangman and chat. I'm sure he would've opened up to you, too."

"Maybe," Dan said, although he highly doubted it. "Anyway, he better not miss registration or he'll be forced to open up to Felix in Advanced Bioethics."

"Be nice," said Abby, but she was smiling.

They filed out behind the other students, grabbing their back-packs from cubbies placed just outside the cafeteria entrance. Apparently you weren't allowed to bring your bags inside because college kids had a habit of making off with a whole week's worth of croissants and fruit cups.

"Seriously, though," said Dan. "This morning Felix asked if I wanted to swap schedules, for a buddy system or something. Then when I finally gave in and showed him the classes I wanted, I could tell he was embarrassed for me. Not enough hard science, I guess."

Abby laughed.

"Yeah, thanks. Laugh at my misery."

Dan sneezed when they stepped outside.

"Bless you."

"Thanks. Hey, I was actually thinking, though, what if we took a class together or something? You, me, and Jordan, I mean. I know you're here for art, but maybe I could convince you to take a history class?" he asked. The dormitories spread out on either side of them, forming an almost perfect ring around the grassy quad. Chairs littered the shade under the biggest tree in the quad, and while the benches lining the path were empty now, he imagined they would all be filled later. He'd overheard a few kids in the cafeteria talking about having a lawn bowling tour-nament after registration.

"Sure, why not. Meanwhile, I've gotta make sure I grab a spot in life drawing. Do you want me to sign you up?"

"Me? Oh, that's right. You've never seen me draw. It's worse than stick figures. Is there something worse? Whatever it is, *that's* my skill level." Dan shook his head, imagining the look on the instructor's face when he turned in his scribbles.

"There will be naked giiiirls," Abby said, drawing out the last word teasingly.

"*And* naked guys," he replied.

"Good point. Ooh! Maybe Jordan will sign up with me."

They passed through the quad and the path divided into two, one leading to the admin building where they were going to register for classes, and the other to the sports center. Up ahead, Dan spied Felix coming from the gym, pale and upright, walking to registration on his own. Dan thought about calling out to him, and really felt that he should. But to be perfectly honest, he was having a good time just being alone with Abby.

"Hey, losers! Wait up!"

So much for being alone. Jordan ran up the path, a sleek-looking leather satchel slung diagonally across his chest. A key chain with a twenty-sided die hung from the satchel's zipper. Jordan looked like he had just rolled out of bed and thrown on whatever was at hand, yet somehow he made Dan feel like the sloppy one.

"Where were you?" Abby asked, slipping her arm through Jordan's. "We missed you at breakfast."

"Overslept. How was the food? Gross, probably." Jordan walked quickly and they had to trot a bit to keep up.

"It wasn't bad, actually," Dan answered, although he wasn't sure Jordan really cared about the answer. Jordan was hard to read, he thought. One minute he was up, and the next he was acting all snide. And then there was the Jordan who was so afraid of getting kicked out and going home. "Although Abby's coffee was a diabetic's nightmare."

"Dan's just grumpy because his roommate shamed him over his class choices this morning."

"Shamed? What the hell? How is it any of his business?" Jordan laughed. "You lost the roommate lottery, Danny boy. Me? I won it. Yi is good stuff. He played the cello for me this morning." Jordan waved to a tall, disheveled guy who was setting up his cello on the grass. "He's getting together a chamber music group to play outside on the lawn. Can you imagine? I mean, can we hurry up and get to college for real, please? I want cello every morning. I want this." He swept his hand out in front of him. "It sure beats living under the Talibans. I'm so ready for it."

"You shouldn't wish away your life," Abby said smugly. "You only get it once."

"Not if you're a Buddhist. Or a ghost. But you're right, who wants to get old? Not me. I'll be handsome, of course, distinguished, but still . . . Wrinkles? Back pain? No, thanks." He tweaked Abby's nose. "At least you'll be gorgeous forever."

Dan couldn't argue with that.

"Dan, on the other hand, already looks middle-aged," Jordan continued, chuckling again. "In a good way! Don't hit me—in a good way! Look at you over there, all quiet and earnest and crap. Wise beyond your years, man, like a hot, skinny Buddha."

"Uh, thanks?" Dan looked at his feet, his face growing warm. He didn't particularly want anybody, especially Abby, thinking of Buddha when they looked at him.

"Is he blushing? I think he's blushing." Jordan cackled and sped up, tugging Abby swiftly along the sidewalk, forcing Dan to hurry to keep pace.

"Leave him alone, Jordan." She turned to Dan with an

apologetic smile. "Don't worry, you don't look middle-aged to me. He's just trying to rile you up."

"From the state of his face I'd say it's working," Jordan said.

"You're awfully chipper this morning," Abby said. "No bad dreams after last night?"

Jordan shook his curly head. "Me? No, I slept the sleep of the innocent. It's probably from being away from home."

Dan thought of his own night and the sleep he definitely hadn't gotten. He seemed to be the only one whom the basement had really affected. He was also the only one who had dug deeper into the asylum's history. He didn't want Abby and Jordan to think he'd gone all obsessive, and was glad he hadn't said anything to Abby. It was time to change the subject before he said something he'd regret later. "So, Jordan, Abby and I were just talking about what classes we want to take."

"Okay . . . ?"

"Well, we were just thinking of some we might take together. You interested?"

"Sure," Jordan said, although he took out his phone and began texting at light speed with only his thumb, turning away slightly to shield the screen from them. Dan didn't give it a second thought; who Jordan texted was his own business.

Talk of courses carried them the remaining distance to registration. Dan's mood lifted with every step. Abby and he agreed on two classes together, but while Abby and Jordan were taking Life Drawing, Dan would be in History of Psychiatry. He probably knew a lot of the subject matter already, but he knew classes at NHCP were designed to push even the smartest kids.

Posted on a wooden pillar off to the side of the admin building were flyers for a harp concert, an L.A.R.P. demonstration, and a casual bocce ball match. The morning mist had yet to burn off, and the students milling around looked almost like ghosts in a dream. A good dream.

"Can you imagine doing this every day?" Dan said.

"Picking classes? No, it's exhausting." Abby slipped her course catalog back into her patchwork messenger bag.

"No, I mean *this*. Walking around campus on a nice day with kids who actually want to be here, going to classes you actually want to take."

"Amen," said Jordan.

"Amen too," said Abby, and she linked arms with Jordan and Dan.

Dan was content with himself for once. He had two new friends and classes he was actually excited to attend. One day in, the summer was looking up.

⨯ ⨯ ⨯ ⨯ ⨯

After registration, the students were split into a few smaller, more manageable groups and funneled into rooms off the main floor of Wilfurd Commons. The director of the program was there to help guide the flow of traffic, waving and joking with a few of the professors who idled out in the hall. Inside their designated room, the friends were greeted by a professor and a red-headed guy who was handing out information on the various services available to them, emergency numbers, and maps of campus. The guy seemed to recognize Jordan, greeting him with a friendly "What's up" before moving on to the next kid in line.

"Haven't we heard all this a thousand times already?" Jordan groused as they took their seats. A dozen or so rows of chairs had been set up in front of a pull-down screen. They sat at the end of the third row, backpacks tucked under their feet. "I mean, I know I read this somewhere already. The pamphlets, the website . . ."

"Some of these kids have never been away from home before," Dan replied. Abby sat between him and Jordan, perusing a neon-green handout.

"Have you?" Abby asked. It was a friendly, conversational question, but Dan froze, not sure how to answer. He didn't like to talk about the foster homes he'd been in before lucking out with Paul and Sandy.

He was glad when the professor motioned for everyone to be quiet, waiting by the projector until the students had stopped talking.

"That's Joe," Jordan said, nodding toward the stocky, red-headed student. "He's a hall monitor on my floor."

"Kinda cute."

"A hall monitor? No way, Abs, that's forbidden fruit. Ha ha, *fruit*, get it?"

"Unfortunately, yes," Abby muttered, rolling her eyes.

"Ahhh, I crack me up," Jordan added, wiping away a nonexistent tear.

"That makes one of us."

The dark-haired girl sitting ahead of them turned and glared, silencing Abby and Jordan with a look. Behind her back, Jordan stuck out his tongue as the professor finally started talking.

"This is Joe McMullan, and I'm Professor Reyes. I know you're all probably very bored with orientation stuff, but this will be quick and painless, I promise."

Her name sounded familiar. Dan reached quietly into his pocket and pulled out his schedule. Scanning the list, he found that she was his History of Psychiatry professor. He tucked the schedule away, fixing his attention to the front of the room again. She was shorter than Joe by at least a head, and looked approachable enough, with ruddy cheeks and a gap in her teeth. She wore all black accented by a chunky necklace of turquoise stones.

"First, a few words on dorm safety . . ."

Dan let his eyes wander around the room. A few seats down he saw Felix sitting bolt upright in his chair. He sighed, thinking he really ought to include his roommate more, and maybe see if an hour or two kicking back as a group would bring Felix out of his shell. But he genuinely liked what he had going with Abby and Jordan, and if Felix made things weird, Dan would be blamed for forcing him into the dynamic.

"Brookline has a rich and complex past," Professor Reyes was saying. "So if you have any questions, ask anytime! History is nothing to be afraid of."

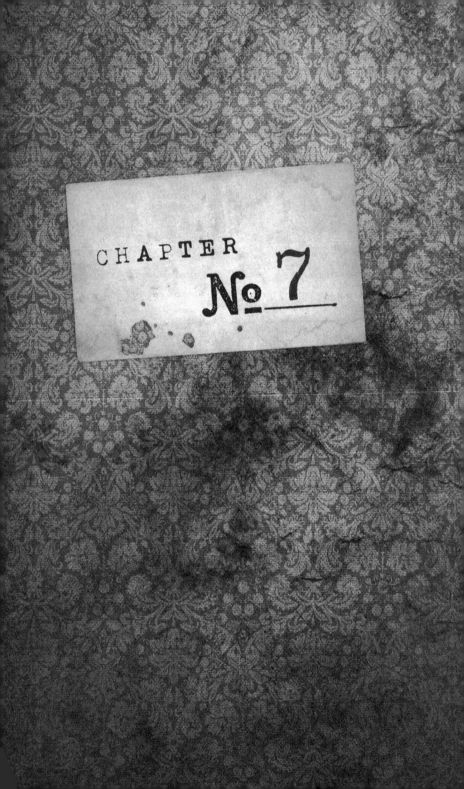

CHAPTER
№ 7

It was wrong, all wrong. Dan was in the wrong place. There must have been some mistake. He didn't deserve to be here. He wasn't crazy, he wasn't. So why was he chained to the wall? He struggled until there was blood on his wrists from where the shackles held him.

"Help!" he screamed, but his voice came out in a whisper.

The room changed. Now Dan was lying on a table in a robe. A key clicked in the door and a waiter wearing glasses and a white serving uniform came in, rolling a tray in front of him. There was a big silver dome on the tray, and Dan could hear something under it tinkling and rattling like silverware. "Your dinner, sir," the waiter said, removing the dome. Underneath were surgical instruments: a scalpel, a clamp, and a hypodermic needle.

Dan looked up, and the waiter's face had changed. Now he was wearing a white doctor's coat and a surgical mask. Worst of all, where his eyes had been there were only black sockets, as if his eyes had been scratched out.

As he reached for the instruments, the doctor said in a gentle voice, "Don't worry, Daniel Crawford. I'm here to take care of you."

an startled awake. Sweat was pouring down his face, and he had grabbed the sheet so tightly that his fingers were cramping. He was still muttering, "No, no, don't hurt me!"

Heart pounding, he sat up. His eyes adjusted to the darkness slowly. He was in his room. There was no waiter, no doctor.

There was only Felix, stock-still, standing beside the bed watching him.

"Ah!" He sank down into the pillows again and yanked the sheet up to his chin. "What . . . what are you doing?"

"You were speaking in your sleep, Daniel," Felix replied calmly. He took a tiny step away from the bed. "Are you feeling all right? The noise was . . . Well, it woke me, as you can see. . . ."

"S-sorry," Dan mumbled. "Just a nightmare. I'm . . . I'm fine, really."

But I'd be better if you backed the hell away.

"I need some air," he added, rolling out of bed. The sheets were damp with sweat.

"That should help," Felix said with a sad smile. "Fresh air always clears my thoughts. I hope it does the same for you."

Dan grabbed his hoodie and raced out the door, wondering if he was fleeing his roommate, the room, or both. He tried to slow down his breathing. *It was just a dream, that's all it was.* He wiped sweat from the bridge of his nose with one knuckle. The photographs had clearly disturbed him more than he'd realized. For the second night in a row, sleep was a lost cause. The hallway was dimly lit and quiet. No one was there, but Dan shivered. What was it about this place that made him feel like he was being watched?

It felt good to get downstairs. But when he got to the entrance hall, the main door was already propped open. Someone had gone out before him and was now sitting on the steps.

"Funny meeting you here," he said.

Abby yelped, surprised. Dan only just managed to dodge the pebble she picked up and chucked in his direction. "Dan! *Ugh.*

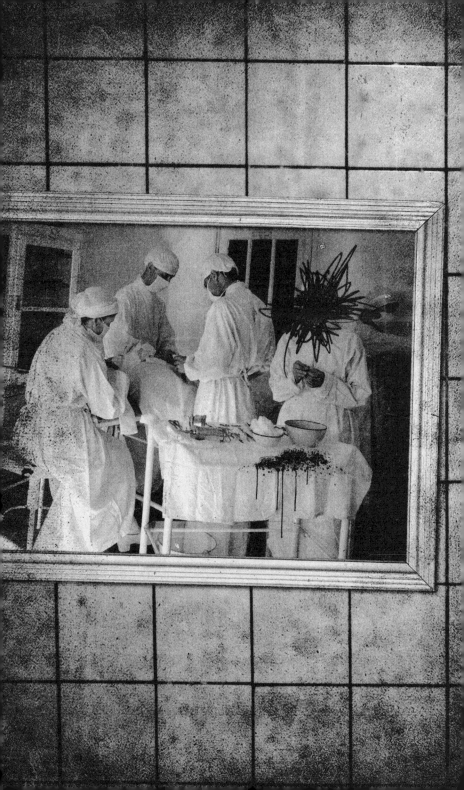

You scared me half to death."

It probably didn't help that his bad dream and sudden waking had left his voice hoarse. "Sorry," he said, sitting down next to her. "Didn't mean to make you jump."

Abby sat with her knees drawn up and her phone in one hand, her arms wrapped tight around her shins. Little fat clouds with smiles decorated her pajama pants.

"You're up late," she said. Her voice sounded ragged, too.

"Couldn't sleep. You?"

Abby looked at him, as if weighing how to respond. Finally, she said, "I got a text from my sister. Well, several texts. Things at home are . . . They could be better." She paused. Dan might not have been a social wizard, but he knew that asking questions was not the right thing to do just now. So he waited for Abby to go on. "My parents don't see eye to eye on much. Pops does corporate jingles and he hates it, but the money's good. Mom thinks he should go back to making real music. *His* music. But it doesn't pay."

"No easy answers there."

"They go back and forth, and every time I get so freaked out thinking that they'll . . . Anyway, Jessy thinks it's for real this time. She thinks they'll really do it." Abby sighed.

"What? Divorce?" *Sensitive, Dan, real sensitive.*

"Yeah." She sighed again, and this time he heard a catch in her breath. He had no idea what to do if she started crying, and he hoped like hell it wouldn't come to that, because he wouldn't know the right way to handle it. "It would kill my sister. Sometimes I think it would kill me, too."

"That really sucks. I'm sorry." He was flubbing this. Epically.

Not that it was an appropriate time to be acting all smooth and seductive or whatever, but surely something deeper was required here?

"I wish they could just keep it together for a few more years until Jessy and I are both in college."

Dan sat in what he hoped came off as sympathetic silence.

"So what about you?" she asked, tilting her head.

"Me? What about me?"

"Why couldn't you sleep?"

"Oh." Dan could feel that familiar instinct to shut down coming on. And he didn't want to darken the mood even more with a detailed retelling of his dream. Still, Abby had shared something private with him, and her eyes looked so big and sad. . . . A fair trade seemed only right. "I had a nightmare."

"Like falling or drowning?"

"Sort of." *No, not really.* But he decided he couldn't tell her about the dream after all. Not that dream, and not the ones he usually had either. She would think he was too strange, and her opinion mattered a lot to him. So all he said was "It was just the kind where you feel so . . . so . . ."

"Powerless?"

"Yeah."

"I know the feeling. That's how it is with my parents, too. Nothing I can do and it totally *blows*." She took a breath and then said, "You know, weird as it sounds, I feel kind of better now. I don't usually talk about this stuff."

"What about Jordan? I thought you two were tight."

"No. I mean yes. Well, sure, but I'm more *his* confidant. His situation is so screwed up. . . . I don't want to burden him with my problems too much. It doesn't seem right, piling more on top of him."

They sat in companionable silence. The grass at the foot of the trees was tall, and pale tendrils of mist wove through the overgrown tufts before fanning out across the lawn. The darkness was lifting slowly as dawn came. "You're a good listener, Dan. You've got this whole wise vibe going on."

"Thank you." Dan smiled. "Wait, this isn't that Buddha stuff again, is it? Because that seriously did not feel like a compliment."

Abby laughed, and for a second Dan really did feel like he had helped. "Jordan definitely could have phrased that better, but I think he was on to something." Still smiling, she scooted closer to him on the stoop. The feathers in her hair were gone, leaving her mass of black curls falling unevenly over one shoulder. For a moment, he thought she was about to kiss him, and he knew then and there he would ask her out on a date.

"So," she said. "You want to know my trick for getting to sleep?"

"Go for it."

"So I close my eyes, right? I mean, that's a given. But I close my eyes and relax, and I pretend I'm a tree—"

Dan snorted, shrugging away when Abby smacked him on his shoulder.

"A *tree*?"

"Shut *up*! It works!"

"Uh-huh. *Sure* it does . . ."

"Fine, smarty-pants. I'm not going to tell you my secret then." Abby crossed her arms and made a *hmph* sound.

"No, please, continue. Come on, I want to know more about . . . about . . . being a tree." Laughter bubbled up through his words no matter how hard he tried to clamp down on it.

"I'm not telling you now."

"Abby, please . . ."

"Ugh. Okay, but only because I like you."

Dan missed part of her next sentence, because she had said she liked him.

" . . . you picture your individual roots, picture them moving down through the soil, going deeper and deeper, focusing on each one, one after another, down, down, cool and safe and surrounded . . ."

Just listening to her describe it was relaxing. Then she reached over and gently pressed her thumbs to his temples. "Every root moving through the earth, shifting the dirt, getting stronger. . . ." He stretched, enjoying the feeling that he could fall asleep.

"Ha. See? I told you it works."

"Not bad, Branches."

"We should probably get back inside," she said, getting slowly to her feet and stretching. "And don't call me Branches."

"Acorn?"

"Not. Funny."

"Whatever you say, Branches." He covered a yawn.

"I'm serious." She glared. "You call me Branches and I'll call you Buddha."

"All right, fine. Truce." Dan followed her inside and closed the door behind them. It automatically locked. They walked to Abby's floor.

"Well, night," Dan said, rocking on his heels.

"Night. And remember . . ." Abby closed her eyes and struck a pose. "Be the tree."

"I'll try," Dan said, watching her back as she headed off to her room.

And alone in his room, Dan did try. But when he closed his eyes, the tree became a vine and the vine became a shackle, and then it was the same nightmare all over again.

CHAPTER

№ 8

The next morning, Dan hardly said two words to his friends. They wouldn't have class together until later in the afternoon, and his restless night meant his alarm had gone to snooze half a dozen times. Breakfast consisted of wolfing down Cheerios and orange juice too fast, and watching Abby put cold spoons on her eyelids. She insisted it would help her wake up and get rid of her sleepless puffiness.

No time to myth bust that. Instead, Dan ran, course list in hand, to his first class, thinking that History of Psychiatry would get him off to a good start. When he got there he saw Jordan's roommate, Yi, and was glad for the friendly face in a room full of strangers. Ignoring the familiar voice that told him it'd be easier to sit alone, Dan went over to Yi and introduced himself.

"How's it going?" he said to Yi as he sat down.

"Eh." Yi shrugged. "Jordan won't stop texting people when we're supposed to be sleeping. I could hear his little clicky-clacky fingers going until like four in the morning."

"He does love that phone."

"Otherwise? I'm glad to have the chance to do something outside of playing the damn cello. I love music and all, but I'm open to another calling. Maybe I'll find it in this class. If nothing else, I'll learn something new, right? That, and we might get to hear some cool shit about our loony bin of a dorm."

Professor Reyes arrived promptly and began handing out the syllabi. She was dressed in all black again, this time with a quartz necklace. Her appearance reminded Dan slightly of the fortune-tellers from late-night infomercials.

He liked Professor Reyes right away, particularly after a student raised his hand and she responded with a gentle, "No, we will not be discussing Brookline Sanatorium, but thank you for asking. If you'd like to do your own study on the subject for extra credit, that will be fine."

The hand went down immediately.

The two hours flew by, and the few times Dan's mind did wander it was to consider what Abby and Jordan might be up to in their drawing class. He sort of hoped Abby was keeping their late-night chat to herself. It's not that he cared if Jordan knew about his nightmares or Abby's parental problems, he simply liked the idea of that conversation remaining something they alone shared.

No harsh, loud bell rang to signal the end of class. Instead, the college's chapel chimes sounded once at a quarter to the hour, and that was the professor's signal to wrap things up. It was a refreshing change. Dan packed his folders away. Buying the textbooks for the classes was not mandatory, and most of the material came in the form of printed-off packets, slide shows, and documentaries. Right on Yi's heels, Dan was quick out the door—then he remembered that this wasn't high school, and he wasn't going to get in trouble if he was late for lunch.

The college had provided everyone with a map, but consulting it made him feel like such a tourist. Outside, the weather had shifted from the slight dewiness of morning to the full heat of a summer afternoon.

Professor Reyes was already out in the courtyard taking a smoke break. He remembered what she had said about a possible extra-credit project and approached.

Professor Reyes smiled at him, finishing her cigarette and flicking it into a nearby metal bucket for stubs.

"Darren, right?" she asked.

"Dan," he corrected, sticking his hands into his pockets. "Daniel Crawford?"

She stared at him for a long moment, then said, "Ah. Got it. I won't forget."

"I was wondering about that extra-credit project?"

"Oh, Dan, I was kidding. You know there are no grades here, right?" The professor laughed softly. "So are you looking for a recommendation, or just sucking up?"

"Well, I—" Dan didn't quite know what to say, embarrassed that she was already thinking badly of him. "This is just sort of my main interest. . . . Psychiatry and history, I mean. So the extra credit sounded cool. I was thinking I might try to do some interviews around town, get a local perspective."

"Good luck with that." Professor Reyes adjusted the briefcase slung over her shoulder.

"I'm sorry?"

"The townsfolk are, shall we say, superstitious? And that's putting it mildly. . . . They've been petitioning to get Brookline leveled for years, but they can't. One, because it's a historical site and deserves to stay put. Two, because there's no reason to tear it down. The foundation is sketchy, sure, but the college is paying to have it redone soon enough." She rummaged in her briefcase until she found her cigarette pack. She lit one, gesturing with it. "So you might come up against some, well, resistance. They'll talk about Brookline, sure—they'll talk your ear off about it—but only about how much they want it gone."

"That's too bad," Dan said, meaning it. "I thought it might make a good paper."

"It would, and you should try for it." Professor Reyes leaned closer, giving him a conspiratorial grin. "Actually, I've gotten permission to do a senior seminar in the old closed-off parts of the dorm. We'll be archiving some of the stuff in there and finally getting it off the school's hands at the same time. Any chance you're coming here next year?"

"I wish," Dan said. "I'm just starting my senior year of high school." Truthfully, Dan hadn't really considered coming to college here. But if he liked all his classes this summer, why not? "Hey, maybe if my interviews go well, you could use the paper for your seminar."

"Sure," she said. "We'll see."

Dan left, giving her a tiny wave as he went. He wasn't sure if the idea of digging deeper into Brookline's history made him excited or afraid, but having it as a kind of class assignment— even an unofficial, extra-fake-credit assignment—at least gave it some validity. Now he could tell Jordan and Abby about what he'd learned without sounding all psycho.

And speaking of Jordan and Abby, they were probably waiting for him at lunch now. He remembered the moment last night when he thought Abby was about to kiss him. Would she remember it the same way? Was she still thinking about him, too?

✗ ✗ ✗ ✗ ✗

It took Dan four days to get up the courage to ask Abby out on a date.

To be fair, it was an amazing four days in which he, Abby, and Jordan basically became inseparable. They ate together, sat next to one another in class, and hung out at night. Of course, this made Dan even more anxious about asking Abby out. His mind went round and round in circles. *Should* he ask her out? What if she said no? Could they still be friends? How would Jordan feel about it? What would it do to the three of them? What if she said yes? What if . . . ?

He was so broody that even Felix noticed something was going on.

"You seem distracted, Daniel," Felix said one day after lunch when Dan had come into the room, flopped down on his bed, and sighed loudly. "Want to talk it over?"

Dan wondered about the wisdom of asking Felix for dating advice—although Felix did seem to be relaxing into the program, too. He still studied alone in their room all the time, spoke like a science teacher, and required ludicrously small amounts of sleep. But his manga magazines had disappeared and he seemed to enjoy doing his own thing.

"Well," Dan said. "I'm thinking of asking Abby out. What do you think my chances are?"

"Ah, yes. I can see why you're so nervous. . . ."

"You . . . can?" Dan waited, although he wasn't sure he wanted Felix to elaborate.

"You *are* facially symmetrical, but suffer from slightly protruding ears. You're not exactly tall, and your lack of muscular definition, well . . . Abby is, on the other hand—"

"Yeah," Dan said, cutting him off. "She's cute as hell."

Felix paused and gave a quick shrug. "I'd say she is, in the popular vernacular, out of your league."

"I thought so, thanks," Dan muttered. He really shouldn't feel put out, considering the source of this judgment, but still . . . it stung.

"But only by a very narrow margin." Felix beamed from his desk chair. "Does that answer your question?"

"Yes," he said. "You've been a big help. Thank you." Dan gathered up his afternoon notebooks and headed out the door.

That phrase, *out of your league*, plagued Dan all the way across campus. Felix was right in a way. Dan had never met anyone like Abby before, someone who lit up his world a little whenever she happened into it.

The first of the chapel bells started ringing, signaling one forty-five and the start of his next class. *Late.* How had that happened? It had been a little after one when he'd left the dorm. Dan sprinted as best he could the rest of the way, arriving outside the social sciences building huffing and sweating. On the last chime, he tumbled into the corridor. Jordan and Abby were waiting by the classroom door.

"There you are!" Abby called. "We thought you weren't coming."

"Just running late. Roommate stuff."

"Sure, we all know you were going for a dramatic entrance," Jordan teased, nudging him lightly. Dan filed in after his friends and shuffled to a seat under the stern gaze of their professor, a tall, middle-aged man with a short goatee and salt-and-pepper hair.

"Well, if it isn't the Hydra," Professor Douglas said, pulling his glasses halfway down the bridge of his nose. "Don't make it a habit, you three."

Hydra. Clever, Dan thought. He smiled.

"Sorry!" Abby said, whipping out her binder at lightning speed. "It won't happen again."

Professor Douglas nodded and turned to the whiteboard.

After class, they walked together back toward the quad. A tall, lantern-jawed kid ran up to them on the path, planting himself in Abby's way and putting a hand on her arm like he knew her.

"Hey, Abby! Jordan." The guy smiled, showing a megawatt, dentist-approved grin. "Y'all want to grab a coffee or something?"

Of course he had a charming Southern accent. Why wouldn't he?

"I'm Dan." Dan stuck out his hand, forcing the guy to let go of Abby's arm.

"Ash," the boy said, gripping Dan's hand like a vise. "Pleased to meet you. So . . . ?" Ash cocked his head in the direction of Wilfurd.

"Sure, I'm down," Abby chirped. "Guys?"

"Sounds good to me," Jordan said.

Dan just shrugged and tried to smile in a way that said, *okay, but it wouldn't be my first choice.* Quietly, hands in his pockets, he dropped back a few paces. Jordan joined him, giving him the sort of deliberate, laser-eyed look that made Dan feel extremely uncomfortable. He wasn't going to say anything. If Abby wanted to hang out with Ash, that was none of his business.

But Jordan didn't let up.

"He goes to Abby's high school," he whispered conspiratorially as he twirled a pencil in his fingers. "She introduced us in drawing class. I guess they run the art club together at their school."

"Oh," Dan replied. "I guess he seems nice enough. . . ."

"But?"

"But nothing." Dan kicked a stick out of the way, sending it spinning into the grass. "He's nice. But maybe that's all there is to him. Anyway, who cares about *nice*? Most people are nice." He thought about his high school. "Nice" kids were a dime a dozen there, and none of them really caught his interest. Not that he much cared. He was at the top of his class, and in a year, he'd be headed to college far away from them all.

Jordan raised an eyebrow. "You don't think you're being a little harsh on the kid? You've known him all of ten seconds, Dan. He's just one of those guys, you know? He gets along with everyone. People like having him around."

Dan kicked at the ground. "I don't get that. How do you do that? Get along with everyone, I mean."

"Try being a little less jealous, for one," Jordan said.

He meant it lightly, but Dan took it to heart. Was he being that obvious? Maybe he should just get over himself and accept that of course Jordan and Abby would have other friends. But for his part, Dan didn't feel like he needed anyone else.

Dan picked at a muffin while Abby and Jordan chatted with Ash. Nobody seemed to mind that he didn't say a word. He tried not to look all mopey, but he wasn't sure he succeeded.

Afterward, Ash left to join a Frisbee game and Jordan said something about meeting up with people for a group project. Dan and Abby were quite suddenly alone.

Abby looked at Dan with a smile on her face. "Cheer up," she said. "You look so serious."

"I—" he started, but then something came over him and he knew he had to say this now or he never would. "Do you want to go out somewhere tonight? Just the two of us, I mean?"

"Yes." She said, smiling, leaving Dan to inwardly celebrate the vast difference between "yes" and "sure."

Tell her it's a date, that you mean it like a date.

"It doesn't have to be a date or anything," he added sheepishly.

It's a date, it's a date, you're asking her on a date. . . .

"Oh," Abby replied, glancing down. "No, right, of course . . ."

"Or it could be a date?"

"Okay . . ." She laughed. "What did you have in mind?"

"Hm?"

"What did you want to do? Get dinner or . . . ?"

"Oh! Dinner, yeah. I heard, um, I heard that place down in town is nice. Yi was talking about it. Brewster's? They do sandwiches and stuff?" This wasn't so hard.

"Brewster's it is," she said brightly. "How's seven?"

"Seven is perfect."

"Great then! Seven o'clock sharp. I'll see you downstairs at seven." Abby shook her head and laughed. "Jeez, could I say *seven* a few more times?"

"Probably."

After that, Abby said something vague about wanting to go to the sports center, and Dan said he needed to get in some study time, so they parted ways in the quad, smiling and waving like idiots. He watched her walk down the path until she was lost among the crowd of students hanging around outside.

Then he walked slowly back to the dorm. His sneakers crunched on pinecones as he ambled on and off the paths, and on one of the nearby lawns he saw a group gathered around a grill—it looked like a barbecue that a couple of hall monitors were getting started early for dinner. He could smell the smoke as it drifted up into the air and disappeared in the light breeze. He could hear the popping of the fire. He was feeling just fine.

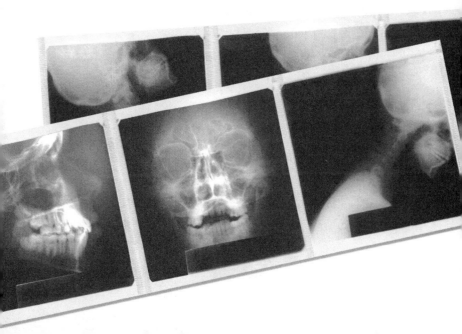

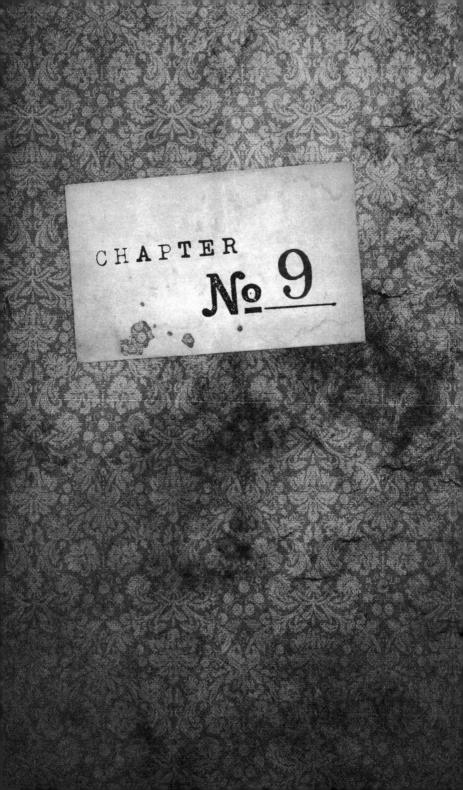

CHAPTER
№ 9

*T*he fact that tonight was a maybe date created more dilemmas for Dan. Like, did he shave? Would that communicate a level of formality that would say too much? Should he keep it informal, so it didn't seem like he was making assumptions? He really hoped it was a date, though. He thought about Abby's eyes: big, consuming, like there was a whole world in there he'd only just glimpsed.

"Idiot," he said. He'd been so lost in his thoughts, he was now probably running late. He threw on a light blue shirt that felt casual but not sloppy. He tucked and untucked it, and even attempted a half-tucked slouchy thing that only catalog models ever seemed to do right. He decided jeans instead of slacks, and definitely no tie—way too formal.

He looked at his clock.

Time seemed to function strangely here. What had felt like hours of wardrobe deliberation turned out to be no more than twenty minutes. He actually had time to kill. Dan sat down at his desk and cracked open his laptop to check his email. There was a long one from his parents that basically just said they hoped he was having a great time with his new friends. Some junk mail. A video from Jordan of a cat running full tilt into a tiny shoe box, and a link to a new band he thought Dan should check out.

For a second, Dan wondered what Jordan would think about this dinner with Abby. Had Abby told him? Dan didn't look forward to Jordan's inevitable jokes once he found out.

Then, an unread message in his Sent folder caught Dan's attention. That was . . . odd. How could you even *have* an unread message in your Sent folder? By virtue of composing and sending the message, didn't that mean he had himself read it?

Dan clicked on the folder, catching a subject line that read "RE: Your inquiry regarding patient 361"—but then his in-box minimized and an error message popped up midscreen. The cursor changed to the spinny wheel of sadness.

"What? Hey!" Dan smacked the side of the laptop. "Yes!" he shouted. "Yes, I would like to restart the browser, you piece of—and thank you *ever* so much for choosing this exact second to crash!"

Finally, the internet closed and reopened a second later, but his Sent folder was minus one mysteriously unread message.

Dan felt his pulse begin to race. *I'm sitting in an old mental hospital, hallucinating emails about patients. Yeah. No biggie. Ready for that date, slugger?*

"I have to get out of here," he said to the room.

Dan shoved up his sleeves and grabbed his keys and wallet. He turned off all the lights except his desk lamp. He never wanted to come back to a pitch-black room again, afraid he might find— well, whatever trick his imagination had played on him that first night. He went out the door, locking it behind him.

Dan hustled down the hall and around the corner, taking the steps to the lower level in long strides. That weird feeling of being watched was always worse in the halls. He chalked it up to the small windows letting in such anemic slats of light. But he couldn't go five steps in here without the hairs on the back of his neck standing up. Maybe it was knowing those photographs were downstairs, just sitting there in that office of horrors. He always seemed to forget about them when he was outside, away from Brookline, but when he was here, they crept back into his mind.

He reached the entrance hall, and there she was, Abby, wearing a low-cut top with spaghetti straps and a skirt. What a departure from her usual slouchy shirts and grandma vests. Shit, he was being such a guy, and she was going to notice and call the whole thing off. . . .

"You okay?" she asked as they started down the path to Camford, the little town that lay a mile away from campus. It was still relatively light out, summer prolonging the balmy twilight warmth. "You look kind of pale."

Pale? Damn. Was it from that phantom email in his Sent folder, or from that shirt of hers? Hard to say. What he did know was that she looked great, and Paul had taught him that this was the sort of thing a guy ought to say to a girl.

"No, I'm fine," he said. "You look neat." Abby glanced up at him, an uncertain smile on her face. Somewhere, his father was having a seizure. "I mean good. You look good. Amazing. You look amazing."

That stupid ghost email had rattled him harder than he thought.

He fidgeted with a button on his sleeve. A thin vapor of fog clung to the ground. Dan had heard Professor Reyes refer to it as "the Brookline soup," this fog that showed up without fail at dusk. Allegedly, it could get almost opaque in the autumn months.

The walk down to Brewster's was uneventful. Not boring, just . . . easy. He liked that about Abby—nothing was overly dramatic or even really mysterious. Game playing, lying, rules—none of that seemed to apply with her. She said what was on her mind—at the moment, an obsession with glow-in-the-dark cats they were engineering in Japan (she wanted one for the cute factor, but more so for the geek factor)—and then said even more about what was on her mind.

"I'm rambling," she said.

"No," he answered. "You make it interesting." He hoped that didn't sound too pathetic. But she just gave him a smile and his heart lifted.

While they waited at the restaurant counter to order, Dan breathed in the intoxicating mix of scents—coffee grounds, pesto, and the flowery loveliness coming from Abby. She must have put on some perfume. She leaned into the counter, rocking from her heels up to her tiptoes as she tried to decide what to eat. Some guy only a year or two older than them took Dan's order, scribbling all of it down without looking once at the paper because he was staring at Abby. If Dan's sandwich came out anywhere near correct, he would be shocked.

They grabbed a corner booth and settled in with their drinks.

Abby sipped her Diet Coke and stared out into the street. The lamps had just come on, making the damp sidewalks glisten. Interestingly, the town proper seemed to be immune to the fog that plagued the campus.

Say something, Crawford. Anything.

"Do you know much about computers?" Dan blurted out. He hadn't planned to talk about the email, but maybe he needed someone else to affirm that he wasn't overreacting, that it was normal to be a little freaked out by what had happened.

"A bit," Abby said as their sandwiches arrived, along with a double espresso for Abby (on the house) that the waiter had just accidentally (yeah, right) made for a mixed-up order (read: Abby). Dan's side of mustard, of course, was nowhere to be found. "What'd you want to know?"

"It's going to sound moronic," he said.

"I promise not to laugh at you," Abby replied. "Not much, anyway."

"How sweet of you." Dan ruffled the back of his hair, which he always did when he was choosing his words carefully. "Is it possible to like . . . I don't know, have someone's email show up randomly in your account?"

Abby blinked across the table at him. "Um . . . isn't that . . . the entire point of email?"

"Oh! No. Shit, see? This is why I shouldn't have brought it up." Dan shook his head. "What I mean is, could the signals get crossed or something? A message someone else sent wind up looking like *you* sent it?"

He was botching this spectacularly.

Abby dabbed at her lips with a paper napkin and tilted her head to the side, considering. One loop of hair came free from her headband, brushing her cheek. Dan fought the urge to tuck it behind her ear. "I don't think so," she replied finally. "Not unless someone hacked your account or stole your password. Why? Do you think a ghost is using your email without permission?" She lifted her fingertips and danced them across the air, making an exaggerated *booOOOOoooo* noise.

"Uh-oh, Dan, haunted dormitory, spooky, scary . . ."

Dan smacked her hand lightly. But she did have a point. He sounded ridiculous. "Never mind. It's nothing."

"No, no. What was the message?" Abby picked up her sandwich again. A sliver of tomato escaped, plopping onto the plate. It looked unappetizingly like a bit of flesh.

"That's the thing, I only caught a glimpse of the subject line. Then my browser borked and when I opened up my Sent folder, nothing was there. It had just disappeared. It's like I imagined it."

"Disappeared?" But for a moment, she looked a little uneasy. At least she wasn't laughing at him anymore.

The waiter interrupted them, this time with an "accidental" cookie.

"Could you not?" snapped Dan, shooting the guy a black look. "We're trying to have a conversation here."

"Whatever, man. It's cool."

Abby covered her mouth to hide a smile and watched the guy slink back to the cash register. "Aww, he's just being nice." She poked the cookie around on its little plate.

"If you say so." Dan crossed his arms and leaned back in the booth. He didn't want to pursue the email conversation anymore; he knew he shouldn't have brought it up.

But Abby wasn't done. "We were talking about your ghostwriter," she said, encouragingly. "Was it a love note?"

"No." It came out a little hot, a little testy. "It was . . ."

It was burned in his mind: "RE: Your inquiry regarding patient 361."

"Go on, I'm ready this time. I won't tease. Scout's honor."

Dan went back and forth, trying to decide how much to reveal.

If he told her about the Sculptor, then she'd really stop laughing. But he was regretting having said so much already. "It was medical. About a doctor's report or something," he finally said. He pulled out his cell phone to look at his Sent folder, just in case the email had miraculously reappeared. It hadn't.

When he looked back at Abby, he saw that fleeting look of fear on her face again.

"Dan . . ." Her lower lip quavered, something he would've found insanely hot under any other circumstances. "What if . . . what if . . ." Abby lowered her voice to a whisper, her eyes wide. He felt his pulse speed up. Did she sense it, too? That this really was no accident, no hallucination, but part of something much more sinister?

"What if . . ." He almost couldn't hear her, as a tremor of fear worked its way into her voice. She was leaning in closer and Dan felt himself doing it too, unconsciously drawn toward her. Abby's voice came out in one rush.

"What if you're in a Scooby-Doo *mystery?"*

"Oh, screw you." Dan rolled his eyes, leaning back hard against the cushioned booth. He should have followed his first instinct—not to talk about it at all. He was actually really hurt by Abby's reaction, especially after she had promised not to tease him, but he didn't want to show it. So he joined her laughter and asked about her studio classes.

And as talk turned from classes to favorite movies to what life was like as a teenager in New York, Dan felt less and less concerned about the email and the visions and the photos in the basement. This is why he'd come to NHCP. This moment, right here.

Then his phone vibrated on the table. He'd forgotten he'd even left it there. He picked it up, meaning to turn it off, but noticed that it was buzzing with an unread email in his in-box. A nervous tingle shot up his back. He pressed his thumb over the new mail icon. The white background flashed up at him, and a subject line reading "RE: Patient 361—question about Thursday's session" popped up for a second before it was suddenly replaced by the buzzing of a text message.

Dan jumped in his seat, nearly dropping his cell.

But it was just a text from Felix.

Hello, Dan. Hope evening with Abby is going well. I have plans in town and will be out late if you wish to use our room. Should return around ten.

Damn his timing. When Dan went back to his in-box, the email had vanished, just like the other one. Even before he checked the Trash folder, he knew it wouldn't be there. He was right.

"Hello? Dan? Earth to Daniel?" Abby waved her hand in front of his face. "Is it from Jordan?"

"Hey, hi, yes, sorry." He put the phone away. "I mean no, not Jordan. Just Felix." Dan tried to shrug it off, but it felt like his skin was on too tight. Any second now he would sweat through his shirt. But he couldn't tell Abby. She looked so happy; this sort-of-date was actually going well. He didn't want to spoil the mood. More to the point, he didn't want her to laugh at him again.

"So," he said, drumming up a smile. "Care to share that ill-gotten cookie of yours?"

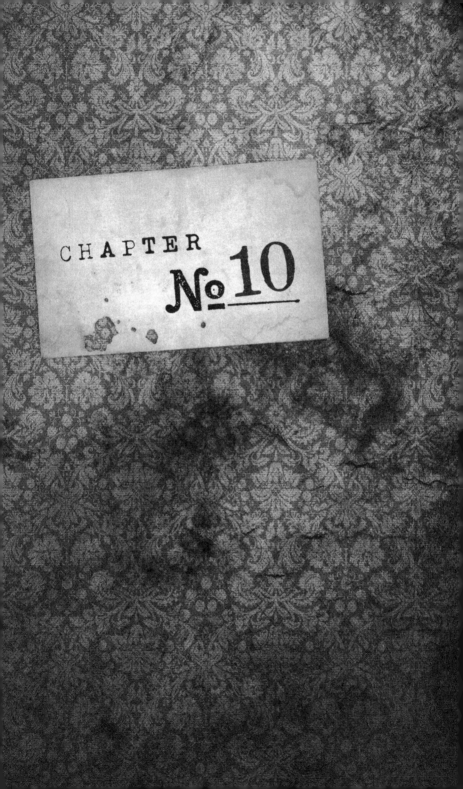

CHAPTER
№ 10

*A*ll in all, with Abby sipping that take-away espresso at his side and the stars just beginning to twinkle overhead, Dan was feeling pretty damn all right. They meandered back to campus at a leisurely pace while Abby told him the latest news from home—her parents had patched things up for now, her dad agreeing to work on a more creative personal project, even going so far as to ask Abby to design artwork for an online fund-raiser to cover the recording costs.

"That's good news," he said, walking her up the path leading to Brookline. He was beginning to wonder if he should kiss her goodnight.

No, no, slow, remember?. . . Mess this up and you lose her as a friend, too.

Of course, if she offered, then all bets were off. They ambled through the entrance hall and over to the main staircase.

"You should link me to that fund-raiser when it goes up. I'd love to contribute."

"Yeah, right." Abby nudged him with her hip. "You don't even know what his stuff sounds like."

"So? I'd love to buy something you did. And it obviously means a lot to you." She stopped at the landing to her floor and turned to look him full in the face. That meant tipping her head back a little to adjust for their height difference. "That's really . . . really . . . Thank you, Dan."

"No problem."

They turned the corner and found the hallway empty except for Jordan. Abby whispered, "Oh, *crap*."

"What?" Dan looked back and forth between them.

"I usually meet Jordan after dinner to study. It totally slipped my mind." Abby squeezed her coffee cup so tightly the Styrofoam creaked. "He's going to be pissed."

Dan knew the two of them hung out plenty but he had no idea the study sessions were some kind of hard-and-fast ritual. They slowed down as they approached Jordan looming outside Abby's door.

"Oh, hello. Do you live here?" he asked.

"Jordan, I'm so sorry." Spreading her arms wide, Abby went in for a hug that Jordan nimbly sidestepped.

"No, no, I'm fine. Really. Just break plans without letting me know, it's cool." He had a disposable cup like Abby's in his right hand. As he sipped from it, she wrinkled her nose.

"Jordan, is there liquor in that?"

"No."

"*Jordan.*"

"Fine! Yes!" He pushed it under her nose. "You're driving me to drink."

Abby reached for the cup, but Jordan backed up across the hall. He tilted it back and drank the rest of what was inside.

Abby's eyes flashed. "I said I was sorry, Jordan. What else do you want me to say?" Dan took her coffee cup while she got her keys and unlocked the door. She gave him a relieved smile. Dan was just happy to be an ally.

"Anyway, why didn't you just call instead of lurking outside my room?" Abby said.

Jordan shrugged, suddenly engrossed in picking at his fingernails. "Don't know."

"I think you do, so spill it," she said, opening the door. Dan expected Jordan to follow Abby inside and start in on them both, but instead Jordan hesitated, eyeing the door suspiciously, as if he thought Abby was waiting for the right moment to slam it in his face.

"What are you, a vampire?" she asked. "Do I need to *invite* you across the threshold?"

"Just wasn't sure I was welcome."

"Don't be ridiculous, Jordan. Get in here, both of you."

Dan stepped in, admiring how cool her room was, with lots of her own art decorating the walls. Most of it was colorful, exciting, and vivid, so he wasn't prepared for the one picture that stood out like a dead rose in a bouquet. The hollow-eyed girl. Taped on the wall above the bed, it was drawn exactly like the photograph. Dan stared at the empty eyes and the scar on the little girl's forehead, wondering why Abby would ever want something that creepy watching over her while she slept. It was hard to look at—and hard to look away.

"Sorry it's a bit of a mess," Abby was saying, seeming not to notice what was really bothering him. She swept some clothes off her bed and motioned for Dan and Jordan to sit down. Pulling out her desk chair, she scooted it along the floor until she was right next to them.

"Now spill, Jordan. What's going on with you?"

Jordan looked only at Abby. "This just . . . being left . . .

Well, it hit a nerve," he said slowly. "I had this friend back home. Blake." Jordan stumbled over the name as if just saying it had made him choke. "We pretty much did everything together, until a few months ago when I finally came out to him. Although come on, how could anyone be around me for five minutes and not know?" he added bitterly. "Anyway, he made himself scarce. Not like a blowup fight or anything. He just . . . disappeared. One day we're fine, buddies, whatever, and the next he's not returning my texts, he's ignoring me at school. . . . He'd pass me in the halls and just look *through* me, like I didn't exist . . . like I was some kind of ghost."

A long silence followed Jordan's confession. Abby glanced at Dan.

"That's not fair," she finally whispered. "We didn't *disappear*. We're not ignoring you. And I'm sorry, Jordan, we both are, but honestly . . . we were sort of on a date."

"You were?"

"We were?" He and Jordan spoke at the exact same time. Dan cleared his throat. "I mean, we were."

"Oh. Good for you . . ." Jordan chewed the inside of his cheek. It didn't sound like much of a congratulation.

"But next time we'll call," Abby said, hurriedly adding, "if we've made plans with you or anything. Okay?"

"Okay." He sounded like a little kid, one who had unexpectedly gotten his way but didn't want to stop pouting.

"Abby . . ." Dan couldn't hold back the question any longer. "Why did you do that drawing?" Abby followed his eyes to the picture of the little girl as if she didn't know immediately which one he meant.

"I don't know, why not?" she said. "She seemed so sad, I wanted her to feel like she was in a safe place. She was clearly lonely down there in the dark and dust. I thought I would just put her somewhere a bit brighter for a while." She looked at the drawing. "Wow . . . I guess I didn't think about how creepy it is." She paused. "Is it weird?"

"Yes." Jordan was the first to answer.

"Really? And you think so, too, Dan?"

Think very, very carefully about these next words. . . .

"I just . . . It doesn't freak you out at all? She's very . . . *unusual*, is all."

Behind Abby's back, Jordan gave him double thumbs-up, mouthing, "Nice job."

Abby paused. "It's like she's speaking to me. Like she needs me."

"No offense, Abby, but that sounds a little cracked," Jordan said.

"Probably," she replied, laughing softly. "I guess *I'm* a little cracked. But blah. We should do something, you know? Get out of here . . . Go somewhere! What do you think, Jordan? Let us make it up to you?" Abby's face brightened as she added, "What do you say we check out the creepy old office again?"

"I don't know. . . ." Jordan looked to Dan for help. "Last time got kind of . . . strange . . ." He trailed off.

Dan wanted to agree with Abby. He wanted to be on her side, and show her that she could count on him. But between this picture on her wall and the weird emails from earlier, re: patient 361, Dan felt like he'd had enough scares for one night. The more he thought about it, though, the more he felt like something from the office was tugging at him. And he had just gone on a first date with Abby—now was not the time to start telling her no.

"Why not check it out," Dan said cautiously. "There's probably nothing down there, but . . ."

"Exactly." Abby reached for Jordan's hand. "It's just a bunch of old pictures. There's nothing to be afraid of."

"It's not about that," Jordan snapped. "I'm trying to make it so we don't get kicked out. So *I* don't get kicked out! I'm not even supposed to be here. It would be a total shitstorm if my parents found out."

"Calm down, guys, I'm sure we can all agree on something else to do." Dan aimed for neutrality, hoping to lower the tension in the room. Besides, he could always explore on his own later.

"But it's two against one—Dan and I want to check it out, don't we, Dan?" Abby said.

"Yeah, but—"

"I mean, there could be a clue down there about those emails you got, your mysterious ghostwriter—"

"Your what?" Jordan perked up, turning to glare at Dan. "What emails?"

"Hey, I hadn't really decided whether I wanted to spread that information around just yet."

"Wuh-hoh, lovers' first spat? And over a 'ghostwriter'? What exactly did I miss?" Jordan sat back down on the bed and patted the space next to him. Dan and Abby both kept standing.

"Dan got a weird email, but when he went to read it, it was gone. Doctor stuff, patient report or something like that."

Dan bristled.

"Maybe it's a data ghost," Jordan said.

"What's a data ghost?" Dan asked.

"It's like a fragment of human consciousness that gets stuck in a piece of technology even after the person's dead . . . a bit of soul trying to reach out before it's gone for good. It can communicate, but only for a little while before it starts going haywire and degrading."

That sounded eerily on point to Dan. Maybe he wasn't crazy after all. . . . Although the idea of an *actual* ghostwriter wasn't exactly comforting. "Is this a real thing? How have I not heard of it before?"

"Oh, no, it's not real." Jordan laughed, dismissing the idea with a wave of his hand. "At least, I don't think so. I saw it on an episode of *Doctor Who*. But it sounds similar though, right?"

"It does," Abby agreed, "but I think Dan was looking for something a little less sci-fi. And if it's *real* he wants, then he'll probably find it down in the basement, don't you think?"

Jordan paced, fishing a die out of his pocket and passing it around between his palms. Abby reached out and intercepted it, hiding it in her fist. "You said it was doctor stuff, right Dan? Maybe something down there is reaching out from beyond the grave or, I don't know, sending psychic brain waves to freak you out."

There was a pause as they all considered this.

Finally, Jordan said, "Dan, if something *unexplainable* is going on, why would you want to go sticking your nose in it? I mean, not that I believe it, but shouldn't you just let sleeping dogs lie? What are you even hoping to find?"

Dan shrugged. From the break in Jordan's voice, Dan could tell that they'd won. Against his better judgment, Jordan would be joining them downstairs.

"I have a feeling I'll know it when I see it."

CHAPTER
№ 11

*I*t didn't take Jordan long to pick the lock this time.

"Once more into the breach?" said Dan, trying to make a joke. No one responded. *Idiot*.

It was as dusty and dark as Dan remembered. He shivered, with cold or excitement he wasn't sure. Probably a bit of both.

Despite having seen it only once before, they moved quickly through the reception area, retracing their previous path to the warden's office.

Dan held the door open until everyone had stepped through.

"So where do we start?" Jordan asked in a nervous whisper.

"I feel like there has to be more to the old wing," Dan said. "Which would mean there's another door around here somewhere."

He sincerely hoped there was more, anyway. It seemed a bit extreme that people in town would want to tear down the whole building over a dusty reception room and a messy office. But there was something else, too, a feeling that the asylum went deeper.

"Look for hidden doors, latches, anything," he said, squeezing between his friends. The beam from the flashlight he'd brought this time bounced along the floor and up the walls as he studied the filing cabinets and bookshelves. Abby drifted to the wall beside the desk and immediately found the picture of the little girl again. Jordan stood frozen as if he'd already seen enough. Dan ignored them and pressed ahead.

He moved from one bookcase to the next, shining his light over the cracks between each one. Dust covered everything, shimmering up into the air at even the lightest disturbance. Going clockwise, Dan eventually ended up at a cluster of filing cabinets that lined the wall behind the warden's desk. The third cabinet in the bunch looked strangely cocked, as if it had been pulled out from the wall and pushed back again, but not all the way. This was it, he knew it. As if to confirm his suspicion, a pair of rusted, broken spectacles hung from a hook on the other side of the cabinet. He reached out to touch them, then stopped. There were fingerprint streaks on the wall behind the glasses, like someone had hung them up with a bloody hand.

"Guys, I think I found something," he said, reaching around to the back of the cabinet and gripping the edge. He pulled, and the cabinet lurched half an inch forward, its metal feet screeching across the floor.

"What are you doing?" Jordan hissed. "Don't break anything."

"Let me help." Abby was at his side, gripping the front right edge of the cabinet and counting, "One, two, three."

They heaved, and the cabinet eased forward a foot, giving them a glimpse of an opening behind.

"No way," Abby breathed. "A secret passage? Is this for real? How did you know to look here?"

"The spectacles," Dan said, pointing to the hook and the glasses.

Abby looked at the streak marks, shuddered, and then seemed to collect herself.

"Just a little farther and I think we can squeeze through," she said matter-of-factly.

"Nope. No, thank you. I am *not* going in there." Jordan shuffled a few steps backward, holding his hands up as if in surrender.

"Suit yourself. I want to see where this leads." She motioned for Dan to help her out, and after one last moment of hesitation, Dan reached for the back of the cabinet and pulled. In two quick tugs, their way was clear.

"Use your flashlight, Dan. I can't see anything."

He went through first, his heart pounding in his ears.

"This must have been a real doorway once, but it looks like someone tried to brick it off," Dan said as he and Abby crouched and walked through to the next room.

"Then who opened it back up?"

Bits of loose brick and wall scattered from Dan's shoes. "Professor Reyes mentioned something about a senior seminar archiving this place. I'm guessing they needed to knock a hole in the wall to get access."

The ceiling and walls opened up, and with a quick sweep of the flashlight, Dan determined they were in a second, smaller office, this one with nothing but two tan filing cabinets and a downward stairwell to the right.

"What's in there?" Jordan called from the other side, making them both jump.

"Nothing much," Dan replied, nearing the cabinets. Little placards with A–D, E–I, and so on down the alphabet were affixed to each drawer. "Just patient records, I think. You can come through if you want."

Jordan appeared from the narrow passage, his eyes wide and spooked. He noticed the dark stairwell and recoiled. "Please tell me you are not thinking about going down there, Abs."

"We haven't even found anything yet," she replied, flashing her phone toward the stairs. "Feels cold. I bet it leads down to a whole lower level."

"Which is exactly why you shouldn't go. Have you seen even one horror movie? Jesus!"

"I just want to see where it goes," she said. "And the stairs don't look too bad." Gingerly, she put one foot on the top stair and transferred her weight to it. "See? Sturdy enough."

"I'll go with you," Dan offered.

"Great. Awesome. You two go into the abyss, then. I'll just be here not getting axe-murdered."

Together, Dan and Abby carefully took the stairs down, testing each step before putting their full weight on it. Dan wanted to think it was romantic, the way they were watching out for each other, but it was a stretch, even before you considered the cold and the moldy smell that grew stronger with every step. At last the stairs ended abruptly, winding around into a narrow corridor. Step by step they crept forward, the corridor pressing in on them, making Dan feel like he couldn't breathe. He wondered how claustrophobic it must have felt working down here—especially if you were trying to push a wheelchair or a gurney along this narrow hall.

Doors began appearing on their left and then their right, staggered every few yards or so. Abby drew up in front of one, flashing her light into the little slot of a window set in the door.

"God," she murmured. "There's still stuff laying around."

"What kind of stuff? Let's see." Dan opened the door and inched inside, frightened of what they might find. He shined his flashlight into the darkness.

Instantly, he felt sick. It was the room from his vision, right down to the operating table and the bloody shackles on the wall. How could he have seen a room he'd never been in? He felt shaky and weak, and leaned against the door while Abby toured around the room with her tiny cell phone light.

"What's that on the table?" she asked, pointing to the rusty stain on the white sheet.

"Blood," said Dan.

"How can you be so sure?"

I have no idea.

"It's so sad in here." Abby looked up at the single window in the room with the bars across it, as if anyone could actually climb through a slit that small and that high. As low as they were, the window must just barely be aboveground, if it led outside at all. "Did they really live like this?"

"This place would make anyone crazy," Dan said with a violent shudder. "Let's get out of here."

He'd meant the basement altogether, but when Abby turned to lead them farther down the hallway, Dan didn't stop her. At last, the narrow corridor opened up into a kind of small rotunda, with two closed doors at the far end of the curve.

Abby approached the left-hand door, shining her phone over it. "More offices?" she said.

"I don't know. . . . I thought the offices were all upstairs. . . ." Dan opened the left door—unlocked—and took a step into the room. It was a mess. The contents of six—no, seven—file cabinets lay strewn across the floor. There were folders, papers, and hand-written notes heaped in waist-deep piles. Like someone had been frantically looking for something and hadn't had time to clean up.

Dan picked his way through the mess, going to a door on the opposite side of the room and peering in. He couldn't help smiling as he shined his flashlight into the next office—jackpot.

"What is this place?" Abby asked. "Maybe it's storage? I mean there's stuff tossed everywhere. . . ."

"No, come look." Dan pushed through to the next room, Abby close on his heels. His light fell over a desk and, behind it, a high-backed chair. This room was as neat as the previous one was messy. In fact, it was so marvelously, eerily intact that a half-finished letter still lay on the desk, abandoned. A fountain pen had long ago bled its innards onto the paper. Dan leaned over the little visitor's chair to get a better look, but whatever had been written on the paper was now obscured by spilled ink. *Damn it.* He felt foolish for the depth of his disappointment. What had he expected to find? Something with a subject line like those ghost emails?

Also on the desk was a small leather-bound folder. Dan picked it up and was about to look through it when Abby said, "Check this out, Dan."

Dan slid the folder into his hoodie pocket and walked around the desk. There were a few photographs in freestanding frames lined up beside a green glass banker's lamp. Abby had one of them in her hands and now passed it to Dan.

A row of nurses in clean aprons and masks all stood neatly posed, with the warden in his spectacles and coat seated in front.

Every single one of them stared straight ahead except for the nurse at the far right; her head was cocked unnaturally to the side, as if her neck had been snapped just before the picture was taken.

Taking a step back, Dan imagined the infamous Brookline warden sitting at this desk, adjusting his spectacles and poring over research or composing a letter, maybe even *this* letter, the one stained with spilled black ink. A second, less rusty pair of spectacles sat on the desk near the photos. Without really being aware of it, Dan reached for them. They felt brittle to the touch and icy, but he held onto them, turning them over until the lenses caught the light and shone behind their layer of dust. *Try them on, Dan.* And so he did. They fit perfectly. He looked again at the photograph of the warden and the nurses, the photograph in which no one was smiling. The glass of the frame reflected his face back at him, overlaid on the photo. With a jolt he realized that he looked like the warden.

He tore off the glasses as though they had burned him.

Then something struck him. He'd seen this man—the warden—before. *Twice.*

"They sure look jazzed to be there," Abby commented. But Dan barely heard her.

"Hey! Guys! Guys? I found something up here!" It was Jordan, his voice echoing down from the floor above, reaching them faintly across the stretch of corridor. Dan set the photo back where Abby had found it, going so far as to reposition the frame in the marks it'd left in the dust. He felt that the last thing he should do was *disturb* a place like this.

They hurried back down the hall and up the stairs, more confident now that they had made the trip once. Jordan was in the

midst of searching through the alphabetized cabinets. With his cell phone tucked between his cheek and his shoulder, he was thumbing through the contents of the top drawer. It was full of yellowing index cards. "There are a ton of files in here," he said. "It must have every single one of the patients. And get this: every single one of them's criminally insane."

Both Dan and Abby craned over his shoulder to see what he meant.

Jordan pulled out one of the cards, and they leaned in to study it. It was for a patient named Bittle, Frank. It had his name, date of birth, and city of origin. There was a box marked "DOA 3.13.1964" that must have meant date of admission. Surely a psych ward wouldn't treat patients who were dead on arrival? Below that box was another that gave Dan a chill: Homicidal. There were small check boxes for Y and for N. On this particular card, the Y had been checked. Yes. Frank Bittle had been a murderer. Under the Recovered box was an N for No, he had not recovered.

Abby replaced the card and flipped through a few more. Every single one had a Y checked for Homicidal. Every single one had an N in the Recovered box.

"Look—this one burned down his own house with his family still inside," Abby said.

"They certainly didn't mention this in the admissions packet." Jordan reached for another of the cards, inspecting it closely. "This guy killed three wives before he was caught and sent here."

Dan's brain was racing. As Jordan and Abby pulled out more cards, he ducked under them and opened a middle drawer in the file cabinet. Maybe he could find a card on Dennis Heimline, a card that might say what had ultimately happened to him. He flipped through the cards quickly. Gabler, Gentile, Gold. *Ah, here was H.* Hall, Harte, Heimline . . . He reached out to pull it—

—and a hand gripped his shoulder.

"Got you!" a voice said.

CHAPTER № 12

$\mathcal{D}$an shouted in surprise. In the glare of a new flashlight, he couldn't see who had grabbed him. He thought his heart would burst.

"Hey! Chill out! Someone's going to get hurt down here."

It was Joe, the redheaded hall monitor from the orientation meeting. *Shit.* Dan felt a bead of sweat slip down his temple.

"A sign and a big lock on the door weren't enough? How did you get in here anyway? Come on out, it's not safe. There's water damage everywhere. Not to mention the rats."

Dan swallowed hard. "There wasn't— We didn't—"

"Didn't what? Think? Now come on, get out of here." Joe turned around, and in a flash, Dan pulled out the index card on Dennis Heimline and shoved it into his pocket.

"Shit," Jordan groaned. "I am so burned."

"I've got this," Abby whispered. "Just follow my lead, okay?"

How could she be so calm? Dan's hands were shaking, and he was full-on sweating. This was *not* him. He was not a troublemaker. He was a reader, a studier, and rule follower. Who was this person who broke into offices and stole things?

Joe waited for them all to get through the passage in the wall, shining his flashlight directly at their feet. When Dan stood up on the other side, Abby looked like she was rubbing her eyes furiously, getting dust all over her face.

"Is she okay?" Dan asked Jordan softly.

Jordan shrugged.

Joe motioned them all into the old reception area. As he corralled them back into the first floor hallway, Dan frantically tried to think of a way to pretend this was all part of his classwork for Professor Reyes. Every excuse sounded more implausible than the last. Joe paused at the door to redo the padlock and said, "Okay, this is what's going to happen. I'm going to . . ."

Suddenly, Abby burst into tears.

Jordan immediately put an arm around her, and she collapsed against his side.

"W-we're s-so sorry, Joe," she sobbed, wiping her tear-stained face. Her tears left actual streaks down her dusty face. "We d-didn't mean to b-break any rules. We w-were just so curious. . . . Please . . . I'm so s-sorry!"

It was, in Dan's honest opinion, too theatrical, and Joe seemed to pick up on that, too, rolling his eyes at her. But then Abby inhaled deeply and burst out with the rawest, most heartbreaking sob Dan had ever heard. Joe looked dismayed, and Dan could see his authority cracking before their eyes. Joe was thinking about what a monster he would be if he reported her.

"It'll be all right," Dan said softly, patting Abby's shoulder. "It's going to be okay. . . ."

"For the love of . . . Just don't do it again, all right? I mean it. Don't." Joe shined his flashlight into each of their faces in turn. Abby nodded furiously when the light was on her. "Now get back to your rooms. *Now.*"

He marched off, muttering under his breath.

"*Sweet* Enola Gay, *that was amazing,*" Jordan whispered when Joe was out of sight. Then he turned and pulled Abby into his arms, spinning her off her feet. "An Oscar moment if ever there was one!"

"Thanks," she said, using the back of her hand to wipe the last of the tears. Without another word, she set off for the stairs. "That was too close."

"Close? Closer than close. We got *caught*," Dan said, feeling as if he was resurfacing from the murky depths of a swamp. And to think, he'd been on a date with Abby just hours before. A nice *normal* date . . .

They reached Abby's door.

"Jeez, I need a shower," she said. She sounded like she wasn't even a little bit fazed.

But a shower did sound great. Dan itched from the dust and dirt that had settled over his skin, and the more he thought about it, the more it itched. He'd be clawing at his skin soon, but he wanted to talk to Abby one last time alone before he went back to his room. He looked at Jordan, trying to signal with his eyes that he wanted some privacy to say good-bye to Abby, dusty or otherwise.

"Okay, on that note," Jordan said breathlessly. "I need to go pray. A lot. I will pray to every freaking god there is in thanks that I did not just get my ass kicked out."

Jordan trotted off up the stairs, one hand in his pocket, the other pulling out his trusty die. Dan heard him whistle a little song as he went, the tune floating up and up before fading away.

When he was sure they were alone, Dan said, "I had a really great time tonight. Before the getting-busted thing, obviously."

"Yeah," Abby replied. Something was distracting her, though. Her eyes went to his shoulder, then to the floor, and then finally to his eyes. "I had fun, too."

"I'm sorry we got caught and that you had to cry. . . . But you were amazing, really. We would've been in huge trouble without you."

"It was nothing." She shrugged. Then she said abruptly, "I'll see you in the morning, Dan, okay?"

He nodded too fast, blowing whatever nonchalance he had hoped to project. "Yeah, of course. Sleep tight, Abby. Be a tree."

They both laughed nervously and looked at their feet. Whatever had been between them earlier this evening—if there had been something between them—was gone. Of course, all things considered, how could it not be?

"Well, good night."

Abby gave him a quick wave and went into her room. A dust bunny hung like a burr in her hair. He should've brushed it away.

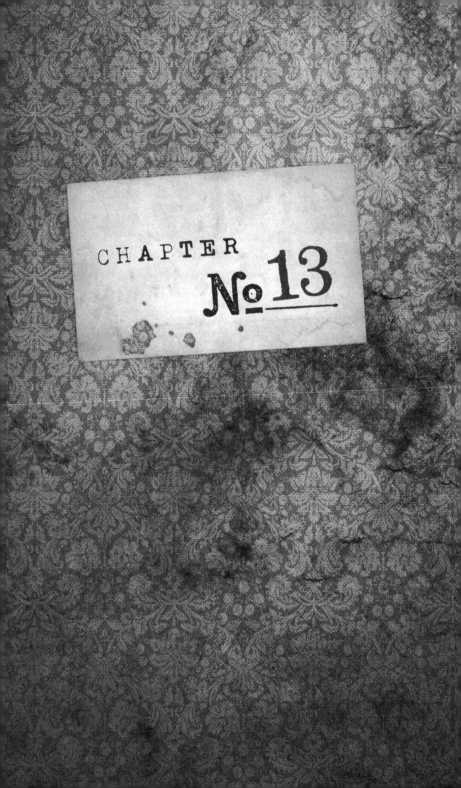

CHAPTER
№ 13

$\mathcal{D}$an was dead tired. As he started to climb the stairs, he couldn't believe it was only a little after ten. But his most pressing thought was not of sleep. With every step he felt his energy surge. He had a card on the Sculptor! And a leather folder to go through! The closer he got to his room, the more wired he felt.

Dan was relieved to find that Felix was still gone. He wanted to look at the stuff he'd taken in private. He pulled out the index card and the folder and put them on his desk. His fingers were repelled by them. The stench of the basement and his itch made him feel unclean. But he couldn't stop.

He took a look at the index card first.

Heimline, Dennis. Alias: the Sculptor
Born: 1935
DOA: 5.15.1965
Reason for Admittance: Serial Killer
Homicidal: Y
Recovered: Y

Y?

Dan was shocked by that last line. A serial killer—*recovered*? How? How would they even know? Then something else caught his eye—on the bottom right corner of the card. Three hand-written numbers. *361.*

Suddenly Dan was clawing at his shoulders, trying to stop the itch. The card sat on the desk, just as it was, but the 361 seemed to shimmer. *Get a grip, Dan.* He really had to calm down. Take a shower. But first he took the card and folder and hid them in the drawer. *With the warden.*

Dan stood in the shower for a long time. Jung had this way of talking about coincidences, one that Dan had always liked. Basically, he said that when people saw a meaningful connection between two moments—a coincidence—the connection wasn't because one moment led to the other, it was because people's brains were always making connections.

The Sculptor *was* patient 361. His discovery couldn't be a coincidence. It was a connection.

Dan fumbled with the towel and his clothes in his haste to get back to his room.

He grabbed the folder and flipped through the sheets of paper inside. Invoices . . . employee evaluations . . . Dan gave every-thing a passing glance, but he didn't stop on anything until he came to a slip of folded paper. The sheet was torn, as if it had been yanked out of a journal or notebook. Dense, cursive hand-writing filled the page.

He sat on his bed and began to read.

very nature of his ailment continues to baffle me, and baffle us all. What is the source of this abnormality? Everywhere we observe plants, animals, systems with a core. Every flower has its seed. Every animal its heart. Every masterpiece its inspiration. Yet the answers I seek elude me. There is a root somewhere in his very nature of his ailment continues to baffle me and baffle us all. What is the source of their aberration? Everywhere we observe plants, animals, systems with a core. Every flower has its seed. Every animal its heart. Every masterpiece its inspiration. Yet the answer I seek elude me. There is a root somewhere in his brain, a twisted root that sprouts madness and malice. I will find it. No matter the cost, no matter the difficulty, I will have it. I will live a truly great life. My colleagues will no doubt hang me, metaphorically, but I say let them hang. Legality, morality, sympathy aside, I will pull madness out by its black root, and I will leave a legacy no man, however sanctimonious, can fault.

A truly great life. That is what humanity deserves. Not an average life, not even a normal one — a life in which genius is not an anomaly but an expectation.

But to desire such things

brain, a twisted root that sprouts madness and malice. I will find it. No matter the cost, no matter the difficulty, I will find it. I will live a truly great life. My colleagues will no doubt hang me metaphorically, but I say let them hang. Legality, morality, sympathy aside, I will pull madness out by its black root, and I will leave a legacy no man, however sanctimonious, can fault.

A truly great life. That is what humanity deserves. Not an average life, not even a normal one—a life in which genius is not an anomaly but an expectation.

But to achieve such things

And there the page ended. Dan flipped it over, perfectly aware that it was blank on the other side, but wanting to know more, much more. Without context, without a signature, the piece of paper wasn't much to go by.

The writer of this page was clearly talking about curing someone who was insane. And he was talking about something unusual, some new treatment that he alone might discover. Dan's mind began to race. These weren't the musings of some random Brookline doctor—these had to be the ideas of its warden. And not just any warden, if he was to believe the conspiracy enthusiast Sal Weathers—*the* warden, the one who had changed Brookline's history and rehabilitated a serial killer.

Rereading the journal page, Dan admired the warden's grand vision. This man was willing to try something revolutionary to cure insanity. He dared to be different, to challenge the status quo. Even if he was rejected for it. Wasn't that a little of what Dan was like—scorning the popular opinion, the popular crowd, and aspiring to something more?

But this note wasn't just promoting intelligence, he thought. This was something a little more sinister. *Genius is an expectation.* Genius was nice and all but you couldn't *force* it on people, could you? Besides, what kind of treatment could do something like that? What could put a *Y* next to Recovered?

He leaned back on his pillow, trying to put the pieces together in his head. The horrible photograph of the patient struggling. This piece of paper by the warden about a mad man. The emails about patient 361. The Sculptor. It all seemed to be adding up. But to what?

Dan grabbed his laptop. When he went back to Sal Weathers' website and clicked "Contact Me," he was totally just looking for an email address. But good old Sal had listed his full details, and Dan was shocked to find an address that wasn't just in New Hampshire, it was in *Camford*.

"One of Professor Reyes's petitioners, I'll bet," Dan murmured. It now made sense that Sal Weathers would be so invested in cataloging and publishing Brookline's sordid history—he was probably hoping to get the place torn down.

Part of him wished Sal lived across the country, or in Cambodia, so that the temptation to visit him wouldn't be so strong. But all signs were pointing to a meeting with this man, and Dan wasn't about to ignore a message from the universe.

"So it's official," he whispered to the computer. "I'm obsessed."

He stood in a cell, waiting. Finally, a group of doctors came in, all wearing masks and gowns. Dan waited for them to hurt him, but they didn't seem to know that he was there. They stood around talking and jotting notes on their pads.

Then Dan heard screaming. Two orderlies came into the room, dragging a girl between them. She was barely ten years old, and her face was familiar—pale, frightened, with big open eyes.

"Okay, fellows, let's get to work on her."

At the sound of his own voice, Dan bolted awake. Even in his sleep he couldn't escape.

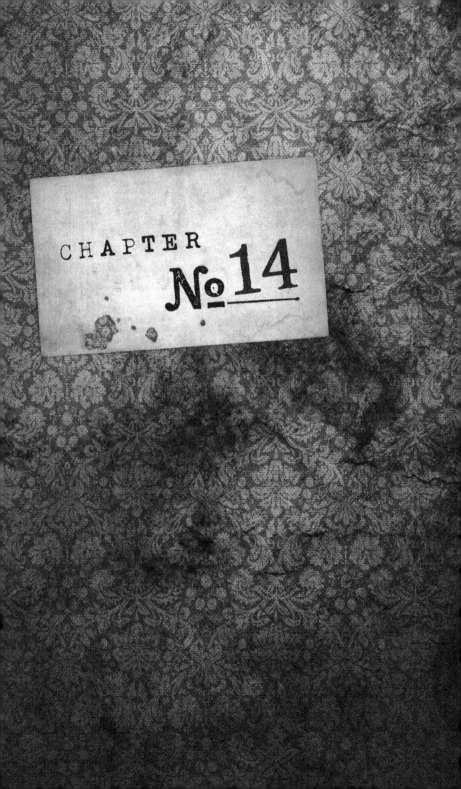

CHAPTER
№ 14

*U*sually Abby beat him to the dining hall, but despite the late night and broken sleep, Dan saw no sign of her or Jordan as he got in line for breakfast.

He heaped hash browns, eggs, and a few strips of bacon onto his plate and grabbed a bowl of cereal from the end of the buffet before heading to their usual spot, a circular table by the far windows. While he finished eating his eggs and bacon, he watched the other students filing in, but Abby and Jordan still didn't come. He started in on his cereal, taking his time with it.

As the minutes ticked by with no sign of his friends, he became increasingly aware of the fact that he was the only student eating alone. He was used to this at his high school but here he felt conspicuous, naked without his friends.

Finally, he spotted Jordan, who looked even worse than Dan felt, if that was possible.

"Hey," Jordan said, sitting down with a *whump*. Big, nasty bags rimmed his eyes behind his glasses.

"You all right? Looking a bit tired there . . ."

"I'm fine," Jordan snapped, sounding decidedly *un*fine.

Dan glanced at the doors again. Abby would know how to make this better.

"She'll show up when she shows up," Jordan said. "Can't you even wait a second to see her?" He bit into an English muffin as if it had personally insulted him.

What the hell?

"Are you okay, Jordan?" Dan risked, knowing Jordan might go for him again.

"I'm *fine*. Jesus, what is this, the Inquisition? Are you on my dad's payroll now?" The English muffin was dying a painful death in Jordan's tightening grip. A piece broke off and landed in his bowl of Cap'n Crunch. Jordan fished it out with his chewed-up fingernails.

They fell into an uneasy game of looking anywhere but at each other. Given his options—get chewed out again or stare at his cereal—Dan chose the cereal. Could Jordan still be angry about last night?

With five minutes until the dining hall closed, Abby finally made an appearance. She dashed to the fruit-and-granola line and grabbed a banana and a bowl of yogurt. Her usual sunny disposition was gone. Her eyes were half-lidded, and her pretty olive complexion was ashen.

She sat down with a quick "Hey," and started eating without another word.

"Hey," Jordan said. "Did you come down with something? You look terrible."

"What are you talking about?" Abby glared.

"Nothing, I was just saying you looked *radiant*. New makeup?"

"Yeah, because sarcasm is exactly what I need right now."

Dan tried to lighten the mood. "Well, sounds like someone woke up on the wrong side of the gurney." He immediately wished he had kept his mouth shut.

Abby looked at him, her eyes flashing in anger. She dropped her spoon in her bowl, splattering yogurt all over her tray. "Actually, Dan, there *was* something important I wanted to talk to you guys about. But I guess it will have to wait."

With that, she grabbed her tray and left the table.

"Congratulations," said Jordan. "That might be the briefest relationship in the history of the universe." Jordan finished his mangled muffin. "In fact, since you're not even technically a couple yet, it's sure to be one of those delightful death-by-silent-treatment endings. *Quel dommage.*"

"What the . . . ? What the hell did I do to piss you guys off?" But Jordan was already on his way out, and Dan ended up saying it to the back of his head.

Dan's mood worsened in class, when the professor showed a documentary he had already seen, which meant he sat for two hours in the dark, distracted, not a word of the film penetrating his brain while he replayed breakfast in his head. Maybe it wasn't fair to expect Abby to be sunshine and daisies all the time. Everyone was allowed a bad day here and there. She might have gotten another disheartening text from her sister. Whatever the cause, Dan decided it was foolish to read too much into it. Abby would tell him what was wrong in her own time, and he would be there to listen when she did. He wouldn't let a bad breakfast spoil things between them.

With that reasonable plan in mind, Dan felt his spirits lift on the walk back to Brookline. Neither Jordan nor Abby had said anything about lunch, so he figured he would try to fit in a bit of studying. Or, he thought, his nerves coming to jittery life, he could make good on his self-promise to visit Sal Weathers. He'd have more than enough time if he hurried.

Felix was in when Dan got back to his room. He was, as always, at his computer. It looked like he was browsing a body-building forum of all things, and Dan noticed that his roommate was sucking down something called Muscle Aid. Which, judging by the strapping, oiled dude on the bottle, was some kind of prepackaged protein shake. Not Felix's usual diet, but then again, Dan had known the kid for a grand total of a week. Still, he thought Felix looked more buff than he had when they first arrived. His shoulders seemed broader somehow. Maybe protein shakes worked after all.

"Hey," Dan said, going straight to his own desk.

"Hello, Dan." Finishing his drink, Felix crushed the plastic bottle in his hand and threw it over his shoulder, and Dan watched, amazed, as it landed squarely in the garbage can behind him.

"Nice throw," Dan said, trying to cover his surprise.

A crisp white envelope waited on Dan's keyboard. His heart beat a little faster. Was it from Abby? An apology, or maybe an invitation to go somewhere and talk?

"Did you see who brought this?" Dan asked, opening the envelope.

"No, it was here when I came in. I assumed you put it there before you went to breakfast."

"Shit. I must have forgotten to lock the door this morning," Dan said. It was a hard habit to get in to. Still, he could swear he'd locked things up that morning.

"That's troubling," Felix replied, not taking his eyes from his computer screen. "Please don't let that happen again."

"Sorry, man. I won't."

Inside the envelope, Dan found a simple card made of thick paper. On it was just a single line of spidery handwriting, a single question. . . .

Q: How do you kill a hydra?

That was . . . distressing. Dan flipped the card over.

A: You strike at its heart.

Q: How do you kill a hydra?

CHAPTER № 15

*W*hat kind of sick joke was this?

Dan looked at Felix, who hadn't turned around or moved a muscle.

"Are you sure you didn't see who left this?" Dan said.

"I'm sure. It's not signed?"

"No, it's not signed." Dan flashed the card at Felix, but not long enough for him to be able to read it.

"Hm. Strange. Do you recognize the handwriting?" Felix continued browsing his current web page, the wheel on his mouse clicking softly as he spun it.

"No, it's calligraphy or something. Nobody writes like this anymore. . . ."

"Calligraphers do."

"Do you know any calligraphers?" Dan snapped.

At last, Felix turned around. He thought for a few seconds and then said calmly, "Not at this program, no. I do have a friend back at school though who's pretty good at it."

"That doesn't help me." Sighing, Dan dropped into his chair and swiveled it around. "Sorry. Bad day."

"I understand, and I hope you find your mystery pen pal."

Sinking deeper into his chair, Dan flipped the card over and over again, studying the handwriting, trying to find some clue in the words. *Hydra*. There were at least fifty kids in Professor Douglas's class who would have heard the clever nickname he had given the three of them yesterday. Dan had no way of pinning down the identity of the writer.

What if Joe, the hall monitor who had caught them in the old wing, had placed the card on his desk? It actually made a weird kind of sense. Joe would want to keep them from snooping around again after hours, and the note was just creepy and threatening enough to make Dan think twice about a repeat of last night. Joe would also, as a hall monitor, have a master key to the rooms, which fit because Dan was *positive* he had locked the door that morning.

The knot in Dan's stomach loosened. Thinking of Joe as the author of the note made the whole thing feel explicable at the very least and perhaps even a little bit funny. *Ha ha, Joe, you got me good.*

But Dan wasn't entirely convinced. He decided he'd bring the card to dinner. If Jordan and Abby had received notes, too, they might be able to figure it out together.

Until then, Dan knew he definitely wouldn't be able to do any real studying. And if anything, the card only strengthened his determination to meet Sal Weathers. There wasn't enough time left in lunch break to make it to town and back, so he decided to skip his next class. He threw his sweatshirt on again, pulled up Sal's address on his phone, grabbed his backpack, and then sped out the door.

It felt good to get out of the dorm. Things had a way of feeling so heavy there.

The weather seemed to be on his wavelength, overcast and chilly despite the fact that it was June. It looked like it might rain. Dan walked briskly, keeping his head down and following the path that led from the dorms back to the academic side and beyond. The paved path dipped, taking a wide curve down a hill. For all the hustle and bustle on campus, Camford always felt rather small and quiet. Today the streets were practically empty; a lone pick-up truck sped by as Dan made it down to the bottom of the hill.

Three blocks, one donut shop, and a car garage later, Dan was at his destination. He snuggled down deeper into his sweatshirt, staring up the drive to a brick, dormered house set back from the road. Pausing, he glanced over his shoulder, his eyes scanning above the tree line. From here, he could just make out the top of the old church steeple, and beyond that, Wilfurd Commons and Brookline's roof.

He fished out a notebook and pen from his backpack, wondering how best to introduce himself.

A simple wicker cross hung in the window of the front door. Dan knocked, suddenly hoarse with nerves, already thinking it had been a mistake to come. Sure, Sal sounded talkative on his website, but would he be so effusive in person? Dan would have to express his own interest in a way that would get him the information he needed.

He knocked again, with more conviction. Finally, he heard a shuffling from inside.

A spotted, craggy face appeared in the window behind the cross, and a second later the door flew open. The scent of cinnamon candles rushed out to meet him. "What are you selling?"

"Selling? Oh! No, nothing . . . I'm from the college," Dan explained. He gestured clumsily over his shoulder to the hill. "I—I was going to email you, but . . . I'm sorry, I know this is sort of strange, but I found your web page. The one about

Brookline? I'm doing a project on it and you seemed like the local expert, so . . ."

Sal stared at him, clearly trying to decide if he was crazy or joking or both.

"Come in," he finally muttered, disappearing into a dark mudroom. A light came on, showing a shoe rack filled almost exclusively with work boots and lady's slippers. "So you found my little report on the internet, huh? Good. That's good. More people oughta know. But I gotta tell you, kid, I don't much like talking about it. None of us do. I said my piece with that page on the internet, and now the only time I want to talk about it is to get that hell of a place torn down. Course, some bitch up at the college won't stand for it, says it's *historical*!"

"I think you mean Professor Reyes," Dan said pointedly. "She's actually planning to run a seminar in the dorm, and then—"

"A *dorm*? So they're housing you kids in it now, are they? That's a real *laugh*." Sal shuffled into the kitchen and Dan followed. He had a feeling he would be leaving with a blank notebook. "This is my wife," Sal was saying. "Don't mind us, honey. This young man's from the college, but he's not staying very long."

The kitchen was cramped, furnished with cheap laminate cabinets and mauve tiles. Dan ducked his head shyly. "Hello." He greeted Sal's wife. She was gaunt, sunken, but Dan saw shadows of a pretty woman gone old and frail. Her thick hair was tied into a bun at her nape and a heavy fringe of bangs covered her forehead. She seemed to be staring at nothing, her hands propped lightly on the island countertop in the middle of the room.

Sal puttered around the island until he found a coffee mug. He checked its contents and then took a big sip. When he glanced back up and saw Dan still standing there, a look of resignation crossed his face. He shuffled over until he was almost right in Dan's face and said in a voice barely above a whisper, "All right, kid. You get one question. What did you want to know so bad?"

Dan hardly knew where to start. He tried to collect his thoughts into one single question.

Finally, hoping that this one question would lead to many answers, he said, "I just wanted to know more about Dennis Heimline." Instantly, he knew he'd said something wrong. Sal flinched, and behind him his wife stopped staring at whatever was so interesting over Dan's shoulder and looked right in his eyes. Dan blundered on. "I, um, well, I was curious about the connection between the last warden and Dennis Heimline, the Sculptor—"

"What did you say your name was?" Sal interrupted, slamming his mug down on the island.

"I d-didn't," Dan stammered, taking a step back. "It's Dan? Dan Crawford?"

It was like a bomb had gone off. Suddenly Sal's wife was screaming, throwing herself down on the island countertop, swinging her arms, and sending Sal's mug and a stack of dishes crashing to the floor. Dan leapt back only to have Sal descend on him, his craggy old face red with blotches. "What the hell kind of sick joke are you trying to pull? My wife is ill and you come in here like that, you damned college kids, always so smart, so clever, eh? Not so clever today—get out! *Get. Out!*"

Dan hardly bothered to turn, backing out as fast as he could without getting tangled up in the shoe rack and the door. The woman's shrieking followed him onto the stoop. Then Sal was at the door, still shouting, "Get the hell out!" as if Dan wasn't trying to do exactly that.

He ran. He ran until he reached the hill and the path winding back up to the college. What had just happened? What had he said? How could Dennis Heimline be such a sore subject when Sal himself had written about the guy?

When Dan reached his room, Felix was gone. A note on his dry erase board read simply, "Departed for gymnasium 1600." Dan rolled his eyes, thinking, *Just another Felix Quirk™*.

He shrugged off his backpack and flung himself down on his bed. Miserable, he rolled onto his back and shoved the pillow over his face. Class skipped and for what? He was no closer to figuring out the link between the warden, the Sculptor, Brookline, and himself than he had been at the start of the day. And now he had the horrified face of Sal's wife to add to the list of things haunting him. And her screams . . .

Dan groaned into the pillow. He had to let it go or he'd drive himself crazy over nothing. Sal was just a nutty old bat who hated the college and everything associated with Brookline. He probably grew up in Camford resenting the kids who could afford a higher education. Wasn't there even a label for that? The townies and the gownies? It wasn't his fault.

Outside, it had started raining. That would make getting to dinner a little less pleasant. But after the afternoon he'd just had, Dan was eager for friendly company, and it was already five minutes till five, so there'd soon be people in the dining hall. He snatched up the hydra note and headed downstairs. As he passed the hallway leading down to the old wing, he felt a sudden temptation to go there and hide, but he pressed on to the main

doors, shaking off the fear that was creeping down his back.

Dan pulled up the hood of his sweatshirt and ran through the downpour to the Commons. He shook himself off when he reached the entrance, then followed the line of students forming inside the cafeteria.

Mac and cheese night. Could be worse. Dan grabbed a tray, his eyes roaming over half-familiar faces as he looked for his friends. He saw Yi come in and wave to a few guys on the other side of the room before getting in line right behind him.

"How's it going?" Yi asked, drumming his fingers on his pastel-blue tray.

"You know, the usual. Studying. Classes." *Threatening notes, psychos.* "Yourself?"

"So amazing." Yi pulled a slip of paper out of his cargo pants and handed it to Dan. *Oh God, did Yi get a strange note, too?* But when he unfolded it, Dan saw it was only a printed-out dating profile for someone with the screen name Chloe_Chloe13. She liked skiing and *Amélie*.

"I'm studying abroad on a scholarship in the fall. Conservatory in Paris . . ." Dan handed the paper back and watched Yi smiling dreamily down at it. "Just a few more months and I'll be swimming in hot, foreign women."

Dan coughed.

"Yeeaaaah, I could have phrased that better." Yi put Chloe_Chloe13 back in his pocket. The line moved forward. "How's things on the Abby front?"

"Hm?" They sidled up to the buffet. Dan slopped macaroni onto his warm plate. "How did you . . . ?"

"Jordan mentioned a date or something. How'd it go?"

Surprisingly, Yi bypassed the mac and cheese and went for the vegan offering, something with lentils and unidentifiable chunks of vegetable matter.

"Things with Abby are good!" Dan managed to croak. Honestly, he didn't know what to think, considering how Abby had been this morning. "And I guess it was a date. We just got dinner at Brewster's, hung out. . . . It was a nice time." Dan dug the big metal ladle into the macaroni again, preparing to take another serving.

"Bullshit. You get any?"

Dan dropped the spoon, and it clattered against the edge of the buffet. He caught it, but not before splattering himself with globs of cheese product. "Crap, that's hot!" He half elbowed, half bumped the spoon back into the tray and tried to brush the neon-orange cheese off his forearm.

Yi chuckled, moving away from the line. "I'll take that as a no."

Swearing, Dan grabbed a dinner roll from the pile and then walked over to their usual table. He dropped into the chair nearest the window, brooding over his steaming plate of food. His time with Abby last night felt private—not something to be discussed casually over the dinner line. Or maybe it was just that he didn't know how things stood, and he didn't want to jinx them by bragging. He rubbed at the splotchy red marks on his skin. They were still smarting.

"Hey."

It was Abby. Her hair was in a damp tangle and her eyes were red. She set her tray on the table and sat down slowly, as if moving through water.

"Hey," Dan said, forgetting his burn.

"Can I sit? I mean, I *am* sitting already but . . ." She looked down into her soup, sighing. "Do you mind?"

"No, by all means," Dan said. "I was hoping you'd turn up."

"Yeah?" Smiling, Abby put her elbows onto the table. "Thanks. I was . . . I was pretty horrible at breakfast. But I have a good excuse, I promise. I wouldn't just . . . I wouldn't just *be* like that."

"It's okay if you were," he replied. "We all have rotten days." He nodded to the window behind them, where the rain fell in noisy sheets against the glass. "See? The weather's feeling like crap, too."

"No, I like the rain. It's relaxing. Refreshing." She gazed out the window. Puddles were forming in the low dips of the grass and along the pathways, and the mist was swirling so that the rain and fog couldn't be teased apart. "I needed a bit of rain."

Dan smiled. Already she was making him feel better. He decided he'd wait for Jordan to get there before mentioning the note, so he and Abby more or less ate in comfortable silence until Jordan stumbled into the dining hall. After a quick breeze through the food line, he sat down with just a cup of piping-hot coffee and a slice of Boston cream pie. He didn't even say hello. Rain and the steam from the coffee fogged his glasses.

But Dan couldn't wait any longer. "I got a note," he blurted, startling Abby and Jordan. He reached into his back pocket and took out the card, dropping it onto the table between them. Jordan picked it up. "'How do you kill a hydra?' What the hell?"

"Turn it over."

Jordan read the back, his face a mixture of confusion and distaste.

"What is this? Where did it come from?" Jordan pushed the card away with a grimace, and Abby grabbed it.

"It was on my desk when I got back from class. Felix didn't see who left it, but someone managed to get into the room even though I'm sure I locked the door. You guys didn't get anything like this?"

They both shook their heads. Dan was dismayed. He hadn't realized how much he was counting on this being a bad joke. Rubbing his temples, he said, "I think it could be from Joe. I don't know who else would leave something like this, or even be able to get into the room. But I was sure he'd have left them for you guys, too." Dan pushed his macaroni into a little hill. "I don't like feeling singled out."

"So what are you going to do?" Abby asked, giving the card back to him.

Dan shrugged. He knew it would be impossible to explain to anyone else why this bothered him so much. He wasn't even sure he fully understood it himself.

"Just ignore it," Jordan said. "Joe's trying to rile you up, that's all. That's what bullies do. Trust me, I know. It's better if you let it slide off your back."

They were silent for a moment. Then Abby said, "There's something else. Your note . . . It's important and all, but I wanted to tell you both something, too. It's what I was going to bring up at breakfast, before I got so . . . well, mad."

She paused. "I'm not quite sure how to say this," she said, twisting her hands around each other. "So I'll just go for simple. Simple is probably best, if anything about this *is* simple."

As she talked, Dan noticed that her entire demeanor changed. Her shoulders sagged, and the light went out of her eyes.

She took a deep breath. "My aunt. My father's sister. She was a patient here."

There was silence. Dan and Jordan looked at each other.

"Um . . . how do you know?" asked Dan.

"Here, look what I found last night." Abby pulled an index card out from her raincoat. It was from the card catalog in the warden's office and looked just like the one for Dennis Heimline. So Abby had taken something, too.

Hands shaking, Abby turned the card around so that both Jordan and Dan could read it. There were just four lines, typed.

Valdez, Lucy Abigail.
Born: 7.15.1960
DOA: 2.12.1968
Recovered: N

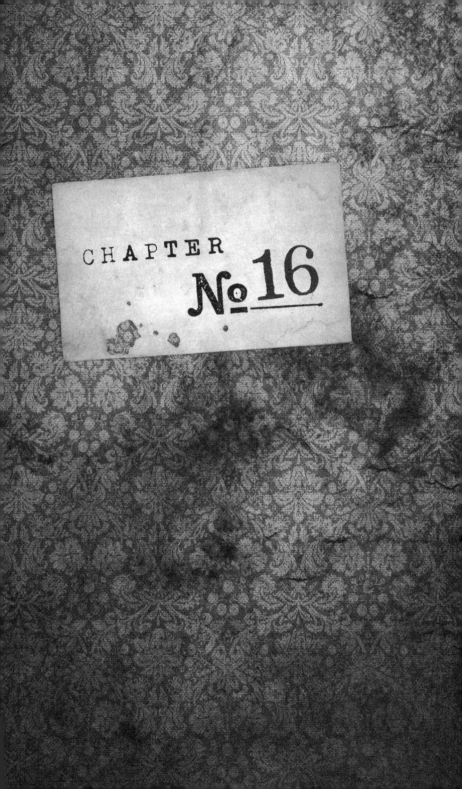

CHAPTER №16

*F*or a moment Dan didn't understand. The words didn't make any sense. Then they slowly came into focus.

Lucy. Abigail. Valdez.

Abby Valdez.

"It's a common-enough last name," Dan said at last, stammering a little. "Right?" He looked up into Abby's wide eyes. *"Right?"*

She shook her head, pressing her lips tightly together. "That's my aunt. Aunt Lucy. I was named after her."

"Come on, Abby," Jordan said. "That's not your aunt, that's just not possible."

Dan sat back, silent, waiting for a reasonable explanation. If one existed.

"I'm afraid it *is* possible." A gust of wind hit the windows, rattling the glass. The rain slapped down on the glass like a shower of pebbles. Abby looked out the window and then back again. She was clearly trying to keep from crying. "My grandparents were really strict on my pops when he was growing up. His sister Lucy never got along with them, from the time she was a little girl. She never listened, she'd talk back, scream, break things, stuff like that. One day there was a huge fight. My pops doesn't know what it was about, he was only five, but he remembers that

Lucy ran out the door and slammed it behind her. That night, he woke up from a nightmare and Lucy wasn't in her bed. Seven years old, and she was gone. Just . . . *gone*. My grandparents acted like everything was normal, and when my pops would ask, they'd get really angry and tell him he wasn't allowed to say her name any more."

Dan was at a loss. The story lined up, but what were the odds? "Maybe it's just a coincidence, the name," he said, not really believing that himself. He just wanted so badly for it to be true.

"A coincidence is you and me both picking pie for dessert," Jordan said. He gestured to the patient card with his cup. "What *Abby* is suggesting is flat-out strange."

"What, you don't believe me?" Abby said. Her voice sounded like she was kidding at first, waiting for Jordan to contradict her. But he didn't. "That's it, isn't it? You don't believe me."

"Can you really blame me? I mean, what are the chances you just randomly wind up here for the summer, at the place where your aunt used to be a *mental* patient?" Jordan sat back, arms crossed. "I think there's something you're not telling us. Or you're just not telling us the truth."

Dan could see Abby's shoulders beginning to shake as she tried and failed to control her breathing. It was too late to intervene, and he couldn't think of a damn thing to contribute anyway. Jordan had a point about how impossible the coincidence was, but Abby wasn't the sort to mess with them for kicks. *Or was she?* a little voice whispered in his mind. How well did he really know her, after all? Her mood in the last twenty-four hours had certainly been unpredictable. He stopped himself. She wouldn't make a joke out of something like this. She just wouldn't.

"Fine," Abby finally said, composing herself. "I wasn't going to say anything, but I guess we're a little past this now."

Dan shared a nervous glance with Jordan.

Abby picked up her spoon and dragged it softly across her bowl as she began to speak. "When I was little, I used to go through my mom's clothes looking for hats and skirts and scarves and stuff to play dress up. She and my pops shared dressers, and one time I found this . . . this box." She inhaled deeply, then pressed on. "I didn't know what it was, but when I opened it and saw a bunch of papers, I—I started reading them. They were all letters. From my grandpapa. He was already dead by then, and my pops never talked about him, except to say what a mean man he'd been. . . . But these letters . . . Grandpapa just kept apologizing. He kept saying he was sorry for sending his little Lucy away. Away to *that place*."

"And let me guess, that place was Brookline," Jordan said coldly. He obviously still wasn't convinced.

"It had to be," Abby replied quickly. "There was stuff about how she was dangerous, and how he had sent her away for her own good. And there was more. . . . Grandpapa kept talking about 'making a trip to New Hampshire.' He never mentioned Brookline by name, but . . ."

"But I can see how you would put two and two together," Dan finished, trying to show at least a little support.

She nodded. "It all adds up. I mean, listen, I didn't think it was possible, either. Part of me always assumed I was imagining it, or had completely read them wrong. After that first time, my pops found out I'd read the letters and moved them all. But I never forgot. And when I got the letter about this program, well, I thought the fact that it was in New Hampshire was a sign."

"A sign of how *ridiculous* this story is," Jordan protested, sinking down lower in his seat. "I mean what, you just thought you'd come work on your art skills *and* find your long-lost aunt at the same time? Kill two birds with one stone?"

Abby looked horrified.

"Jordan . . ." Dan warned.

But Jordan barreled right on ahead, gesturing first to Dan and then to Abby. "Let me guess, you guys made this up together, thought you'd have a harmless laugh at my expense. Well, ha ha. Very funny. It's not working, okay? I am *not* that gullible."

"Jordan, why would I make something like this up? It's too sick. . . ."

Jordan shrugged. "Who knows? Attention? Fun? Take your pick."

"God, you're such an asshole sometimes!" She clenched her jaw and looked at Jordan as if she had never really seen him before.

"Let's all calm down and just think for a minute," Dan said, hating to see the anger between them. "First of all, Jordan, I have to ask—do you really think I wrote this note to myself? For attention?"

Jordan sighed. "I don't know anymore, man. You. Abby. I don't know what's going on. I feel like you're trying to make me look stupid. Like the two of you are ganging up on me."

"Okay, and Abby, do you think there's *any* chance this could be a different Lucy Valdez?" he asked.

"No," she replied firmly. "I know it's her, and I bet there's more evidence somewhere in the old wing about what they did to her."

Jordan snorted.

Suddenly Abby slammed her fist down on the table. Both boys jumped in their seats. Dan's plate rattled, his hill of macaroni crumbling.

"What would it take for you to *trust* me?"

Jordan didn't say anything.

"I trust you," Dan said in a placating murmur.

"Uh-huh, Peeta Mellark over here believes you. In other news, rain is wet," Jordan said. "Color me sur-freaking-prised." Taking his coffee and pie, he left without another word. The rain and the sounds of the dining hall rose up to fill the silence left by Jordan's angry departure.

"Are you all right?" Dan asked.

"Would you be?"

"No. No, I guess not."

"Then there's your answer." She took a spoonful of her minestrone. "Ugh. It's cold."

Dan scrambled for something helpful to say. All he could think about was how, if Abby could keep such a big secret so well, there might be any number of things she still hadn't shared. Not that he was any better. "You know what? About Jordan? I think he's still upset about the date thing. He's probably worrying that we can't be a duo and a trio at the same time, you know?"

"Hm? What? A duo?" Abby frowned, staring off into the middle distance. "Oh, right. Yeah, maybe. Maybe that's it."

Dan didn't want to take her response as personally as he did, given the fight she'd just had with Jordan, but she'd really turned cold there at the mention of the word *date*. Everything seemed to be slipping out of control. His new best friends were quickly withdrawing—from him and from each other. He had to find answers and hold the group together, or they'd be total strangers again. Then the hydra really *would* be dead.

"Don't worry, we'll figure this whole thing out," he said.

"I know *I* will," Abby said coolly. "I'm going back into that office. One way or another."

CHAPTER
№ 17

The next morning it was time to pick a new set of classes, which meant that Dan had already been at the program for a full week and counting. In some ways, he couldn't believe that it had been that long, but by and large, he felt like it had been much, much longer.

Dan planned to wait for Abby and Jordan at the admin building to see if there were any classes they wanted to take together, but when he got there, he saw that Abby was already moving from table to table in the art department area. She gave him a quick wave and then kept on going. Dan felt a pang of rejection, but pushed it down.

"So I might have been out of line last night."

It was Jordan. He grabbed Dan and pulled him over to the Theoretical Mathematics table.

"*Might* have been?" Dan asked.

"Yeah, yeah, I know you're on her side," Jordan began, "but I swear I'm looking out for both of us. Between you and me, I've seen girls like Abby go through this kind of identity meltdown thing before. This whole story about her 'aunt' will blow over, you'll see."

"That doesn't exactly sound like an apology," said Dan. Anyway, what did Jordan even mean, "girls like Abby"?

"Fair enough." Jordan inched forward toward the professor's table, where the sign-up sheet waited. "Listen, Abby's great, I love her and everything, and shame on me if this thing with her aunt is for real. I just can't get wrapped up in a bunch of drama right now. I'm here for math, not la la crazy ghost hunting. I could've handled it better, though, that's for sure. Anyway, what I'm trying to say is I'm sorry I was a jerk last night. And about the hydra thing: it's probably like you said, just Joe being an asshole."

"No harm done," Dan replied with a shrug.

"You sure?"

"I'm sure."

"All right, then." They'd made their way to the front of the line, and Jordan signed his name on the clipboard in the tiny scrawl of a true mathematician.

"I'm going to head over and sign up for Twentieth-Century German Lit," Dan said.

Jordan stuck his finger in his mouth and made a noise like he was choking, then smiled and went off in the opposite direction.

It wasn't until the end of the morning, after waiting in one course line after another, that Dan acknowledged the sad truth: the three of them hadn't chosen a single class together. Dan waded among all the students hanging around outside, and he finally found Abby finishing up a conversation with some people he didn't know. He waited off to the side until she noticed him, and then with a wave to her other friends, she came up and immediately started talking about all the new classes she was excited to take. Advanced Portraiture, Impressionism, Graphic Novel Illustration. Jordan eventually found them, and his list of classes proved similarly alienating—Multivariable Calculus, Real and Complex Analysis. . . . Dan could solve for zero, but this went far beyond a fundamental grasp of numbers. He gazed down at his own schedule—history, literature, more history. . . . None of it matched up.

As they were talking, Dan noticed that as friendly as their conversation might sound to an outside listener, Abby never once actually looked at Jordan, and Jordan kept directing his jokes at Dan. It was hard to deny now: in the space of a few days—a few *hours*, really—their whole easygoing dynamic had changed. Is this what it always felt like, getting close to people?

✗ ✗ ✗ ✗ ✗ ✗

The new class schedule meant a new routine, so Dan went from building to building, map in pocket, relearning his daily pattern. He hardly saw Jordan or Abby. They didn't even share a common lunch hour anymore. True, they still met for dinner every night, but the conversation was now full of inside jokes from their different classes and stories for which the other two "just had to be there." Jordan had said he'd apologized to Abby, and the fact that they could still sit at the same table seemed evidence of that. But she seemed distant, and pointedly avoided any mention of her aunt. Dan wondered if she still planned to go back to the warden's office. He personally had no desire to ever go there again.

On Friday night, Dan arrived in the dining hall to find Jordan waiting at their usual spot. Three legal pads sat on the table next to his food tray, each one covered in his messy scribbling.

As Dan moved closer, he saw the scribbles were numbers and equations—the kind of equations that had enough letters to look like sentences. Jordan didn't seem to notice Dan's approach but stayed bent over one of the pads, his hand moving at lightning speed across the page.

"Homework?" Dan asked, taking the seat across from Jordan. He couldn't remember ever seeing Jordan working outside of class, let alone on a Friday night.

"You could say that." Jordan scratched his right temple with the dry end of a pen. "One of my teachers mentioned this problem that's supposed to be unsolvable. But the thing is, there isn't a proof yet that *shows* it's unsolvable. So I'm working on either the proof or the solution, whichever comes first. Call it a pet project."

"Or OCD." Dan meant it as a joke, but Jordan's head flew up, his unruly mop of hair springing out in all directions.

"Excuse me?"

"Nothing," Dan said quickly.

Jordan bent over his paper again.

Then, with dinner in full swing and Jordan favoring numbers over Dan's company, Abby arrived. She hit the salad bar and grabbed a glass of orange juice, but instead of joining them, she took a detour to a nearby table where the art kids congregated. Dan thought of them as the art kids because they chain-smoked, dressed like Broadway extras, and wore ironic grandma glasses even though maybe only one in five of them actually had bad eyesight.

Jordan had apparently noticed, too, despite being nose deep in math. "They think they're it," he said.

"I didn't know she hung out with them." Dan cringed. He sounded and felt so stupidly high school. Us versus Them. Outcasts versus In Crowd.

"Hi," Abby said when at last she came over. She sat down, placing a sketchbook on the seat next to her. "I was just showing Ash and Patches some of my new work."

"Patches?" Jordan said, looking up.

"Yes. Patches. Is there a problem with that?"

Mayday, Mayday.

"Nope." Jordan snorted, low enough to sound like a cough. He brought his attention back to the legal pads. "No problem at all."

Abby shifted in her chair, sitting with one leg crooked under her. Despite her expectant face and the paper flowers woven into her braid, she was troubled. His heart sank when she said, "So I was thinking tonight might finally be the night. What do you say? Feeling up to sneaking around?"

"I don't know. It's been a pretty long week." He wished they'd never gone into the old wing. It was changing them all somehow. It was changing *Abby.* Dan pressed on. "I was hoping we could just watch a movie or something. Something light. Besides, if we get caught again—"

"We won't get caught," she said flatly, ignoring the rest of what he'd said. She dug into her salad, eating so fast Dan couldn't imagine she had time to taste it. "So what do you say, meet me at the bottom of the stairs at eleven?" She stopped assaulting her food to look at him, her gaze unwavering.

"Um . . . I'm not sure . . ." Dan replied, not knowing what to say.

"Jesus, Abs, give the guy a break. He obviously doesn't want to go." Jordan flicked his eyes from Dan to Abby, a smirk on his face.

"Thank you *so much* for joining the conversation, Jordan. I *was* going to ask if you wanted to tag along, but I'm sure crunching numbers is more fun." Abby stabbed a cherry tomato with her fork. The fork scraped hard against the bowl, sending a nails-on-chalkboard shiver down Dan's spine.

"Yeah, it probably is. Maybe you can get your superawesome art buddies to go instead," Jordan shot back.

"Maybe I *will*. At least they won't go all *A Beautiful Mind* on us."

"You wouldn't even *begin* to know what is happening in my mind," Jordan said. "Thanks to your stupid office I've been having these dreams. *Nightmares.* Like something got inside of me when we were down there and it's been trying to claw its way out. But what would you care? You're too busy thinking about yourself to worry about anyone else."

Abby opened her mouth and shut it again.

It was up to Dan to say the right thing. "What sort of nightmares?" he asked gently.

"I don't want to talk about it." Jordan pushed a hand through his tangled hair, smearing ink across his forehead. The poor guy had never looked so unhappy. He took off his glasses and wiped them on his shirt. Dan knew better than to press him.

After a minute Jordan sighed. "Wait, I do want to talk about it." He looked around nervously, as if to make certain that nobody was eavesdropping. "It happened the night you guys went down into that basement—the night Joe caught us. I've had the same dream every night since then. *Exactly* the same. I keep dreaming that I'm in this . . . cell. And there are these doctors all in white looking down at me, only they don't have faces. They have voices and hands and tools, but their faces have holes for eyes and noses and mouths. Then they put all these straps on me, lock me down, and . . ." Jordan's shoulders sagged. He reminded Dan of a wounded animal. "They show me pictures. And they shock me. They shock me over and over again. There's this white, hot pain and I can hear my parents talking somewhere behind the doctors. They're saying, 'He'll be better now. He has to get better now.'"

"That's horrible," Abby whispered. "I'm sorry, Jordan."

Jordan nodded, staring down at his equations.

Dan was frozen. He knew from Professor Reyes's class that they used to administer electroshock therapy to homosexuals in order to "cure" them. Did Jordan know that, too, or had he dreamed it out of nowhere? And how about the fact that Jordan's dream was so similar to the one he'd had. Was it yet another not-quite coincidence? Were they tapping into some Jungian collective unconscious? What was the connection?

Jordan gathered up the legal pads and tucked his pen into his jeans pocket. Then he stood, gave a half smile, and picked up his tray. He hadn't touched his dinner.

"I need a nap. I'll see you two around. . . ."

Jordan wove his way through the tables, ignoring a few kids who called greetings to him as he went.

"I guess that means he won't be going back downstairs with us," Abby said, returning to her salad.

Dan was shocked. "That's a little harsh, don't you think?"

"Well, it's true!" Sighing, Abby let her fork drop into the bowl and leaned back against her seat. "And the only reason you're upset is because you obviously don't want to go either, so why not just say so?"

"It's not that I don't want to go with you. . . ." Dan struggled for the right words. "I just think maybe this whole thing is far beyond being too weird. You're worried about your aunt, I totally get that. You want answers. I get that, too. It's just that—"

"You don't need to help me, Dan. I can do this on my own." Abby snatched up her sketchbook.

"I want to help," he said. "I want to help Jordan, and I want to help you, too, and I . . ."

I still want answers.

"Then *help!*" She caught her foot on the bench as she turned to leave and tripped. Grabbing a hold of the table before she could tumble to the ground, she dropped her sketchbook. Dan leapt forward to try to catch it.

Too late. The sketchbook hit the floor and fanned open, revealing page after page of dark, twisted drawings. Some loose sheets scattered. Reds, blacks, touches of blue and gray—with a central figure huddled at the center of every piece. The white shift she wore and the vacant look in her eyes gave it away.

It was the girl in the photograph. The girl Abby had drawn in her room. But there was something more going on in these illustrations. Suddenly Dan knew what Abby was thinking.

"*Lucy,*" Dan murmured. "You think the girl in the picture is Lucy Valdez. . . ."

"I've just been inspired, that's all." Abby grabbed the sketchbook and gathered up the loose pictures.

"I think maybe you should be looking for inspiration somewhere else." *Shit.* That hadn't come out the way he'd wanted it to.

"What would you know about it? You're not an artist, Dan. You're— I don't know what you are. You hold things in. You never share your own opinions. Do you really believe me about my aunt? I don't even know. You get some weird email and a threatening note, and you say you want answers, but you won't even go down to the basement with me. What *are* you, Dan? Whose side are you on?" She turned and stomped away, not giving him a chance to respond. He wanted to answer, to say *something*, but she was already with her friends at the art table and the last thing he wanted was to have an audience while he tried to explain his worth.

Anyway, what would he say? She was right—he *did* keep things to himself. He didn't like to take risks; he was cautious. He was closed in. There was so much he hadn't told her and Jordan. But she'd seen something in him before. Was that gone?

What was he? she'd asked. He was many things right now. And he felt like he was being pulled in a million conflicting directions. He definitely wanted to be with Abby, and that felt like the strongest, clearest direction. But fear of what awaited them in the old wing flooded his body. When they went down to that place, something bad happened to them—and to their friendship.

Dan cleaned up the table, his face hot with embarrassment. He took his tray and walked out of the dining hall without looking at Abby and her new entourage.

Outside, the crisp air felt like a blessing. He paused and glanced over his shoulder, through the windows and into the dining hall. Abby had her back to him, but he could tell by the shake of her shoulders she was laughing.

Dan walked slowly back to Brookline, his thoughts heavy, his heart even heavier.

When he got to his room, he slipped into his bathrobe and trundled down the hall to the bathroom. One of the showers in the cubicle behind him dripped, the droplets pinging the drain with an uneven rhythm. As he washed up, he remembered what the warden had written about "twisted roots." Where did insanity begin? With paranoia and insecurity like Jordan's, or with a strong-minded obsession like Abby's? Should he be worried that their behavior marked the first signs of something more serious?

They are walking the line between genius and insanity. You know the line well.

When he lowered his hands from his face, Dan saw he had scrubbed his skin almost raw. He dried off with his towel, and then paused in front of the mirror. He always chose this same mirror. It had deep black scratches in the upper right-hand corner that looked vaguely like a word, and each night he'd decide it spelled something different. Tonight, it looked like *HELP*.

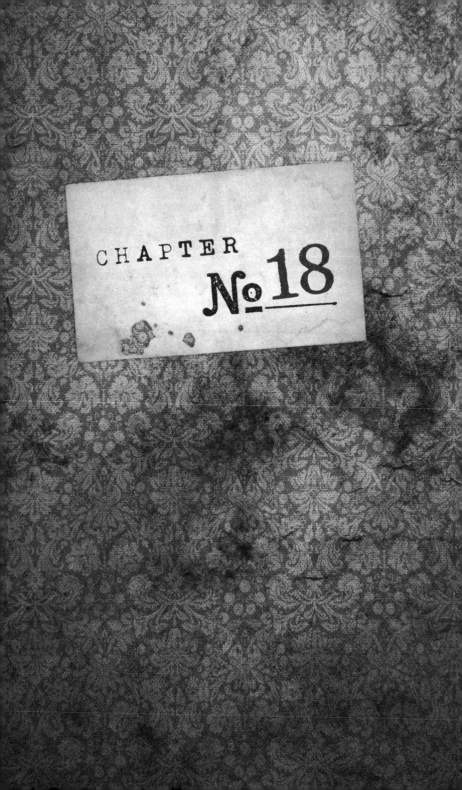

CHAPTER
№ 18

"Maybe you'd feel better if you went for a run. I have so much more energy now that I've started exercising. Have I mentioned that, Dan?"

Dan glanced up from his reading. "Only five times," he muttered. "Today."

"The point stands," Felix replied from the floor. He was in the middle of his billionth set of push-ups.

For the past few days, Dan had basically kept to his room, watching TV shows online and occasionally reading materials for classes. He hadn't heard from or spoken to Abby or Jordan since that night they'd all blown up at one another. At dinner, Abby sat with her new art friends, while Jordan had apparently stopped coming to dinner entirely. So Dan had started sitting with Felix, listening to how much his roommate was enjoying all of his classes and how he wished the program were longer than five weeks. At least *one* of them felt that way.

"Seventy-five," Felix counted. He paused, out of breath, and switched to a kneeling position. His palms were red from the floor. "You're welcome to join me at the gym this evening. It might really cheer you up, take your mind off of things."

Dan had to admire his determination. Protein shakes and daily trips to the gym were quickly turning Felix's once spindly physique into *Fight Club* material. He was still wiry, but Dan wouldn't want to pick a fight with him in a dark alley.

"Thanks," Dan said. "Not sure the gym is my scene, though."

"You never know unless you try."

Felix stood up and went to the closet. He pulled on a T-shirt and a Windbreaker, then packed a sports bag with a roll of clean white socks and a water bottle. "At least get out of the room, Dan," Felix told him when he got to the door. "Take a walk. Get some fresh air. You can watch *Battlestar Galactica* at home. Don't let this temporary setback ruin your whole summer."

"Uh. Okay?" Dan watched Felix slip out and close the door. "Thanks, Oprah."

But of course he was right. Dan got off his bed, shut his laptop, and changed into clean clothes. Just as he reached for his cell phone, it started buzzing so violently it nearly fell off his desk. Dan dove for it and was relieved to see *MOM* on the display.

"Hello?"

"Hi sweetie." His mother's voice was almost completely drowned out by the sound of TV in the background.

"Speakerphone?" he asked with a chuckle. "Really?"

"Your dad wants to say hello, too. No big deal. So how is it going? Do you still love college?"

Her enthusiasm was always infectious, and Dan found himself smiling despite his bad mood. "It's not really college, you know that."

"I know, I know, but still . . ."

"Is that Dan? Hi, Danny boy!"

"Hi, Dad." He pinched the bridge of his nose, pacing from

one end of his bed to the other. "So yeah, I'm doing fine, guys. Everyone is supernice, and the classes are great."

"How is Abby?" his mother asked. Of course that'd be the first place her mind went.

"She's fine, really an amazing artist. And it turns out Jordan's like, a math prodigy."

"Oh, good!" More than happy, Sandy sounded relieved. "Well, just wanted to call and let you know we sent a package with some goodies. I think it should have gotten there already, but I didn't know what the mail situation was like where you are. There's enough in there to share with Abby and Jordan, too, if they like Little Debbies and candy as much as you do."

"Thanks, Mom."

"I hope you're not studying all the time," his father said. "You enjoy yourself this summer, all right?"

"I will," Dan said, meaning it. He glanced around for his coat. "But listen, I should get going and look for that package, it's pretty dark out already."

"Okay, Danny, and let me know when you get it. We miss you! We miss you every day."

"Thanks, guys. I miss you, too."

Hanging up, Dan pulled on his jacket and left the dorm for the first time all day. The evening was pleasantly cool. He walked through the quad, where Yi and his orchestra friends were out playing music on the grass. Dan took a moment to stop and listen. For the first time in days, he felt his mood lifting.

He made good on his promise to his parents and set off toward the academic side. It would be nice to have something from home, and plus Dan was hungry enough to eat a whole box of Little Debbies himself.

Out on the lawn in front of Wilfurd Commons, a resident advisor led a group of students through yoga poses in the grass. Dan skirted around them and walked to the side entrance of the building. A convenience store—student union next to the cafeteria housed post office boxes for each student.

Dan found his box in the middle cluster, number 3808. Crouching, he peered into the tiny glass window and was surprised that it was actually quite full. He used a little key he'd been given on move-in day and opened the door to pull everything out. Sure enough, there was a green piece of paper telling him he could pick up his package at the mail desk. There were also some flyers from the school, mostly information for students interested in applying to the college proper. There was a sketch Abby had done on the back of an assignment. He remembered seeing her doodle it during class. It showed the three of them in full suits of armor, standing on top of a fallen mound of books with "SCHOLASTIC VICTORY, HUZZAH!" written boldly across the top. Dan tucked the drawing away with a smile. He didn't know when she had put it in his box, but maybe it was a sign that she was ready to be friends again. He decided he would call her when he got back to the dorm.

Finally, there was an envelope that simply had "3808" written on the front in thick black ink.

Oh no, not again.

CHAPTER
№ 19

an almost threw the envelope away. Who knew what threat it contained? But in the end he had to know. With a feeling of dread, he opened the flap.

Insanity is relative. It depends on who has who locked in what cage.

The spidery calligraphic handwriting was the same as the hydra note. This time it wasn't fear but anger that shot through Dan. Someone was trying to freak him out, and it was working.

Dan glanced around. Nobody was there, but he couldn't escape the prickly feeling that *someone* was watching. He threw the school papers in the trash and put the note in his jacket pocket. He retrieved his package from the store clerk with a shaky hand, then practically sprinted out of the building.

Once he was back in his room, he grabbed the note out of his pocket and sat down at his desk. He Googled the sentences. It sounded like a quote, not something off-the-cuff. His suspicions proved right. The top few results showed that the line was Ray Bradbury's—from some radio play he'd written.

So now what? He'd assumed finding the source of the quote would be helpful, but it wasn't. Whoever had put it in his mailbox

Clarity is relative.
It depends on who has who
locked in what cage.

had already left one ominous note *on his desk*. They'd been in his room. . . .

Dan spun around in his seat. Of course no one was there.

Think. Think! You're missing something, something right in front of your stupid face.

Rummaging through his desk drawer, Dan unearthed the first note. He held the two of them side by side. He looked at the spidery handwriting, the paper, the ink—everything matched up perfectly. Other than that, he couldn't tell much. He couldn't even say for sure whether the notes had been written by a man or woman.

So, to sum up everything he knew— a nameless, genderless stalker with a fondness for Ray Bradbury was out to terrorize him.

He thought about calling Abby or Jordan but decided not to. The notes were for him, not Abby or Jordan. Someone was trying to get at *him*.

Dan ate microwave popcorn from his care package for dinner and then huddled under his blanket. He couldn't stop shivering. His mind was going around in little circles.

He pulled out his phone and thumbed through his contacts, finally hovering over Dr. Oberst's phone number. If anyone could hear him out without judging him, it would be her. And she had told him to call her *any time* this summer if things got bad.

But what would he even be calling to tell her? If he told her about how he'd imagined *real* rooms before he'd seen them, she'd probably ask for a therapy session—but the notes? How could those be his fault?

Dan had never doubted himself as much as he did in that second. What if he was the "twisted root" at the heart of everything that was going wrong?

He threw his covers off, jumped out of bed, and took the two notes from his desk. He ripped them in half, and then in half again. He refused to let someone else string him along like this. He refused to let someone else keep him caged in his room, in his mind.

He was going to go with his gut on this one. And his gut was telling him he would find answers in the basement.

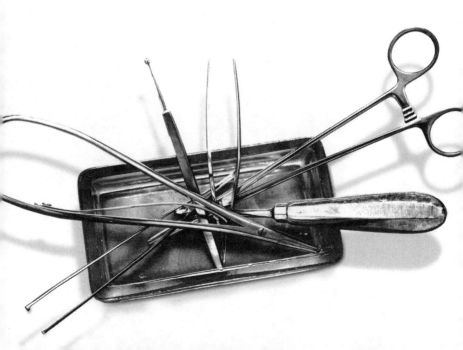

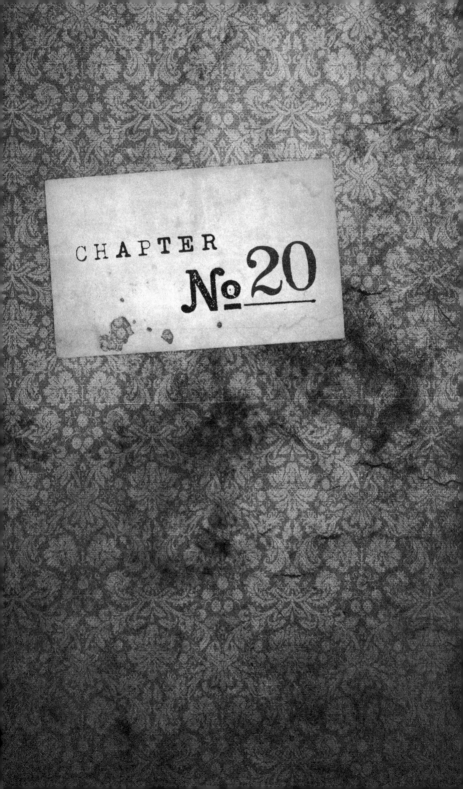

CHAPTER № 20

*D*an knew it was not his best idea, sneaking into the basement by himself. To start with, the door would be locked. One of the hall monitors might be standing guard. But he wasn't going to overthink this. Thinking hadn't gotten him anywhere.

Out in the hall, the lights were too bright. He longed for the cover of total darkness. At least nobody was around. They were probably all at dinner or out doing their own thing like Felix.

Still, Dan didn't want to get careless. He sneaked over to where the vending machines were and was about to turn the corner to the warden's office when he saw a dark silhouette appear at the end of the hall. Footsteps. Voices. For a terrifying instant, thoughts of the Sculptor or another of Brookline's killers returning to stalk the halls made his body tighten up all over. He pressed himself against the wall, hoping he would blend into the shadows.

"They should just trade him and do everyone a favor," said a male voice. Dan let out his breath, not even aware he'd been holding it. It wasn't a ghost; it was Joe.

"Whatever, man."

Dan didn't recognize the second voice. Probably another hall monitor. Were they patrolling the halls, making sure no one went down to the basement? Dan stood there for what felt like forever, until, finally, he saw Joe and his buddy go out the front door. He waited a minute or two more just to be safe, and then he turned the corner to the old wing. Luck was on his side—the heavy door was not only unguarded, it was unlocked. Probably Joe hadn't snapped the padlock shut all the way the other night, Dan convinced himself. Still, he couldn't shake the feeling that the door was ready and waiting for him.

Dan slipped inside and the stale air wrapped itself around him like a welcome. He had forgotten how dark it was down here. He clicked on his flashlight, but without anyone to break the silence, the darkness was exponentially scarier.

Dan plunged through the reception room and into the outer office, the one with the scratched-off letters on the glass. He retraced their steps from last time, pausing to check that the photos were still stacked neatly on the desk. From its frame on the wall, the photo of the struggling patient seemed to be taunting him. *The Sculptor, patient 361.*

Dan crouched behind the file cabinet and climbed through the secret passage. Without hesitating, he pointed his flashlight at the stairwell and hurried down, knowing that if he waited he might lose his courage and turn back. The lower hall was still a mess. He cautiously navigated the chairs and gurneys. The last thing he needed was to break his neck tripping over a piece of furniture. It'd be awhile before anyone found his body.

Dan moved past the empty cells. It felt like something might jump out of every one.

He moved quickly now, anxious to get to the pristine inner office. Apart from his thumping heartbeat and quick breaths, the hallway was eerily silent.

Steps away from the rotunda room and the office beyond, his foot collided with something small but heavy. It rolled noisily away into the darkness, and Dan focused his light on the floor, following the little trail whatever it was had left through the dust, across the floor, and into one of the open cells.

In the middle of the room, Dan reached up and risked pulling the old string attached to the ceiling light. A single, naked bulb clicked on, buzzing and flickering for a moment before bathing the cell in a faint, yellow glow. It was barely enough to see by, but it was better than his flashlight.

Dan looked around. This was one of the many cells he and Abby hadn't explored. There was a table and a bed, but nothing else. He squinted, turning in a complete circle. What had he kicked and where had it gone?

Then a soft, high-pitched chime started up from under the bed. Dan stumbled toward the sound, as whatever it was crackled faintly and then began to sing.

No, not sing—play music . . . Dan crouched, the hairs on his forearms standing up as the broken, off-key tune of a music box filled the room. He didn't recognize the melody. It sounded so old he wasn't sure anyone alive would. Dan fished under the bed until his fingers ran over the ridged metal surface of the box. He nudged it out carefully, then picked it up to examine. There were two broken springs sticking out on either side. Standing on top was a little porcelain figurine, a ballerina. She was in a dancer's pose, her arms curved gracefully above her head. Her fingers ended in dangerously sharp points, and the look on her face was eerily smug, as if she were relishing a secret.

Dan listened to the painful crawl of the song as the notes wound down, the mechanical tune dying a lingering death. Finally, it stopped, and the room fell silent once more.

He tipped the box over and found an inscription etched into the bottom.

To Lucy: On your birthday with love.

Dan stared at the words for a long time, hoping maybe if he just waited they'd change or disappear. This couldn't be the same Lucy, could it? Abby's Lucy? If Abby's story had been true, it didn't seem like Lucy's parents would have been the type to send a birthday present. Maybe it was a gift from the warden himself. Either way, what was it doing down here? Did it mean that Lucy had . . . died . . . or just left it behind?

Dan kept worrying the question like a sore tooth. One thing he knew for sure: he would not be sharing this discovery with Abby. She would go out of her mind worrying about what it meant.

He set the box back down on the floor and turned to leave the cell behind him. But suddenly, the disjointed song started up again, getting louder and clearer and faster as it played. Dan thought about smashing the box to stop it, but he chose to flee instead. That box had meant something to someone, once.

Dan continued down the hall, coming to the rotunda off which he and Abby had found the inner office. This time he took full stock of the space, shining his flashlight all along the wall and finding a small doorway across from the office. He took hold of the knob and turned. The door wasn't locked, but it didn't budge either. It had swollen shut in the dampness and gloom. Putting all his weight behind it, Dan turned and pushed as hard as he could. The door shrieked a protest, but open it did, and Dan only just caught himself from a nasty fall. Lowering before him was another set of stairs.

CHAPTER
№ 21

$\mathcal{D}$an was looking into a yawning void. How far under the earth did this place go, anyway?

The cold rushing up from the space below was shocking. His sweatshirt wasn't close to being warm enough; he should have brought a damn *parka*. And couldn't they have built the stairs a little wider? A safety inspector would have a heart attack—these stairs were steep, narrow, and had a sheer drop on both sides, with only a tiny pole of a railing to hold on to.

Clutching the rail in one hand and his flashlight in the other, Dan took the first step. Three stairs, four, ten. At fifteen steps, he reached a small landing, but he still couldn't see the floor with his flashlight. Just more and more stairs, pitched at a nightmarish incline, leading into the bowels of the basement.

One more landing, twelve more steps, and at last he reached the bottom. He shined his flashlight up and around, watching as the meager light failed to find the top or even sides of . . . What, a cave? A vault? He couldn't be sure, but he could tell it was enormous. Coughing, he listened to the sound bounce and echo for a solid minute before finally fading away.

He slowly walked forward into the huge space. There were wooden posts that ran from the floor to the ceiling. Otherwise, the hall he was in seemed completely empty.

Finally, he reached a square arch leading into yet another space beyond. Dan suddenly felt like laughing—he'd been creeped out by the expansiveness of the cell level and the warden's secret office, but this was something else, something he could hardly fathom, even as his eyes fed him the information. It was like a palace down here. What could it have been used for?

But this was the last room; it had to be. Shining his light all around, he found a rusted metal box screwed into the wall beside him, and he carefully nudged open the front panel. The rusty hinges squealed, and the echoes in the chamber reverberated endlessly.

He'd hit the jackpot. There were switches in the box, and lots of them. Dan flicked the biggest one and was rewarded with a low hum, then a buzz, and finally a quiet pop as the lights came up. Only a few worked, and one exploded overhead in a shower of glass and sparks. Dan ducked instinctively, and then gasped.

He was looking down into an operating amphitheater.

In the very middle of the room was a raised wooden platform, and standing dead center was an operating table. It was covered with a smooth sheet, originally white, now gray with dust. There was a padded pillow at the top. Leather straps, buckled, trisected the bed. Around the main table stood a few smaller tables on wheels. They had surgical instruments on them.

Encircling the platform were stepped rows of chairs, like in a sports arena. *The stands.* As if watching someone's surgery was some kind of amusement . . .

With a sickening lurch, Dan realized he'd seen this room before, too, in another nightmare. In his dream, he'd started out *on* that table.

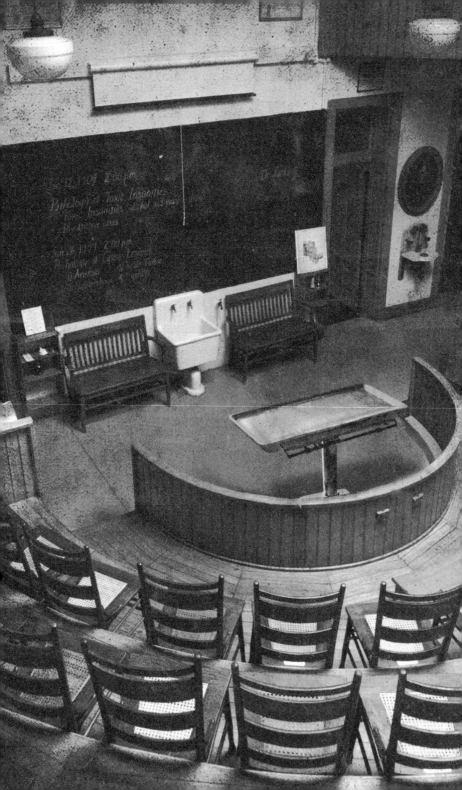

He moved slowly down the stands, drawn to the platform. He walked a complete circle around it, his eyes never leaving the table. How many killers had been treated here? Had little Lucy been strapped down for surgery while people *watched*? Dan thought of the scar on her forehead that suggested a lobotomy. If it had been that, and she had survived, poor little Lucy wouldn't have had much of a life.

Why on earth would an operating amphitheater be built so far underground? Were they concealing something?

A small desk and filing cabinet at the very back of the room caught Dan's eye. They'd both been pushed into the shadows as if they wanted to be overlooked. Dan's heart raced. If patients were operated on here—if Lucy Valdez had been operated on—there would surely be records of it. If he was lucky, those records might not have gotten lost in the shuffle when Brookline closed.

But as he approached the cabinets, his head felt suddenly heavy, like it had been stuffed with wool. He blinked once . . . twice. . . . The floor didn't feel so sturdy anymore.

He stood over the table, ready, confident. This was his moment. He had an audience, and he would not disappoint them. This was his chance to prove that his methods, however unorthodox, worked. He was the warden, the trusted father of the Brookline family, strict but ultimately fair. Daniel looked down at his clean white coat and the instruments in his hands, sanitized and gleaming. Everything was prepared.

Necks craned as each man tried to get a better look. Before him, strapped to the operating table, was a young boy who liked to set fires. When Daniel blinked, it was someone new, someone else who needed fixing—a cruel widow who had poisoned six husbands, a pretty young girl with fiery red hair.

Blinking again, he found the most wretched creature of all. He looked at the man's waxy face, slack now from the sedatives. This man was broken, but he wouldn't be broken for long. He could be fixed, they could all be fixed. . . .

Dan—the warden—started. Sudden sounds . . . A pounding like thunder . . . Footsteps overhead . . . His vision blurred, spinning out of control. Not now! They couldn't come for him now. The authorities would never understand what he was trying to do.

Dan . . . Dan . . .

They were calling his name now, they were coming for him.

"Dan! Hello? Dan, are you all right? You're scaring me, snap out of it!"

Snap, snap, snap.

Dan was cold all over and realized with a jolt that he was lying on the floor. Abby's face materialized above him through the fading blur of the vision. For a moment, he was relieved, but then he felt instantly ashamed. What would she think if she could see inside his head?

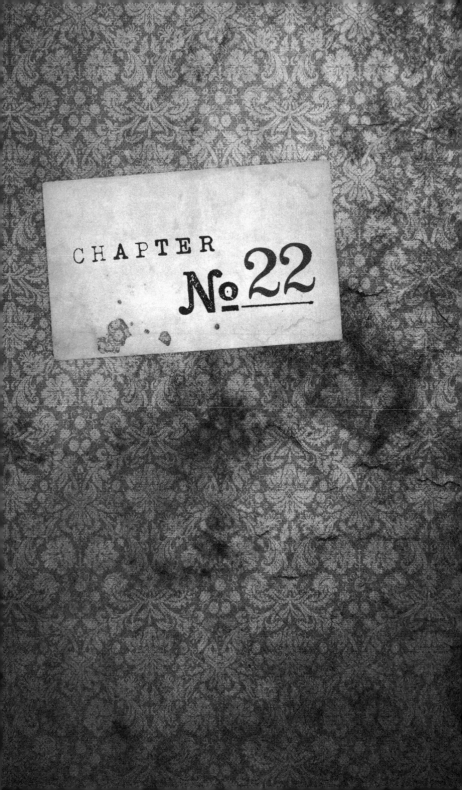

CHAPTER
№ 22

"*I*t's me," Abby said. She was kneeling beside him. "It's okay, you're all right now, you're all right."

"How long have I been out?" he said, touching a sore spot on his head where he must have bumped it. He saw that he was on the floor near the file cabinet, surrounded by scattered papers.

"I don't know," she said. "I just got here and you were lying on the ground."

She looked so concerned that it made him feel better. And maybe it was the relief of seeing her worried face, or the relief that it was her and not some ghost of the past made real—Dan didn't know and he didn't care—but suddenly he reached up, pulled her in, and kissed her.

It surprised them both.

"Oh. Well," Abby breathed. She tasted like Altoids and cherry lip balm. "I guess we can stop pretending to hate each other now, huh?"

"I guess so," Dan replied.

She smiled up down him. "And . . . can we just pretend I never said that stuff about you being a weirdo?"

"Wait a minute, what stuff?" he asked.

Abby swatted him lightly on the chest. As nice as it was to see her smiling and laughing again, Dan really *didn't* remember her calling him a weirdo. Had he blocked that out, or did she mean she'd said it to some of her art friends? Or to *Ash*.

Dan shook his head. He wasn't going down that road. Not anymore. He had kissed her and it was as good as he could ever have hoped.

"We should get out of here," Abby said. "This place gives me the creeps."

She helped Dan get up. His head hurt, and he felt more than a little dizzy.

"Hey," he said suddenly, "what are you doing down here anyway?"

Abby looked a little embarrassed. "Um . . . I went to your room after dinner, just to see you and apologize for the way I've been acting. You weren't there so I got worried that you'd come down here by yourself. I guess I just wanted to make sure you were okay."

Dan reached out and took Abby's hand, and she gave it a squeeze. They walked up the stepped rows. Back at the top, Dan stopped to flick off the lights. He turned around and took one more look at the now-dark chamber.

Two bright spots glowed from the far corner.

Just a trick of the eye. Just imprints of the lightbulbs left behind. Not the eyes of men watching. Dan shut the door quickly behind him.

"What's the hold up?" Abby asked.

Dan moved next to her, shaking his head. "Nothing," he said softly. "Nothing. Let's just get out of here. Are you hungry? I've got some amazingly stale snack cakes up in my room."

"Sounds delicious," Abby said, leaning into him. "It's a date."

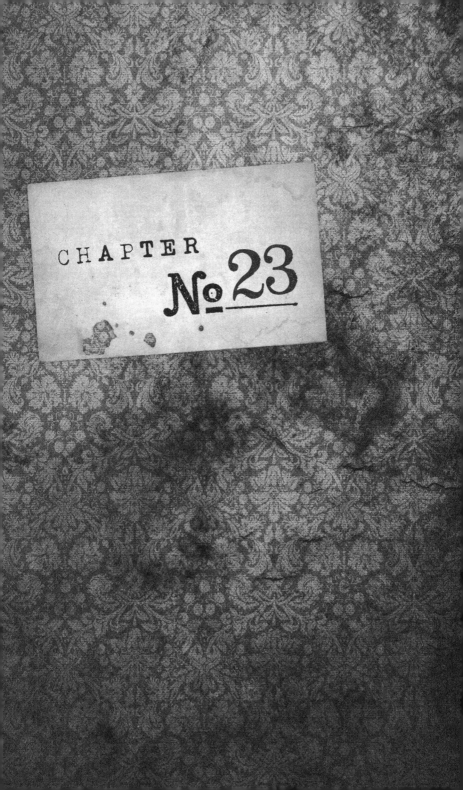

CHAPTER
№ 23

When they got to the final door, Dan felt he was done with the basement for good. What mattered now was Abby, and how warm her hand felt in his own. They would fix things with Jordan, and he would finish the summer with his best friends, out in the sunshine, away from all this gloom.

Dan's euphoria was short-lived.

Something had gone terribly wrong on the first floor. Police were swarming everywhere, and the entrance hall was flooded with students. One girl was crying hysterically. The lights made Dan's eyes hurt after the blackness of the basement.

Exchanging a worried glance, Dan and Abby did their best to blend in with the crowd. A tall police officer crossed in front of them, almost bumping into them. He barely spared them a glance and rapidly moved across the hall, shouldering students out of the way. The crowd parted for him slowly. He reached the crying girl and took her by the shoulders, talking to her gently.

"What the . . ." Dan and Abby tried to see what was going on, but the crowd was just too dense to move more than a few feet.

Another police officer rushed in through the front door. Dan could see the flashing blue-and-red lights of the police cars parked outside. It looked like there were four or five of them.

"Move out of the way!" the officer thundered. "This is a crime scene! Move outside, now!" She and the tall policeman started herding the kids outside onto the lawn. The students shuffled slowly, bottlenecking at the front door. Dan and Abby moved along with the crowd, following the officer's instructions.

"Police?" Abby whispered. The color had drained from her face.

"Let's try to find out what happened."

Outside, a third policeman was now talking to the crying girl. Everyone else stood in groups, conversing in hushed whispers. Dan finally spotted Yi and Jordan. Jordan didn't look too good. He glared at Dan and Abby and then disappeared into the crowd.

"What's going on?" asked Dan.

Yi looked at Dan with surprise. "Your roomie found a dead guy on the stairs. One of the hall monitors. Jake . . . George . . ."

"*Joe?*" Dan blurted out, and Abby covered her mouth.

"Yeah, that's it. Joe. Your boy Felix was coming back from a late-night run and found him. It looked like he'd been dead for a while."

A while couldn't have been that long, surely. Dan had seen Joe in the halls just before he went into the basement. That was what, an hour ago? Maybe less? Dan needed to figure out how long he'd been down there.

Yi was saying, "At least, that was what it looked like when I saw him."

"You saw him?" Abby said, horrified.

Yi nodded. "Just a glimpse, after Felix started screaming. Eyes open, wide open. Just . . . staring. It was so freaking creepy.

191

Jordan saw him, too. Joe was standing, propped up in the stair-well with one hand on the railing, and another holding his cell phone. . . ."

Like a sculpture . . .

"Hey," Yi said suddenly, startling them both. "Where were you guys anyway? How is it you didn't know?"

"We weren't doing anything," Abby said too quickly. Then she glanced up at Dan.

"Yes," he said, "that sounded as guilty as you think it did."

"Crap. All right, fine. You're *right*." She looked at her feet. "We were making out, okay?"

Dan wasn't going to argue with that exaggeration. He liked it quite a lot, in fact. It was a clever cover, too—this way no one would know they'd actually been exploring the old wing.

"In the old wing?" Yi asked.

Abby shrugged.

"You two are weird as hell," Yi muttered. Then he said, "You know, I'm worried about Jordan. Seeing Joe definitely freaked him out—I mean, it's freaked *all* of us out. But he wasn't look-ing too good before. These days he hardly talks to me, and he's always working on math that I'm pretty sure is not even for a class."

"Do you think his nightmares are getting to him?" Abby asked.

"Yeah—he keeps waking up in the middle of the night. And I think there might be stuff with his parents, like they found out he was here or something. Anyway, I get the feeling it's way worse than he's letting on. I just hope he's got a place to go back to, you know?" Yi paused. "Are you two keeping an eye on him?"

Abby and Dan exchanged a worried look. Since they'd all gone their separate ways, they had no idea that Jordan had gotten this bad. Dan felt guilty—he should have checked on Jordan, even though Jordan had withdrawn.

"Yeah, we're keeping an eye on him," Dan said. *We are now, anyway.*

More policemen arrived. They began sectioning off the students, arranging them in smaller, more manageable groups. Probably for interviews.

Shit, why did he feel so guilty?

"Dan, buddy? You feeling okay? You just got a little green. . . ." Yi punched his arm lightly.

"Me? I'm fine."

"What are you talking about?" Abby demanded, looking up at him. "Clearly, none of us are fine."

Two cops, the tall one and the police officer who had moved everyone outside, reached where they were standing and herded their group over to a tree.

"Better come up with a believable story," Yi said softly. "Before Mulder and Scully over there get a go at you. You don't want them knowing you were in the forbidden zone."

Yi turned to talk with another kid, but Dan could hardly move. What if Yi was right? Were they really going to be interrogated? *Of course they're going to question you, someone was* murdered.

"We weren't in the old wing," Dan said, grabbing Abby's arm. "We were in the second-floor lounge, the one by your room. We have to get our story straight or they might think we had something to do with . . . with . . ."

He couldn't bring himself to say it.

"But we weren't anywhere near the second floor." She looked at him strangely. "Why would we need a story?"

He took her by the forearm, tugging her away from the other students. "Just trust me, okay? Think about it—we were both out wandering late at night. Joe's a big guy, so they probably won't suspect you could overpower him, but the two of us—"

"Hey, I resent that," Abby said, yanking her arm out of his grasp. "I might be a little on the petite side—"

"Tiny."

"Whatever. It doesn't matter, Dan, I'm stronger than I look. And it's not like you're some kind of muscle-bound hulk, so I don't see why *you'd* be a suspect and I wouldn't."

"Why are we arguing about this?" he whispered. "You're Wonder Woman, okay? You're . . ."

"Say I'm Black Widow."

"Abby—"

"*Say it.*" She crossed her arms, cocking one hip to the side.

"You're Black Widow. Times ten. Happy now? And Jesus, why aren't you more freaked out?"

"I *am* freaked out," Abby squeaked, giving him a little shove. "I'm seriously freaked out. This is what I do when I'm freaked out. I babble. Inanely. I babble inanely to distract myself from the freaking out!"

"Okay, okay." He hoped nobody had heard that. They both sounded guilty, even if they weren't. Well, not guilty of *murder*, just guilty of having poor judgment and a blatant disregard for the loose curfew rules. He knew that at least. Right?

"Poor Felix. I hope he's not too traumatized," she said, turning to search the crowd. "Do you see him?"

"No," Dan said. "I'm sure he's being questioned by the police."

"Gird your loins." Yi was back. He slid up to them, talking out of the corner of his mouth. "I got Mulder and Scully on my six."

Dan took a deep breath, preparing to unleash a whole mouthful of bullshit on officers of the law. They separated him from Abby, the policewoman taking her aside while Dan went with the tall guy. The whole process was surprisingly quick and painless. He was asked standard questions—where he was, what he heard and saw, if he could remember any strangers around the dorm that day. Dan answered vaguely, mentioning he was on the second floor with his friend, that he had seen Joe "earlier that day" but hadn't noticed anyone suspicious loitering in Brookline.

"Thanks," the cop told him when the questions ran out. "If you see anything strange, anything at all out of the ordinary, you tell someone. Okay, son?"

"Okay. Thanks, sir."

Dan wandered away, numb. He had just lied through his teeth to a cop. Why? Exploring the basement wasn't the same as murder, it just wasn't. He had to keep reminding himself of that over and over again. *Forget about your freaking alibi, whoever did this is still out there.*

The officer finished speaking to Abby a moment later. As Dan waited for her, he heard one of the cops talking to another in low tones.

"Probably some bum," he was saying. "They're always getting blind drunk and wandering up on to campus. We'll find him in a bush outside, just you wait."

Dan wondered how a stranger could get into the dorm, considering the front doors locked automatically from the outside.

"Could I have your attention please?" Dan recognized the director from the first couple of days. He had been all smiles then. Now he looked ragged, still rumpled from sleep, and shaken to the core.

"If I could have your attention," he repeated, standing on the first step of the entranceway. The students quieted down and the police officers moved away.

"Thank you. All right, I know it's been a difficult night for everyone. First thing in the morning, your parents will be notified of the situation. Right now, we need to do what's best for you, our faculty, staff, and of course what's best for Joe McMullan's family. The police will conduct a full search of the building tonight, and an officer will be stationed on each floor to make certain you are all safe. I'm sure many of you have questions, and I'm happy to stay and assist you however I can. To the rest of you, be safe and vigilant, and cooperate fully with the Camford Police. And let us keep Joe's family in our thoughts tonight."

At this, the sound of crying rippled through the crowd. In front of Dan, two girls clung to each other, sobbing. Students swarmed around the director, shouting questions until he ordered them to calm down and speak one by one.

Dismissed by the policewoman, Abby walked over to Dan.

"I don't think she even wrote down half of what I said. Whatever, I'm so ready for bed it's not even funny, although I don't suppose there's any way I'm going to fall asleep." She shuddered. "I wish this were just a nightmare that we could wake up from. Anyway, see you tomorrow?"

She took his hand and squeezed it. Dan squeezed back. "Yeah. Try to get some sleep. We'll talk tomorrow. Text if you need me."

With heavy steps, Abby followed a police officer who was leading the students to a back staircase to their rooms, since the main stairs were cordoned off with police tape. The body had been moved, but for the time being it was still a crime scene. Dan trudged up the stairs behind her, beyond exhausted, wishing he had a moment to properly remember their kiss and forget that he was at Brookline altogether. At Brookline where a murderer was wandering free.

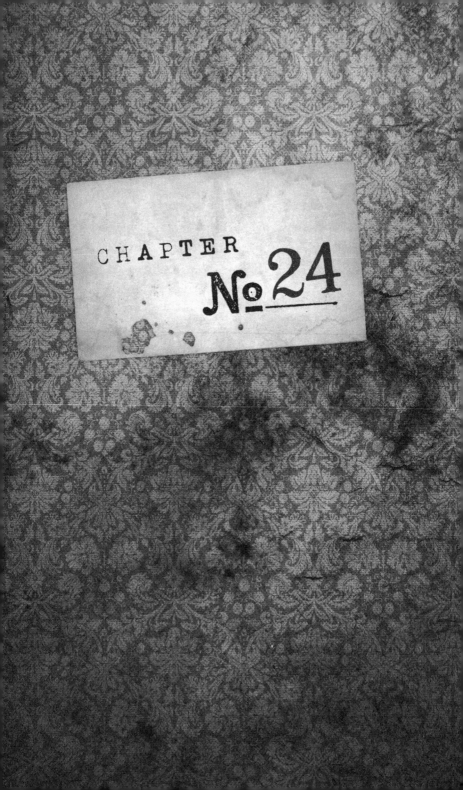

CHAPTER
№ 24

*F*elix was not in the room when Dan got there. *Still being questioned by the police,* Dan thought. He was just wondering if they'd let Felix come back that night at all when the door opened, and Felix walked in. He immediately went to his bed, curled up on it, and hugged his knees to his chest. He was still wearing a T-shirt and running shorts. He looked vulnerable and scared.

"Oh God, Felix, I'm really sorry," Dan said. "Nobody should have to see something like that."

On the bed, Felix was shaking, rattling the whole bed frame.

"Do you want to talk about it?"

Felix shook his head. It looked like if he opened his mouth he would start crying.

"If you need to talk or anything, you know where to find me. Anytime."

Felix didn't respond.

In a fog, Dan went through the motions of brushing his teeth and getting ready for bed. A police officer patrolled the hallway. His hand was on his holster. It made Dan walk very carefully down the hall.

Back in the room, Felix had, surprisingly, fallen asleep. Dan turned off the light and got into bed in the clothes he was wearing. He didn't want to risk waking Felix by changing. Besides, it wasn't like he would be able sleep anyway. As he lay down, he heard a crunching noise. He reached into the pouch of his hoodie and pulled out a few sheets of paper. He had no idea how they got there; dimly, he remembered seeing a set of cabinets in the operating amphitheater, but he had passed out with that vision before reaching them. Was this another memory gap? Weird, though, because he really couldn't remember even making it across the room.

He had an odd thought. What if Abby had put them in his pocket while he was still unconscious? He knew that there had been papers on the ground when he came to. Did she read them and already know about Lucy? But surely she would have said something if she did. And he couldn't think of any reason why she would have put the papers in his pocket.

There was enough light coming through the window that Dan didn't need to switch on his bedside lamp. He smoothed the crumpled papers on his pillow. They were the same kind of memos that he'd already seen.

Dan reached the last piece of paper. The handwriting jumped out at him.

The warden.

> *A flash of inspiration this morning over breakfast—there is, I think, a way in which my ideas can live on forever. All men seek immortality in their own way, either through a legacy of children carrying their name and genetic material, through architecture, through science, and this now is simply my search for a legacy like no other.*
>
> *The work will be grisly, true. I've no doubt about that. Yet Michelangelo had his secret cadavers, and so too must I, an artist of a different sort, risk and sacrifice. . . .*

A flush of inspiration this morning over breakfast — there is, I think, a way in which my dear can live on forever. All men seek immortality in their own way, either through a legacy of children carrying their name and genetic material, through architecture, through science, are these now it simply my research for a legacy like no other

[ ] The work will be grisly, true. There no doubt of that. Yes Michelangelo had his secret cadavers, and so too must I, an artist of a different sort, risk and sacrifice. I always knew that would — great sacrifice. It will require of savage beauty, and a far But sacrifice then went too, and how dear And how dangerous.

So the warden had been performing grisly "sacrifices" on his patients. In order to create a legacy for his name. Dan thought back to the index cards they'd looked at in the warden's office, so many of them with *N* under the Recovered box. How many operations had failed? How many patients had been needlessly subjected to pain and terror all for the sake of the warden searching for a kind of immortality?

Dan kept reading:

I always hated that word—sacrifice. It conjures images of savages beating drums around a fire. But sacrifices there must be, and how dear. And how dangerous.

That was the end of the entry. But there was more writing on the back, in the warden's now familiar handwriting. And at the bottom, a signature. Two words: "Daniel Crawford."

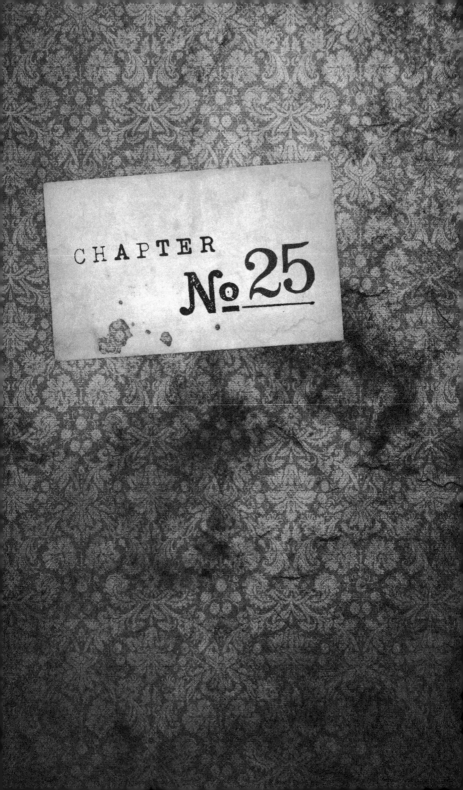

CHAPTER
№ 25

*T*he police found the man who'd killed Joe the next day, in a bar downtown with Joe's wallet and a garrote. The director held a meeting in Wilfurd Commons to tell the student body that they were safe now, but that if any of them wanted to go home, they would get a full refund. Classes would resume the next day. There would be counselors standing by if students needed someone to talk to.

Dan found Abby and asked her if she wanted to go for a walk. The yard outside Wilfurd lacked its usual mob of kids playing Frisbee or lawn bowling. Everyone on campus was in a somber mood. They decided to get away from the campus for a while, so they took a path that led to the forest. As soon as they had gone a couple of yards, the air got cooler and the light dimmer from the riot of trees arching over them.

"How is Felix holding up?" Abby said after a while.

Dan shrugged. He didn't really know. "He wasn't there when I woke up, and I didn't see him in the Commons. Maybe he's seeing one of the counselors."

"How about you? Feel ok?" Abby slipped her hand into his.

"Yeah," Dan lied. *Tell her, tell her everything. Stop holding everything in.* But really, how could he tell her? *Hey, so it turns out there was this one warden behind all the horrible shit here, and oh, guess what, we have the same name.*

Oh, and I've been having these dreams like I'm seeing through his eyes. No biggie.

At least Dan finally knew why Sal Weathers and his wife had gotten so angry when he'd told them his name.

"Jordan's not answering his phone," Abby said, interrupting his thoughts. The pine needles crunched under their feet. "I texted him last night when I got to my room and again this morning. I assume he heard the news that they found the guy, although I'm not sure he's left his room. I got one reply: 'busy with homework.' I don't get why he's being so strange. So unlike the kid I met on the bus."

"Maybe he needs to be alone for a while. I mean, he *saw* the body."

"Maybe . . . but I keep thinking about what Yi said, about us watching out for him. I'm just worried, you know? I worry," she said. "I'll try him again later. Can't hurt to try, right?"

✗ ✗ ✗ ✗ ✗ ✗

Dan didn't see her for the rest of the day. Back in his room, he found himself staring at the wall, his thoughts in a jumble. When his phone rang in his pocket, he nearly jumped out of his skin.

Chill out, Dan, it's just your parents.

He picked up the phone, already knowing what was coming.

"Oh, Danny, we just got off the phone with your program director who tells us that a boy has been *killed* right in your very dorm, what is going on, do you need us to—" His mother's voice came out in a panicked rush.

He jumped to interrupt her. "Hey, hey, listen—they *caught* the guy, okay?" He realized he was almost shouting and lowered his voice. "I'm fine. We're all safe now. They've got counselors and stuff and they caught the guy who did it."

"The director said they had a 'suspect in custody,'" she said shrilly. "He didn't sound nearly as sure as you do."

Dan had to sound sure, not just for his mother, but for himself. It was hard to ignore that while he'd been out cold having a vision about the Sculptor, two floors up Joe was being, well, *sculpted*.

"If they really thought we were in danger, they'd shut down the program and send us home." Dan spoke with as much authority as he could muster, desperately hoping Sandy would take him at his word.

"I suppose that's true. I'm just . . . I'm just heartsick thinking of you there. You're with your friends? You're okay?"

"I'm okay. And Abby and Jordan are, too." *Sort of.* "I promise."

"Okay. Well, if you're sure . . ."

"Hey, while I have you guys on the phone, can I ask you something?"

"Of course, Danny. Let me just put you on speakerphone." He heard a click and suddenly it got very loud on the other end.

"Hi, Dad."

"What do you need, Danny?" Paul asked.

Where to start? "I just had a question about my . . . family history, I guess. I mean, the stuff before you guys. Stuff from when I was younger. I was looking up some of the history about this place—'cause you know, the dorm used to be a psych ward and all—and it turns out the warden here was also named Daniel Crawford." *Careful now . . .* "I thought that was an, uh, interesting coincidence. Do you know if there's any possible relation?"

"Dan," his father said soothingly. "I mean, really, do you need us to come get you? We can get on a plane right now and come get you. It's no problem."

"What? No! That's not what I—"

"I'm serious. The whole thing doesn't feel right to me. You should come home, you're not, you know, always so good with stuff like this," his father said. It had been awhile since Dan had heard him sound so worried.

"Danny, sweetie, your father is just concerned, we both are," his mom added. "Do we need to call Dr. Oberst? If you think this might trigger some sort of episode . . ."

"But I didn't say anything about wanting to come home—"

"Psych wards and wardens and . . . What about you, Danny? It doesn't sound like you're taking care of yourself!" It was his dad again, and from the sound of it, he was working himself up into an angry froth.

"Calm down, Paul. Danny, we're worried about you, that's all. We're just trying to tell you that if you want to leave, we think that would be a good, rational decision. We always knew that this might be too much for you—"

"Look, never mind. Don't call Dr. Oberst. Don't worry about me. I have to get going." He hung up the phone over their protests.

Paul and Sandy had always told him that the most they could give him about his birth parents was "nonidentifying" information, like the fact that they'd been college educated and healthy and had no other kids. But apparently, all you had to do was check a little box saying you didn't want to divulge your identity, and suddenly it took a good reason and a court order to get anywhere.

Frankly, Dan had never really cared to know who his good-for-nothing parents were. Paul and Sandy were more than great; they had come to feel like family.

But suddenly, finding out his history felt like the most important thing in the world. The missing piece in this maddening puzzle—the link between Dan and a ruthless killer. Of all the places he could have ended up this summer, it couldn't be a mistake that he'd chosen this one.

Brookline was his destiny. It was in his blood.

CHAPTER № 26

*D*an tore through his desk drawers, searching for the photo of Daniel Crawford. The scratched-out eyes were still burned in his mind, but the rest of the details had grown hazy, and he needed to give it a closer look. When he'd dumped out the entire contents of his drawers onto his bed and the picture still hadn't surfaced, he started to feel a tightening in his chest. No matter how many times he sifted through the pile, he simply couldn't find it.

The photo was gone.

He *had* seen the photograph, hadn't he?

Yes, yes, he was absolutely sure. He had even questioned Felix about it, which was how he learned about the old wing in the first place.

Maybe Felix had taken the photograph for some reason. Dan couldn't imagine why, but it was better than the alternative—someone sneaking around in his room, planting spooky pictures and taking them away. He reached under his bed where he had hidden the folder, half expecting it to be gone, too.

But no, there it was, exactly as he had left it.

He wanted to make sure he hadn't missed anything last time. Maybe he'd even put the photo in here without remembering it. He opened the folder. There, right on top of the stack of papers, was a note in now dreadfully familiar handwriting. This one wasn't even in an envelope.

In a mad world, only the mad are sane.

Dan hurled the folder across the room. Papers went flying. "I can't take this anymore!" he shouted. A moment later there was a knock at the door, and a guy from the room next to his, Thomas, stuck his head in.

"You okay, man?" he said.

Dan nodded, too upset to say anything coherent.

"Because, you know, if you have anything you want to talk about, I mean, about Joe and all, they have counselors . . . or I could, you know, if you need it. . . ." His voice trailed off.

"No, man, it's really okay, thanks for asking," Dan said, puffing out his cheeks in what he hoped looked like a smile.

Thomas closed the door with a shrug.

Dan didn't want help and he definitely didn't need other people's pity.

At dinner, Abby was withdrawn. She slumped in her chair, chewing her nails and holding a staring contest with her mashed potatoes. Dan was still mulling over the little he knew about his mysterious stalker. While everyone in the cafeteria was noticeably more subdued than usual, Dan felt like all the sadness in the room originated at his table.

Finally, Abby spoke. "So I was thinking we must be terrible people. I mean really, really terrible people."

"I . . . Hm. That's not what *I* was thinking, but go on."

"It's Jordan," Abby said, sliding down even farther in her chair. "I feel like we've completely failed him."

"How? You've been texting him like crazy. He knows we're reaching out."

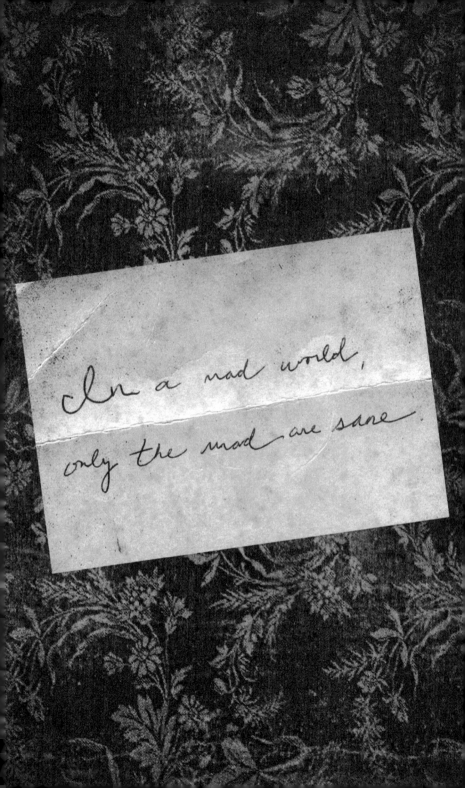

"That's not enough. We should go see him. We have to get through to him; otherwise we're no better than his family, or that guy from his school who ditched him."

"Abby, if he wants to be left alone . . ."

"But he *doesn't*. We all process stress differently. I think he's hiding, like he thinks he'd be a burden or something if he told us what's going on. I want him to know that's not true at all."

"I know, but I still worry about invading his space. Maybe you should just text him again."

"Sometimes, Dan, friends have to take a stand and say: Hey, idiot, we're here for you no matter what. We're not going to disappear when you get grumpy or angry, we're in this for the long haul. We're in this for each other."

"See, that's why I like you so much," he said, surprising both of them.

"What do you mean?"

"Nothing. You're right. We should go see him," Dan said.

"I have figure drawing till nine o'clock—that seems like such a long time away. Do you think you could go after dinner, and I'll come join you after class? It would mean a lot."

"Sure, no problem. I'll tell him what you said, although I might leave out the 'hey, idiot' part. Hope you don't mind. . . ."

"No," she said with a laugh, "that's probably a smart idea. Thanks, Dan. See you later?"

Dan nodded, waving good-bye as she grabbed her tray and left for class. He walked out of the Commons a few minutes later and followed the well-worn path back to the dorm. Just two more weeks of classes, and then they'd all be going home. He wasn't sure how he felt about that. At least Pittsburgh wasn't too far away from New York. He bet it was an easy trip by train.

Two police officers still monitored the entrance hall. They were there to provide peace of mind, but they only made Dan uneasy, as if there was something unresolved that the students weren't being told. The tall cop who had interviewed Dan nodded to him in greeting as he went by. Dan tried not to read anything into the acknowledgment.

Nobody was out and about on Jordan's floor. Dan had noticed that most students had chosen to stay outside and away from Brookline as much as possible that day. That only reinforced Dan's feeling that Jordan would be in, since he seemed so determined to avoid human company.

There was no answer when Dan knocked on Jordan's door. He knocked a little louder and waited, then pressed his ear to the door, wondering if maybe Jordan was in there but just refusing to answer. But no, he couldn't hear anything inside the room. On a whim, he tried the doorknob. The door swung open.

No one was inside. The room was freezing. Yi's side of things looked normal, if a bit messy, but Jordan's half was covered floor to ceiling with torn scraps of yellow legal paper, all filled with his frantic writing. Dan stepped in the room and walked over to one covered wall. He leaned in to take a closer look. This was math on a level he couldn't begin to understand. He wondered if it even made sense to Jordan.

"The unsolvable problem," he murmured.

The surface of Jordan's desk had disappeared under a mountain of yellow paper, too. Laying on top, though, were two photographs that had been printed on regular computer paper. These photographs . . . Dan picked them up. They were both shots of Abby, Jordan, and him together. The three of them stood in a row, arms around one another, grinning from ear to ear. When had they taken these? He had no recollection of posing for either one, and that frightened him immensely. He'd never had such big gaps in his memory as these.

Almost as troubling as his apparent amnesia was the fact that Dan's face had been X-ed out so thoroughly in both pictures that the paper had been torn.

"What are you doing here?"

"Shit!" Dan whirled around, dropping the photographs. "You scared me half to death, man!"

"Do you think I care?" Hair wet, holding a towel, Jordan had clearly just returned from the shower. He jabbed a finger at the door. "Get out!"

"Wait, Jordan—I just wanted to see if you were okay. That's all! I didn't mean to—"

Jordan grabbed Dan by the arm, and dragged him a few steps. "I don't care what you meant to do! Get the hell out!"

Dan sprinted for the hall, cringing when he heard the door slam shut with a bang behind him. He fumbled for his phone, sending off a quick text to Abby. It read simply "Jordan v. mad."

That was rage, real rage, and Dan seemed to be the reason for it. But why? What on earth had he done? Why would Jordan hate him so much?

Wait, could *Jordan* be his stalker?

Now *that* was paranoia.

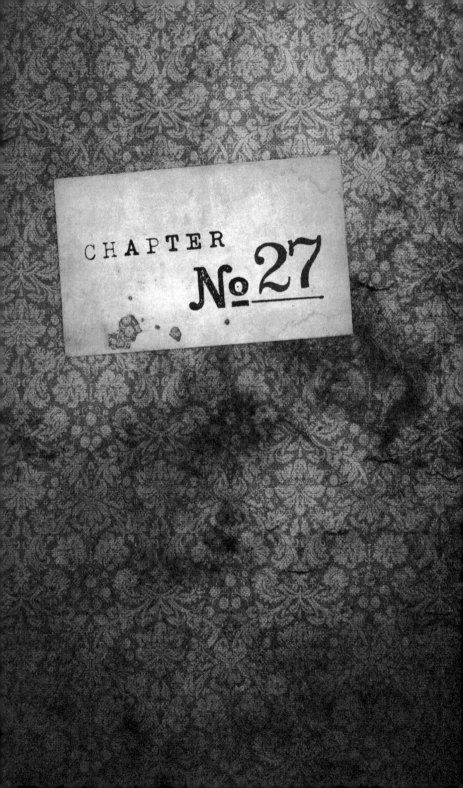

CHAPTER № 27

Dan smelled mint. His office always smelled of mint. The young secretary left a tin of peppermints on his desk every morning and he ate them throughout the day. Julie was her name. Pretty and young—too pretty and young to already be working in a place like this.

A half-finished report sat on the desk before him. This side of things, the paper-pushing side, always annoyed him. That's what assistants were for, damn it all, but they couldn't be depended upon for anything. Sucking on a mint and adjusting his spectacles, he went back to the business at hand.

Where was he? Ah, yes. Writing.

Each victim had been strangled, although some had struggled, the signs of which were evident in the bruises and cuts they sustained. Reportedly, the victims posed to dance looked remarkably convincing, as did those set around the rest of the bar, sitting and standing. Good God, the planning it must have taken to achieve this. . . . A corpse reaches its peak stiffness at approximately twelve hours after death. To kill the patrons of an entire bar and then wait among the dead for hours . . . I admit, even I was skeptical that treatment could help a man so deeply, deeply troubled.

Happily, repeated insulin shock treatments and two weeks in the Dark Room have somewhat improved the patient's temperament. He seems almost docile. I have nearly accomplished something astounding with the man. There will be

Each victim had been strangled, although some had struggled, the signs of which were evident in the bruises our cats they sustained. Reputedly, the victims posed to dance looked remarkably amusing, as did those set among the rest of the bar, sitting or standing. Good God, the planning it must have taken to achieve this ... the corpse reaches its peak stiffness at approximately twelve hours after death. To build the patrons of an entire bar and then wait among the dead for hours ... I admit, even I was skeptical that treatment could help a man so deeply, deeply troubled.

Happily, repeated insular slab treatments and two weeks in the Dark Room have somewhat improved the patient's temperament. He seems almost docile. I have really accomplished something astounding with the ___ man. There will be more sessions, the next one on Thursday, and further monitoring of his behavior.

                                        Dave Conger, Ward

more sessions, the next one on Thursday, and further monitoring of his behavior.
Report complete, he signed his name.

Daniel Crawford, Warden

He considered the signature and signed it again. And again. He wrote his
name faster and faster, pen flying across the page. Daniel Crawford, Daniel
Crawford . . . The page disappeared in front of his eyes. He could see the
dancing corpses, hear the record wheezing softly in the background. It played
the tune of Lucy's music box. And then he was falling down the rabbit hole,
falling, and he . . .

. . . woke from his nap with a start. Dan hadn't even known
he'd fallen asleep. What was the dream? He concentrated before
it faded away. . . . He was seeing again through the warden's eyes
as if they were his own. It felt so real. He even remembered
writing the report, in the warden's own hand. If he thought
hard enough about it, he could taste the peppermints.

Dan rolled out of bed, still decidedly groggy. On the bedside
table, his phone lit up with a picture of Abby. Her text message
appeared underneath.

Class over. They're handing out ice cream in quad. Want update on
Jordan. Meet me in 5?

In five? Damn, no time to shower. Dan checked his breath,
cupping his palm over his mouth and blowing. It . . . could have
been better. He tracked down a beat-up, old pack of gum in his
backpack, but just tasting the mint made him feel sick.

What else would Daniel Crawford ruin for him?

The lure of ice cream had apparently emptied the dorm, both of students and the police. Dan jogged through the silent hall to the back stairs. At the second floor, he grabbed the handrail as usual and swung around it to the next set of stairs below. But a dark shape startled him, and he stumbled, nearly colliding with the lump in the stairwell. He dodged it just in time, sliding to the right and grabbing the opposite handrail.

At first, he assumed it was just a backpack someone had dropped, or maybe a bucket one of the maintenance workers had left. But no, the shape was bigger and—oh, God—it was *human*. There, with one arm on his legs and the other slung over his head, was Jordan's roommate, Yi. For a second, Dan's limbs refused to cooperate. He couldn't move.

Oh, God, he's dead, oh, God, he's dead, he's dead. . . .

Then Dan knelt, taking Yi by the shoulders and shaking him gently. *What did those safety pamphlets always say? Don't move someone who's fallen because you might make things worse?*

"No, no, this can't be happening. It *isn't* happening," Dan whispered, carefully searching along Yi's T-shirt. He pressed his palm to Yi's chest and waited, a hysterical laugh of relief escaping when he felt the thump of his heartbeat.

"Yi! Yi, can you hear me?" He shook him again. No response. Dan yanked his cell phone out of his pocket and frantically dialed 911. Would campus security be better? They'd be closer, that's for sure. Where had those cops gone anyway?

"Yes, hello? I need help. I'm at the Brookline Dormitory on campus. Sorry, um, Camford, New Hampshire College. My friend is unconscious. It looks like he was attacked or maybe he fell? I don't know. He's breathing, but I can't wake him up, but there's definitely a pulse. . . ."

The operator insisted he stay on the line, and while it was probably just a moment or two before the police arrived, it felt like a lifetime. He kept his hand on Yi's shoulder, telling him over and over again that it would be okay, that he'd be okay, that everything was all right. After a while, Dan knew he was babbling, words tripping out of his mouth as he tried not to panic. He tried not to notice that one of Yi's ankles was neatly crossed over the other leg, as if Yi had just sat down on the stairs to take a rest. Finally, the police officers arrived. One of them helped Dan up, patted him on the back, and told him to wait downstairs.

More cops arrived, and more, and then the paramedics. Dan answered their questions in a daze. No, the stairs weren't slippery; no, he hadn't moved Yi at all; yes, he'd called the second he found him. No, he didn't know anyone who would want to hurt Yi. They sat him down on a bench in the front hall while the police secured the doors. Nobody from outside was allowed in, and police posted to each floor told the students still in their rooms to stay exactly where they were.

Through the windows in the entrance hall, Dan could see students gathering around outside and peering in, trying to figure out what was going on. By the time he thought to look at his phone, he had six missed text messages, all from Abby.

Police just freaked out and went inside. Where r u?

and

Dan? r u ok? What happened? Do u c the cops in there?

The messages became increasingly panicked, until the final one was just a mess of exclamation points and question marks.

"I'm fine," he texted back. "Found Yi. He fell down the stairs or something." Dan glanced up from his phone. The paramedics were carrying Yi on a stretcher, a blanket wrapped tightly over his chest. "Taking him to ambulance now."

As soon as the paramedics reached the doors, two cops sprang forward to usher them out and control the crowd waiting to get a look. The noise that flooded in from outside was deafening, one mass of shouts and crying and the blare of ambulance sirens.

Abby texted back in a flash.

Whoa! Poor Yi! I c them taking him to the ambulance now. u holding up ok?

Dan was grateful for her concern. "Fine," he shot back, even if that was only half-true. Because while the police questioned him and paced around and questioned him some more, all Dan could think was that Yi had looked so still, still as a sculpture.

From their questions, it became clear that the cops didn't feel Joe's murder and this incident were related. For one, Yi was still alive, and for another, the apparent murderer was in their custody. But gazing around at the faces of the students outside, Dan knew they were all thinking the same thing—Brookline wasn't safe.

"Son?"

Dan's eyes lifted slowly from his cell phone to the police

officer standing in front of him. He didn't remember his name, although he knew the officer had introduced himself at some point during the questioning. Dan simply didn't have the energy to remember.

"You're free to go," the officer said, nodding to the doors. "We want everyone out for now. They asked that you all gather in the dining hall."

Abby was hovering right outside the dorm, dodging officers who were trying to herd her away. When she caught sight of Dan, she came running.

"Hey! You . . . you're really okay?" She gave him a big hug.

"That helps."

Nobody was doing a very good job of getting people to leave the scene. There was simply too much commotion. Dan looked into the blaze of siren lights, finding that even professors and townsfolk had been roused by the excitement. Clusters of students whispered under the trees, and Dan spotted a few familiar faces—among them some hall monitors and professors, including Professor Reyes, and—*wait, what the hell*—Sal Weathers's wife. Her gaunt face was even more ghostly under the blue flashes of the police car lights. Professor Reyes was pushing through the crowd and flagging down an officer. She seemed to be shouting at him, arguing. When Dan tried to spot Sal's wife again, she was gone.

They joined the stream of kids going into Wilfurd.

"It's all just too awful to think about," Abby said. "Do you think he'll be okay?"

"I don't know. I mean, he was breathing, but he was unconscious. It could've been a fall, I don't know. I just hope he's all right."

Inside, students zoomed around helter-skelter. Some of Abby's art friends raced up to them, bombarding Dan with questions. *Oh, right. I was there. I found him. Of course everyone knows.* Finally Abby intercepted, asking them to give him space.

"Thanks," Dan said to her when they left. "I'm not sure I could handle more questions right now. The police already grilled me."

The hall monitors had moved the ice cream inside, and set it up on the buffet table so students could help themselves. There was also a young woman in a crooked hairnet who was making milk shakes.

"Is this supposed to make us forget?" Abby asked, rolling her eyes. But then she spied Jordan standing alone by the windows. She pinched Dan's elbow. "Let's get him something. He and Yi are close. He must be devastated."

"He wasn't so thrilled to see me when I went to visit," Dan said. "In fact, I got the impression he was really pissed off at me."

"Yeah, I saw your text," she answered quickly. "I still think we should say something."

"Sure, yeah. Let's just . . . approach with caution, you know? I don't feel like getting my head bitten off again right now."

They waited their turn to grab a shake for Jordan. Dan overheard the kids in front of them discussing their plans to leave. His heart sank. Did this mean the program was over for good? He suspected the only reason things hadn't shut down after Joe's murder was because they'd apprehended a suspect so quickly, but another incident . . . Well, it was easy to see why people were drawing a connection.

Milk shakes in hand, Abby and Dan approached Jordan. His

notepads and pen were nowhere in sight. He'd gone back to carrying his many-sided die, turning it in his palm as if he were trying to polish down the corners. He stared out the windows into the quad, still wearing his blue bathrobe and a pair of brown suede slippers.

When Jordan saw them, he said defiantly, "I don't want it. I don't need your pity party."

"Then we'll go. We'll leave you alone," Abby replied. She put the milk shake on the table next to him. "But we wanted you to know we're here if you need us." She turned to leave, nodding for Dan to follow her.

"Hang on a second." Jordan took the milk shake, cradling it in both hands. There were big circles under his eyes; his hair was unkempt. The lights from the police cars outside reflected off his face, tinting him red, then blue, then ghostly pale.

For a moment, Jordan kept his eyes on the cup in his hands. Then he slowly lifted his head to look at them. "Thanks. For the milk shake and . . . thanks."

"So how are you holding up?" Dan asked.

Jordan sighed. "It doesn't feel real. I mean, *maybe* he fell, but did you see all those cops? There's no way he just fell." He took a long slurp on the milk shake. "What did Yi do? He's a good guy, a little talkative, but good."

The program director arrived, informing them in a quavering voice that the dorm had been thoroughly checked and they could now return to their rooms. Nobody seemed eager to leave the dining hall.

"Come on," Abby said. She put her hand on Jordan's arm. "Let's head back to your room."

"I can walk there myself."

Here we go again. . . . Dan braced himself for the blowup.

But Abby ignored the tone. "I know you can, stupid, you've got legs. But let's go together anyway. Nobody should be alone tonight."

CHAPTER
№ 28

*T*he walk back was silent, and it was with heavy steps that all three reentered Brookline. *The dorm has never looked so ugly before*, Dan thought, *so hulking and dilapidated*. Now it was the scene of a murder and a possible attack, to say nothing of the grisly experiments it had once hidden away.

Jordan led them down the hall to his room. As he dug for the key in his pocket, Dan wondered what Abby would say when she saw the room papered in Jordan's mathematical scrawl.

But when Abby stepped into the room behind Jordan, there was no surprised gasp, no cry of horror. The room was clean. Not one piece of yellow paper was in sight, the desk and bed were bare, and there were even a couple of posters on the wall. There was also no sign of the mutilated photographs.

Dan looked at Jordan, but Jordan had slumped on the bed and was staring down at his feet. For a moment, Dan doubted his memory. Could he have just imagined the way the room had been? The photographs? Surely it was strange that Yi hadn't mentioned anything about the paper explosion to Dan and Abby when he told them about how worried he was about Jordan. Or maybe Jordan had cleaned up to freak Dan out deliberately. There were those two photographs he'd defaced, after all. Now that Dan thought about it, maybe Jordan was the one hiding the scratched-out picture of the warden.

But could Jordan really be behind all the shit that was happening to him? It was the second time that night Dan found himself asking this question.

Abby put a kettle on Jordan's hot plate, then joined Jordan on the bed.

"Okay, so I know we're all feeling a little freaked out and distraught right now, but there's something I need to tell you guys," she said. She pushed a loose strand of hair behind her ear, easing into her next words with that delicate earnestness that Dan found so endearing. "My aunt Lucy is still alive."

A grown-up Lucy? So she hadn't died after the operation?

"But how did you . . ." Jordan trailed off.

"Find out?" Abby finished.

Dan wanted to know, too. Abby had clearly been doing her share of snooping, and she'd managed to keep it incredibly well hidden. They had that in common, then.

"You know that tiny little church on the way to Camford?" Abby said. "Dan and I passed it when we went to dinner that night, and I thought, well, maybe they'd have a record of Lucy. I mean, supposing she *had* been here as a little girl, I figured she couldn't have gone far when Brookline closed."

"Okay . . . ?" Dan said, marveling at her calm rationality.

"I went yesterday afternoon. The pastor there was in his office—he's this nice old man, even shorter than I am—and he was very helpful. I told him I was looking for information on my lost aunt who lived in Camford in the late 1960s. He got out the old baptism registry, and we just started going through the names."

Jordan was aghast. Dan hoped he was hiding it better, but he felt the same way.

"There she was, 1973. Baptized with a whole group of kids from the Camford orphanage when she was thirteen. The orphanage is long gone, of course, but the important thing is she made it out of here and stayed in Camford. Like I said. *Et voilà*."

"Oh my *God*, you actually found her? Did you *talk* to her?" Jordan blurted out.

"No, I didn't quite find her. Not yet, anyway."

"This is a lot to take in," said Dan. "I mean . . . you're sure it's her? You're sure it's your aunt?"

"There's no doubt in my mind," Abby replied. "The name . . . the location . . . the timing . . . Do you know what Occam's razor means? It means if there are lots of possible explanations, the simplest one is probably right."

"Who are you and what you have done with Abby?" Jordan said, and Dan laughed before he could stop himself. But when Abby just continued to stare at them, Jordan finally threw up his arms in a shrug. "Oh, what the hell. After everything that's happened, I'm pretty much willing to believe anything at this point."

Dan agreed. They were way beyond coincidences. And maybe now that they were all being so honest, Abby and Jordan could help him put his own puzzle pieces into place.

"Look, guys, there's something I need to tell you, too. I—" He faltered. He'd never be as bold or open as Abby. "I did some online research on Brookline."

He took a deep, centering breath. "Yi told me that when Felix found Joe he was propped up in a weird position. And then tonight, when I found Yi in the stairwell, he was posed strangely, too. It wouldn't matter, but there's mention of this guy on the page that I found. . . . He was one of the patients here who was a murderer. A serial killer. He would kill people and then set them up in these tableaux, posed like statues. . . ."

Reportedly, the victims posed to dance looked remarkably convincing.

"Dan, what are you saying?" Abby asked.

"He was called the Sculptor, and he was here, at Brookline. I . . . also found a card about him in the old wing. That time when Joe caught us. According to the card he was cured, but according to the website no one knows what happened to him. What if he's still around? I mean, it would make sense, wouldn't it? Just like you said about Lucy: Why go far when he could just use his old home as a hunting ground?" Dan wished he hadn't phrased it that way. The thought of being hunted by that monster . . . God, could the *Sculptor* be his stalker? Did he somehow find out a kid was coming here who had the same name as the warden, the man who had performed bizarre experiments on him?

"You have to go to the police with this," Jordan said.

"And tell them what? That a man who was treated here years ago is back for revenge?" It sounded absurd coming out of his mouth. "Why would they believe me?"

"I don't care if they believe you!" Jordan shouted. He stormed to the door, throwing it open. "Yi was attacked. My *roommate* was attacked. Joe was *killed*. Anything you know, anything that might help . . . We owe it to them to tell the cops."

"Jordan's right," Abby said. She gave Dan a sympathetic smile. "You don't need to mention the old wing at all." It was like she'd read his mind. He felt a little guilty that she knew the real reason he was apprehensive to approach the cops.

Dan finally nodded. "You're right. I could just point them to the stuff I found online."

Not to me. Not to Daniel Crawford.

"It's something, at least," Abby agreed. "Let's find an officer now and get it out of the way."

In the hall, it didn't take long to track down a roaming policeman. Jordan and Abby flanked Dan as he approached, as if they were worried he might retreat.

"Excuse me," Dan said, a bit sheepishly. Police always made him nervous, even when he hadn't done anything wrong. The cop turned. The name stitched on his uniform was "Teague." He was short, broad through the shoulders, and had a brown mustache that was just beginning to turn gray. "Excuse me? Hi. I'm a student at the program here. . . . I just wanted to bring some information to your attention, Officer."

"Oh. And what would that be?" the cop said, crossing his arms over his chest.

"Well . . . It's just that I was doing some reading about Brookline online. Out of curiosity, you know, to learn more about the school and so on."

"A serial killer lived at the asylum," Jordan burst out. *No turning back now . . .*

"Go on," Teague said with a nod.

But Dan could already tell this was pointless. The officer had that look on his face, the skeptical one where a smile wasn't a smile but a subtle hint that, while he might be listening, he wasn't the least bit interested in taking a bunch of freaked-out kids seriously.

Careful to leave out anything he had learned from his trips to the basement, Dan told the cop everything he knew about the Sculptor. He mentioned the similarity between the murders back in the sixties and what had happened to Joe, and now Yi.

"I'll make a note of it," Teague said when Dan finished.

"You didn't even write anything down," Jordan pointed out tartly.

"*I'll make a note of it.*" The cop gave Jordan a long, cold look. "Look, I've lived in Camford all my life. We know about the Sculptor, okay? You couldn't grow up here and not hear about all the crazies who were sent here. *Especially* that man. Dennis Heimline. That's a name I won't forget." He tugged down the edge of his uniform and leaned closer to Dan. "He died in '72, the same year this place got shut down."

Dead? Had Sal Weathers gotten his wires crossed? Dan wasn't sure who he trusted less, a crazy self-defined historian or a local cop. But it would make sense that the police would have kept tabs on Heimline.

"It could be a copycat," Dan suggested. "It's not hard to find out about the Sculptor online, anyone could look it up and mimic the crimes."

The cop sighed, waving him off. "Look, kid, we got our man from last night in custody. This thing tonight? It was an accident. Boy slipped, fell, what have you. So this?" He gestured at them. "What you're doing, is scared talk. You should go see one of the counselors, and stop chasing ghosts."

CHAPTER
№ 29

*T*he next day, classes were canceled, leaving Dan to spend most of the day in the quad watching the students who were leaving the program. Abby had several friends who had chosen to go, and she wanted Dan and Jordan there with her for the farewells. He hadn't expected such a simple task to end up exhausting him, but standing there while person after person gave him frightened or pitying looks really ground down his nerves. They wore their thoughts plainly: they thought he was insane to stick with the program.

Felix chose to stay. Dan welcomed his companionship. He couldn't fathom sleeping there alone.

Drained as he was from the long day, Dan should have fallen right to sleep that night. But even though his body was tired, his mind was restless. He kept going in and out of sleep in half-hour stretches.

Finally, the clock on Dan's nightstand read 2:57. Felix snored in the neighboring bed. The open window let in a chill breeze that blew the curtains around. Realizing he'd never get to sleep at this rate, Dan decided to get a snack from the vending machines. Careful not to make a sound, he slid out of bed, pulled on a flannel shirt, and grabbed his phone and his wallet. He decided not to change his sweatpants, reasoning that if a cop saw him it would seem less suspicious if he looked fresh out of bed. He could always claim to be a sleepwalker.

He shut the door softly and moved down the hall. No cops in sight. On tiptoes, he crept silently down the stairs to the first floor, willing himself not to think about Yi and Joe. He peered down the corridor, but again, no cops. Where were they all? He had just reached the vending machines and reached in his pocket for change when a heavy hand landed on his shoulder. He turned quickly, and let out a gust of a sigh. It was only Jordan.

"You scared the crap out of me, Jordan." And that was an understatement. Dan pressed his palm against his chest, feeling the hammer of his pulse.

"Sorry, man. Didn't mean to. I thought you'd know it was me. Anyway, what'd you want to see me for?" he whispered.

"What are you talking about?" Dan was confused.

"You invited me here . . . ?" Jordan sounded irritated. "I thought it was *important*."

"No, I definitely didn't . . ."

"It's three in the goddamn morning. I don't feel like messing around," Jordan muttered. "At least come up to my room, so the cops don't catch us."

When they were safely back upstairs, Jordan took out his phone. He flipped it open and showed Dan his message in-box. Sure enough, there was a text sent from Dan's number asking Jordan to meet him at the vending machines at three o'clock to discuss something urgent.

"Satisfied?" Jordan asked.

What could he say? Dan blinked at the message, his heart sinking. He had absolutely no memory of sending that text; in fact, he hadn't even considered asking Jordan—or anyone—to meet him. He'd decided to get a snack only a few minutes ago. How could he have possibly planned for this?

"I swear, Jordan, I didn't send that." He sounded like he was pleading.

"Check your phone."

"*What?*"

"Check it. Now. I want to see your sent messages." He held open his hand, waiting for Dan to produce the phone.

"I don't know what this proves," Dan muttered. But he remembered the strange emails that had shown up on his phone, so he wasn't even surprised when he saw the message in his Sent folder. It didn't matter because *he hadn't sent it*. He was sure. But Jordan wouldn't believe him.

"This is bullshit, Dan," Jordan hissed. He took off his glasses and rubbed his eyes with the heels of his palms. "I really can't deal with whatever you're up to right now, whatever game you're playing. Yi is in the hospital, I'm sleeping all alone in this creepy freaking dump, and now you're doing . . . whatever this is!" Jordan rubbed his head. "I think you should leave now. I need some sleep."

Suddenly making his friend believe him was more important to Dan than anything. He needed *someone* to tell him he wasn't losing his mind.

"Jordan, you have to trust me. I didn't send this. I don't know who did, but—" Dan looked again at his phone, and Jordan's, which may as well have been surgically grafted to his palm since he was never without it. Could he be behind all the unexplained messages?

No, it was a ridiculous idea. Impossible. Dan was just grasping at straws now and looking for anyone to blame. *Anyone other than yourself.*

"But it's in your phone so you're clearly full of it. Why are you even bothering to deny it?" Jordan was asking. "What's the point?"

"Look . . . This is stupid. I didn't send you that text. I'm going back to bed."

"Yeah, run away, Dan. Real mature."

Dan left in a frustrated huff. The dorm was empty as he returned to his room, no sign of cops or hall monitors. When he unlocked his door and stepped in, he knew right away that something was wrong.

No Felix.

Before he had time to process this, the phone in his hand leapt to life, vibrating and lighting up. He nearly chucked it across the room in surprise. He looked at the screen, hoping the message was from Jordan or Abby. Instead it was from an unknown number. Dan's hand trembled as he opened the message.

You can be one of them, too. You can be immortal. Bend you, pose you, with a smirk or a frown. I'm waiting on the fifth floor, Daniel, to sculpt you.

"No way," Dan whispered. He held the cell phone close to his face, as if reading it from a different angle would change the words somehow.

You're not going, of course. You're going to do the smart thing and show this to the cops. Someone is trying to screw with you.

His mind jumped back to Felix. Where was he? Dan had a sinking feeling. Felix must have woken up, found him missing, and gone looking for him. But what if he'd accidentally found the Sculptor instead? Could *he* be on the fifth floor? Dan had to find him—before it was too late.

His mind was made up. But he wasn't stupid; he'd get a cop to go with him, even though the cops thought the Sculptor was dead. He had proof now that the Sculptor was alive and well—and out to get him.

Anyone could have written that message, a pesky voice reminded him. *Even you said there could be a copycat. . . .*

Either way, Dan thought, this was the person responsible for Joe and Yi. Real deal or copycat, he'd find out who was behind it all.

But when Dan left the room for the second time that night, he discovered that there were still no cops. He checked the second floor and then the first, backtracking all the way to the vending machines. There must have been an emergency in town or something. The Camford police force wasn't exactly huge. Dan took one last lap of the first floor, but it was silent. There was no more time. He would have to go alone, or risk Felix becoming the next victim.

Dan raced up the stairs, actually hoping to make enough noise to rouse someone. Maybe the cops were on the fifth floor already. But when he reached the top of the stairs and turned the corner, Dan knew that was just a foolish hope. The floor was silent, and someone had cut the lights.

Dan groped along the wall for a panel of switches but could only find one.

The wind outside howled, and the overhead eaves, old and probably rotting, groaned in answer. Dan passed one door on his right, clenching his fists to fight the nerves tingling at the base of his spine. He had just enough light to see that the room was empty. The next room was empty, too, and the next, and the next. But suddenly, Dan heard a voice in that last room, and he moved stealthily toward it.

"Please . . . P-please don't hurt me."

Felix.

He quickened his pace.

"P-please . . ." It was Felix again. Dan had never heard anyone whimper like that, a young man reduced to a frightened little child.

Dan stepped as softly as he could. If anything was going to give him away, it would be his labored breathing. His throat had tightened so much, each suck of air came in with a wheeze.

Pressing against the wall, he inched his head around the corner, dreading what he would find. Whatever he expected, it wasn't a man who was six foot three and carrying a crowbar. He was standing over the slumped body of Felix.

Dan must have made a sound because the man turned to look at him, passing his crowbar from hand to hand. He was wearing black gloves. Dan couldn't stop looking at them. Murderers wore black gloves.

Do something.

Dan had never been a hero or an athlete, but an instinct he didn't recognize, one that came from a deep well of anger, drove him into the lounge. He charged, shouting, looking Rambo in his head but probably drunken buffalo in reality. It didn't matter.

The man with the crowbar staggered back in surprise, falling to the floor when Dan crashed into him, hard. Dan heard a loud crack and hoped he'd busted one of the guy's ribs. He brought his knee up, aiming to connect with the man where he knew it would really hurt. But the man parried Dan's blow with a kick of his own. Hands as tough as steel wrapped around Dan's forearms and pulled them apart. Dan was no longer pinning the man down. The man rolled over and shoved him to the floor.

"You little shit," he hissed.

"Help!" Dan screamed as loudly as he could. But the man's hands were pressed so heavily on his chest that it sounded like a whisper.

Dan's head smacked the carpet, paper-thin padding over concrete judging by how much it hurt.

His vision swam, blacks and blues and purples all meshing together, inseparable. This was it. He was going to die. Time seemed to slow; moments stretched apart like tufts of cotton being pulled farther and farther until he heard shouts and the sound of feet pounding down the hall.

"Damn it!" said the man. Jumping up, he ran to an open window and disappeared through it just moments before two cops barreled into the lounge, guns drawn.

Their voices bounced, muted, as if his skull had become an empty echo chamber. Dan tried to sit up, but his head just hurt too damn much. He fell back to the floor.

"Can you hear me? Hey! Are you all right? Did you hit your head?"

He stared up at the officer. Teague.

"Are you okay? Can you stand?"

That remained to be seen. At least his vision was starting to piece itself back together. Dan tried to nod. *Ow.* Bad idea.

"The window," he slurred, trying to point the cops to where the man had escaped.

"Call an ambulance," an officer was saying to his partner. He was kneeling at Felix's side. "This one needs to get to the hospital. He's been hit." A blanket appeared from somewhere and the cop draped it over Felix. "Can't have him going into shock." Another blanket was wrapped around Dan's shoulders.

"Mm fine," Dan insisted. "The man . . . through the window." A moment later, Teague helped him to his feet. The cops let him regain his balance, and the ache in his head gradually subsided as they waited for the paramedics.

The ambulance came, and they put Felix on a stretcher. He was stirring as they left the room, and trying to sit up. Soon Dan heard the sound of an ambulance moving away.

Dan stood on wobbly legs while they took his name and room number, and contact information for his parents.

"The guy is getting away," he said desperately. "You can still catch him if you go now—he's probably still on the roof."

One of the cops ran over to the window and checked around outside. Finally, he turned back to them with a shrug.

"There's no one out there," he said. "And it's a good fifty foot drop down to the ground."

"He's out there!" Dan shouted.

"Whoa, whoa, calm down, buddy," Teague said. "Start at the beginning. What are you doing up here in the first place?" Teague took out a notepad and pencil.

Dan wanted to cry.

"I got up to go to the bathroom," he said, not wanting to touch the thing with Jordan and the mysterious text message. "When I got back to my room Felix was gone. He's been frazzled lately. He was the one who found Joe in the stairs. . . . The Sculptor sent me this weird poem thing and told me he would *sculpt* me if I met him on the fifth floor. I was scared Felix was with him, so I went looking. I didn't want him wandering alone at night."

"Uh-huh," Teague said. He motioned for Dan to continue, but then a third cop strode up to them. She handed Teague a phone. Felix's phone.

"I think you should see this," she said. "And you need to confiscate this kid's cell."

Dan swallowed around a knot, the hot, sick feeling in his gut enough to make him want to double over and hurl. Both cops stared at him, waiting.

"What's on Felix's phone?" Dan asked, stumbling over the words. When had it gotten so hot in the room? He was sweating bullets. "Please, I'm sure I can explain if you just—"

"Yeah, I'm *sure* you can. Your phone, please."

"But—"

"Your *phone*." Teague narrowed his eyes. "I'm not going to ask again."

It was no use protesting. Maybe this was for the best. His outbox probably had a message like "HELLO FELIX I WOULD VERY MUCH LIKE TO BASH YOUR BRAINS IN WITH A CROWBAR." Somehow, it would happen. Then he'd be taken to jail and locked up. At least then he couldn't get into any more trouble. He'd be left alone with his thoughts, and that would finish him off without ever needing a trial.

Then Dan remembered he had a message from the Sculptor in his in-box. Now the police would have to believe him. And they could trace the number!

Dan handed Teague the phone. It would all be over soon.

Teague found his sent messages quickly. "Bingo," he said triumphantly. "'Fifth floor lounge, 3:30, I've got something cool to show you.'" He clucked his tongue softly. "Just what was on Felix's phone. Sounds friendly enough, kid. What went wrong?"

"I didn't send that," Dan snapped, ballistic. "I didn't. I swear to you. . . ."

"Do I look like an idiot?" Teague asked.

"Check my in-box!" Dan burst out. "I told you there's a message there from the Sculptor telling me to meet him here!"

Teague looked at him strangely, but clicked on the in-box. There was a pause. "Nothing there, kid. No mysterious message. And like I said before, the Sculptor is dead."

This was getting worse by the second. The sweat had soaked through the front of Dan's shirt. He wanted to curl up and disappear.

"Why don't you tell me what really happened."

Dan took a deep breath. "Honestly, I don't even know any more," he said. Teague narrowed his eyes. "I tried to find a cop before I came up here but no one was around."

"Kid, we've got cops on every floor."

"There wasn't one when I left my room!" Dan shouted. "All I know is I got to the fifth floor and heard Felix crying out for help. So I came in here and there was this huge guy with a crow-bar. I ran at him."

"Go on," said Teague.

"We were fighting, and then he heard you guys coming and he jumped out that window." Dan pointed to it again, feeling especially stupid.

Teague looked at Dan and slowly shook his head. "Okay, kid, let's go along with you for now. Let's say there's this mystery man who climbs out of a window on the fifth floor after attacking your best friend. Have you ever seen this man before?"

"Never," Dan replied, locking eyes firmly with Teague.

The cop hesitated, looking Dan over and chewing the inside of his cheek. "You know, the weird thing is I almost believe you. You're either in the middle of one hell of a frame-up job or you're a damn good liar.

"Anyway, I suggest you keep your nose clean until we can sit you down and go over this again. I'm not going to take you to the station now, but I will if I have to. Until then, you'll have an officer with you at all times."

"Wait—"

"At *all* times." Teague touched his forefinger to his nose and then pointed it at Dan. "You understand me?"

"Yes, sir," Dan murmured.

Adjusting his cap, Teague nodded, satisfied. Dan hardly felt the grip of the officer assigned to him. Felix would spend the night at the hospital, with an officer waiting patiently to question him, while Dan was manhandled back to his room. A feeling of numb dread settled in his bones. "I'll be right outside," said his jailer. "So don't try anything funny." The irony of his room being used as a cell did not escape him.

The whole night, the whole *day*, now seemed like a dream. Particulars melted away, details disappeared. What had the man with the crowbar looked like? He couldn't really remember now. Would Felix be able to corroborate Dan's story? He didn't know. He'd have to wait and see.

He climbed into bed without feeling the mattress or blankets. It was strange to think that he was a suspect—that the police thought he had attacked Felix. Did they think he was responsible for Yi's attack, too—and, oh God no, Joe's murder? If they discovered he'd been blacked out in the basement, what would they say? All the evidence was against him.

Outside the door, he heard his guard pacing slowly back and forth.

I have to fight back, Dan thought, squeezing his eyes shut.

His mind churned. Why would the Sculptor have a crowbar? That was a blunt weapon, a clumsy one. The Sculptor was smarter—crueler—than that. It frightened Dan that he could come to that conclusion so easily. He didn't know the man, but he was beginning to understand, or at least recognize, his evil. And what did that say about him?

Insanity is relative. It depends on who has who locked in what cage.

Dan rolled onto his side, staring at the clock. If this was a fight against madness, he felt like he was losing. Maybe he already had.

CHAPTER № 30

"I take it she's your police escort?" Abby asked, eyes wide with fascination.

"Yeah." Dan didn't need to look over his shoulder to know Officer Coates—that was her name—was standing three feet behind him.

"So what happened last night?" Jordan asked. Morning light streamed in through the cafeteria windows over his shoulder. The line for pancakes was usually out the door, but it was significantly shorter today. Almost a third of the program's students were gone. "I mean, *after* you texted me."

"I didn't text you," Dan replied automatically. Thinking hurt. He'd hardly slept. His head was stuffed with sleepy wool. He choked down a second cup of coffee and waved to Officer Coates. She rolled her eyes.

"I'm lost," Abby admitted, holding up a hand. "Did he text you or not?"

"Jordan got a message from me, it was in my phone, but I can't remember sending it . . . because I didn't." It sounded ridiculous enough that he didn't blame Abby for her skepticism.

"Nope," she said. "Still lost."

"Me, too." Dan forked his pancake apart into three pieces and scooted them around in the lake of syrup on his plate. He wanted food to taste good again. He wanted life to make sense again. "Anyway, the same thing happened but with Felix. I don't want to go into it. . . . The whole thing's a gigantic mess."

"You don't want to *go into* it? But there's a cop following you around. You don't think that might warrant a bit of explanation?" Abby watched him intently from across the table.

Dan knew that he hadn't been fully forthright with them about things. He was no longer entirely sure why. As much as he liked the *idea* of having best friends with whom he could share anything, it was like all he knew how to be was alone, apart.

"Maybe your phone is haunted," Jordan said bitingly. "Maybe we should perform an exorcism."

"Don't worry," Abby cut in. "This is all just a misunderstanding, I'm sure of it."

I wish I was so sure.

"Ha! Dan, not worry?" Jordan cackled. "You're better off telling a duck not to quack."

"Thanks, you two. You always know how to make me feel better."

✗ ✗ ✗ ✗ ✗

After breakfast, Dan walked to class with his friends, with Officer Coates following ten feet back.

"What do they think I'll do?" Dan wondered aloud. "Run? Where would I go?"

"It does feel a little excessive," Abby agreed, glancing back at their tail. "At least she's giving you space. I'm sure it could be worse."

Dan appreciated that Abby was determined to find the silver lining in everything that morning; he needed a dose of her optimism in his life. They split up when they reached the academic buildings, Jordan heading to one of his math classes while Abby walked off to the art building.

Dan wasn't prepared for the humiliation of attending class with an armed escort. Officer Coates waited outside his classroom, but even so, he felt the burn of accusing eyes on him. The remaining students pointed and whispered with zero subtlety. Dan could do nothing but put his head down, take notes, and try not to burst into flames from the embarrassment of it all. It didn't help when he got passed a note that said, "Go home psycho."

Halfway through the lecture, Dan lost all ability to concentrate. He listened, not really understanding the words, and his hand continued to move, but he had no idea what he was writing.

When class was over, Dan looked down at his notes and bit back the urge to shout. The last few sentences weren't in his normal script, but he recognized the looping penmanship immediately. *The warden's.* It wasn't enough that the warden was in his head; now he was in his *body*, too. He collected his things at lightning speed and ran out the door. If he didn't get some fresh air, he was going to be sick.

Officer Coates stood in the sunshine waiting, and two other officers, including Teague, stood with her. Chatting with the police were the last two people on earth he expected to see.

"Mom? Dad?" Dan hugged his backpack to his chest.

"Sweetheart!" His mother ran over and wrapped him in her arms. He was surprised by how good the hug felt, and he actually had a hard time letting go. Part of him wanted to cry.

"You're okay," Sandy said, hugging him harder. "You're okay, you're okay."

"It's good to see you, Mom," he said.

"Let's take this inside." Teague motioned toward the admissions building down the path. "We should have this conversation in private."

This was the moment Dan had been dreading since last night. His parents walked him north up the hill, the officers following a few steps in their wake. Dan couldn't seem to stop shaking. It didn't matter that he believed his own innocence, it would be impossible to convince anyone else once they found out how messed up he was. . . .

"You just tell us if we need to call a lawyer, kiddo," his father whispered to him. They were right outside the admissions building now.

Dan frowned. "Let's hope it doesn't come to that."

"Inside, please, if you'll follow me," Teague said, charging ahead.

Dan hadn't been inside the admissions building before. It had that venerated old college feeling, with a high ceiling and slender windows and wood paneling on everything. In the front hall was a leather couch and an antique chair. Dan imagined anxious students waiting here, hoping that their college interviews went well. College seemed like a petty concern at the moment.

The police escorted them past the waiting area to a small room on the right. Teague and his parents went first, with Dan bringing up the rear. Officer Coates and another cop waited outside the door.

He was now shaking so bad he could hardly sit down without knocking over the chair.

"Okay, let's have a chat about last night. Why don't you start from the beginning," Teague prompted.

His parents and the officer sat on one side of a conference table, all facing Dan. It felt like an inquisition.

Dan told the story about his searching for Felix and finding the man with the crowbar. When he described the man pinning him to the ground, he thought his mother was going to faint. Finally, he got to the part where the cops had barged in and started accusing him of the worst.

"The thing is, I really don't remember sending those messages. I know they're in my phone, I *know* that, and I know it sounds ridiculous, but I swear: I didn't write those texts."

His parents shared a worried look, and his father cleared his throat.

"Officer, I don't want you to take this the wrong way," his father began gravely, "but what you have to understand is, Dan has always had, shall we say, difficulties. He came to us from the foster system after he'd already lived in a few other places. He's been a great kid since then, I don't want you to misunderstand me, but, well, he's always needed a little extra attention. A few trips to a psychologist . . ."

"Therapist," his mother corrected.

"Therapist," his father agreed.

The officer nodded along with the story. Dan hated talking about this stuff with his parents at all, but in the presence of someone else, a cop? It was embarrassing, frankly, and in this case, incriminating. Teague glanced at him from time to time, and he could swear he saw the officer's jaw setting by degrees, getting stiffer as Dan's guilt solidified in his mind.

"His therapist tells us he has some issues with memory—"

"Mild dissociative disorder," Sandy cut in.

"But that they don't pose any problem for him having a normal, healthy life. He's not a dangerous kid, Officer. If he sent some text message to his buddy and then forgot about it, I'm sure it was meant to be totally harmless."

Dan gripped the chair, struggling to look calm. How bad would it be if he blacked out right then and there?

That unreliable memory of his . . . How could he tell his parents that it had gotten much, much worse, in just a matter of weeks? That maybe he *wasn't* completely harmless?

"Now Mr. and Mrs. Harold, I can't help noticing that Dan doesn't share your last name. Why is that?"

His parents exchanged another look. Dan wanted to sink into the floor and die.

"Well, Crawford is the name he came to us with," his father said.

"We gave him the choice, just like our social worker said we could," his mother said defensively. "Dan had already lived with so many families by that point. I think he just wanted to keep one thing the same—one piece of himself."

"Hm," Teague said. He turned to address Dan directly. "Are you aware that you have the exact same name as the last warden of Brookline asylum?"

Dan nodded. "I read about him recently, yeah."

His parents, bless their hearts, said nothing. He had asked them about it on the phone, but now they kept silent, perhaps sensing, as Dan did, that Teague saw the strange connection as some sort of proof of his guilt.

"It's not that unusual of a last name," his father said. "And lord knows Daniel is common enough."

"But what about Dan's birth parents?" Teague asked, finally looking away from Dan. "There must be a quick way to check if there's any relation."

"I'm afraid it's anything but quick," his mother admitted. "We don't get to see that kind of information at all, and you'd need a court order to get it yourselves. But I can't see why it's so important. So what if Danny *was* related to this warden? What does that prove?"

"You don't think it's a rather alarming coincidence?"

"I think a coincidence is *exactly* what it is, and that's my whole point," his mother said testily.

Dan hated to see his parents get angry, even if it was helping his case.

"Did the . . ." His mouth had suddenly gone so dry it was hard to speak. "Did the guy who killed Joe ever confess?"

Teague stared, taken aback. "Actually, no, he didn't. He insists it was a wrong place, wrong time sort of thing. Still, he had the victim's possessions and a murder weapon on him and he can't explain that." Teague snorted, giving Dan a look that said, "Lucky you." The officer leaned an elbow on the desk between them. His brow lowered and Dan knew he should have kept his mouth shut. "Why do you ask?"

"Just . . . curious." Dan hoped he could keep it together for a few more minutes. He felt like if he didn't get to the bottom of this mystery now, it would plague him for the rest of his life.

It was Thursday. There were now ten days till the end of the program. "I want to finish out the program," he said calmly.

"We're not done questioning you yet," Teague replied, tugging his mustache. "How you answer those questions will determine whether you get to stay or not."

"Fair enough," Dan said.

His father looked ready to argue, but his mother nodded. "We'll stay in town, Danny. Just in case."

Dan couldn't fully explain why he wanted, *needed*, to finish this program, when there were so many reasons why he should run far, far away, as fast as he could.

Dan ending up at Brookline this summer wasn't a coincidence, it was a connection. And he was going to leave Brookline cured if it killed him.

CHAPTER
№ 31

$\mathcal{T}$hankfully, although Teague grilled him for three more hours, nobody else seemed to think Dan was guilty. He had no motive to hurt Felix, no history of violence, and when the cops searched his dorm room, they found nothing of interest. Most importantly, Felix had woken up in the hospital and sworn that he didn't think Dan was behind this.

Dan was totally drained by the time he was allowed to go. He walked his parents to their car and declined their invitation to eat dinner with them in town. He just wanted to be back in his room already.

Dan hadn't gone two steps on the path toward Brookline when he saw Professor Reyes pacing next to an ash bin. She waved, cigarette in hand, beckoning him over.

"Not in cuffs, I see," she said by way of greeting. Her brown eyes twinkled behind the thin veil of smoke that drifted up from her lips. "That's a good sign. Looked like your parents were pretty worried about you."

"Oh, they're fine, it was just a little tense in there."

Her necklace was made of opals today, as fine and white as bone. "I don't know the particulars, but you seem like a good kid." She shook her head, pursing her lips to blow a jet of smoke up and away from them. "Brookline just has a way of taking a hold on people—always has. It's the self-fulfilling prophecy of madness. If someone tells you you're crazy enough times, eventually it becomes true. It's that old psychiatrist's joke: insanity's all in your head."

Dan looked at his shoes, tempted to tell her that no, some conditions were in fact very real. "I'm not sure I know what you mean."

"All I'm saying is, people in town don't want Brookline gone just because of what happened there fifty years ago." Professor Reyes dropped her cigarette and stamped it out. The wind picked up her short dark hair, tossing it in front of her eyes. "Good luck, Dan. I hope you don't need it."

✗ ✗ ✗ ✗ ✗

Abby and Jordan waited outside his door for him. They had even snuck out a pie from the cafeteria, hiding it under a Windbreaker. Rhubarb with extra whipped cream. His favorite.

They piled into his room. Abby pointed to Dan's bed while Jordan sorted out the dessert for everyone. "Come and sit," Abby said. "I have news and we want to hear all about your date with the cops."

"Thanks," Dan said, taking a bite out of his pie. "It's been a hellish day."

"The cops work you over?" Jordan asked.

"They were pretty decent, actually. My parents were there, which helped."

"Seriously?" Abby said anxiously. "They're not making you leave, are they?"

"No, I can finish the program. So at least there's that. And Felix saved my ass, too. I guess he told the cops he 'didn't think I was a threat.'"

Dan decided not to tell them about the rest of it. Right now he needed them on his side.

"Dan, I'm so sorry," Abby murmured, shifting her chair closer. "But at least you're not in trouble. That's good, right?"

"It is, yeah. So what was your news?" Abby lit up. Dan was grateful for a reason to stop talking about himself and she looked ready to pop with excitement.

"The news is that I've decided to come clean about Lucy to my father," she said, bouncing in her chair. "It's time he knew about her, that I've picked up the trail. He deserves to know the truth. I mean, I would want to, wouldn't you?"

"Wow," said Dan. He couldn't tell if it was the exhaustion or something else keeping him from matching Abby's excitement. "Are you sure that's a good idea right now?"

"What?" Abby asked slowly. "Why would it not be a good idea? She's his sister! I'm hoping he might even want to help me find her."

"You don't think it's sort of coming out of nowhere? I mean, the shock and all . . . What if he doesn't believe you?"

"I'd freak if it were me. I mean, it's been so many years. . . ." Jordan added.

"No, it has to be this way," Abby replied with a little nod of finality. "I'm not going to keep this from him, I just can't. It wouldn't be right."

"Maybe this is harsh," Jordan responded. "But as your friend, I feel it's my duty to state for the record that I think your idea is pants-on-head crazy."

"And as your . . . other friend . . . I'm sorry to say I second that motion." Dan raised his hand in the air.

"Well, neither of you gets a say!" she shot back, shoving her pie aside. "It's my decision, and it's *my* father. I just thought you guys would be happy for me. With everything that's happened at this horrible place, I thought this could be something good to come out of it." She stood, dusting off her hands. "I'm calling him," she said, adjusting the zipper on her paint-splattered sweatshirt. "He's going to know the truth about Aunt Lucy. Tonight."

Abby turned and swept out of his room in a huff. Jordan cocked an eyebrow at him, as if to say, what, you're not going after her?

But Dan was exhausted, and after his long day of questioning, he was dying for a moment alone. Plus, there was something he desperately needed to check. Something he'd been trying not to think about since class that morning. Jordan seemed to get the hint.

"Well, you know where to find me, I guess," he said, letting himself out and closing the door behind him.

Immediately, as if he were ripping off a Band-Aid, Dan reached into his backpack and pulled out his class notebooks. He flipped to the page of notes he'd taken today, when he'd caught himself writing in the looping script of the warden. On the bottom of the page he'd written:

Insanity is doing the same thing over and over again and expecting different results. —Albert Einstein

Fighting the urge to throw up, Dan tore through the rest of his notebooks, scanning the pages for any more disturbing asides.

Sure enough, he found a sentence in his History of Psychiatry notes attributed to Aristotle. It was possible Professor Reyes had put this quote up on the board for them to copy down, but he definitely didn't remember writing it, and the script wasn't his:

No great mind has ever existed without a touch of madness.

Dan leapt to his feet, tossing the notebooks off him as if they carried a disease. All these notes . . . on his desk . . . under his bed . . . No wonder it had seemed like he had a stalker every-where he went. He'd written these notes—"delivered" them himself.

"*Mild* dissociative order," Dr. Oberst had said. "Harmless lapses in memory," she'd said. What did she know? She was no better than the doctors who'd been at Brookline fifty years ago. At least their treatments had gotten results.

Now Dan was faced with the fact that he was blacking out for long stretches of time, forgetting text messages, notes, even pic-tures with his best friends. And, oh yeah, who could forget the little fact that every time someone had been attacked, there'd been a mental gap he couldn't account for—unconscious in the basement when Joe had been killed, napping in his room when Yi was knocked out, and sending ominous text messages when Felix was nearly bludgeoned with a crowbar.

These lapses in memory seemed far from harmless to him.

But Dan wasn't ready to believe that he was a cold-blooded killer. He was channeling the warden, not the Sculptor, and as strange as it was to find comfort in that fact, Dan had to admit he'd rather find creepy notes in his possession than a garrote any day.

But what about the birth parents?

Officer Teague's questions still reverberated in his ears. He'd been so sure that Dan was related to the cruel warden, that it had something to do with why Dan was here. Dan had let his mother cast it off as a coincidence, but he knew that nothing about this summer had been coincidental. Being here was his destiny. It was his destiny to solve the mystery of what happened to the warden, and the Sculptor, and Lucy.

Dan remembered that Abby had visited the old church and found Lucy in the records. Maybe the records could work the same magic for him. Occam's razor or whatever the hell you wanted to call it.

It couldn't wait another minute. He refused to accept another restless night, another nightmare-riddled sleep.

Grabbing his flashlight and the closest thing to a weapon he had—a pair of scissors—Dan stepped outside and into the night.

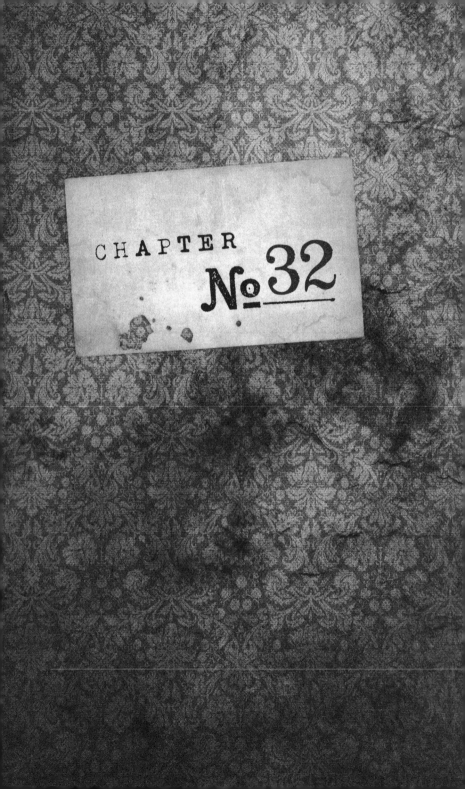

CHAPTER
№ 32

*N*ot only was it beyond dark outside, the perpetual mist had turned into an oppressive drizzle. Dan felt the dampness soaking through the cuffs of his jeans. That, combined with the ever-refreshing clarity that came with distance from Brookline, made Dan pause. Would the church even be open at eight o'clock on a Thursday?

But he felt like he had to try. He needed to know if he was crazy, possessed, or the victim of an elaborate framing job, and right now his only lead was his possible connection to Warden Crawford.

Rounding a curve in the path, Dan was relieved to see there were lights on in the church. Off to the right was the dense tunnel of trees through which Dan's cab had driven on that very first day.

Dan broke into a jog as the drizzle became a steady rain. There was a tiny awning over the front doors of the church, and Dan huddled under it as best he could, first trying the door handles, and then, when they were locked, pounding loudly with his fists.

"Coming! Coming!" came a faint voice.

The doors swung inward to reveal a kindly-looking old man in a suit and tie. He came up to about Dan's shoulders, and he smiled warmly even though Dan had clearly just interrupted him.

"Well come in, come in, I can't have you catching your death on the church doorstep."

Dan stepped into a small vestibule with just enough room for a few long tables. He could see the open sanctuary through the arched doors beyond.

"Now what brings you to Camford Baptist on this rainy Thursday, young man? I don't think I've seen your face in Sunday service."

"No, I—I'm a summer student up at the college. I mean, I'm still in high school. I'm in the college prep program."

"Ah, NHCP," he said, enunciating each letter to show he was in with the lingo. "I know it well. My granddaughter attended the program a few years ago now."

"Oh, cool," Dan said. He felt sort of awkward barging ahead with his questions, but the man seemed content to stand here in the entrance and talk. "Well, sir, I'm sorry to bother you so late, but a friend of mine was here a couple days ago, and she said you helped her find some stuff about her aunt?"

"Ah, you must mean Abby. Yes, lovely girl. Reminded me of my granddaughter, actually."

"Well, I was sort of hoping you could help me with the same thing, I guess. I used to have family in Camford, too."

"Is that so?" The pastor eyed Dan strangely, like maybe he didn't believe him. Dan decided he should take a page from Abby's book and just put everything out in the open.

"The thing is, I'm not sure, to be totally honest. I was a foster kid for a while and then I was adopted by my current parents, but there have been some weird things this summer that make me think I might have stumbled on my birth relatives here in Camford."

"Let me guess—Daniel Crawford?" The pastor's demeanor had turned solemn, almost icy.

"Dan," he said defensively. "How did you know?"

"It's a small town, Mr. Crawford." And then, when Dan simply continued to look at him, he added, "Mr. Weathers is in my parish."

It took Dan a second to realize he meant *Sal* Weathers.

"Oh, that. Yeah, my trip to his house didn't go very well. But Sal—Mr. Weathers—thought I was playing a joke on him or something, and I wasn't, I swear. My name really is Dan Crawford, and I really did want to know about Brookline."

"I believe you," the pastor said placatingly, his mouth a grim line. "But I think to Mr. Weathers, the idea that you might not have been joking would be even more frightening."

"Oh. I see."

"Do you? How much do you know about what really went on up at Brookline?"

"I know a lot more than they're telling us," Dan said defiantly.

"Indeed."

It was almost like they were in a poker game, each of them trying to guess at what the other already knew. Finally, the man sighed; if their talk was a game, he was folding.

"Well, I admit I was just a boy myself when Warden Crawford took over the asylum, but the rumors of what happened under his regime are legend. Inhuman conditions at the best of times, tortuous experiments at the worst. Not exactly memories we townsfolk are eager to relive."

Dan slumped, feeling chastised.

"I *do* remember the warden's family, though," the pastor continued, and Dan snapped to attention. "Oh yes, he had a family. No wife or kids of his own, but the Crawford boys were

Camford natives, and Daniel was the oldest of the three. By the time he returned from medical school to take on the role of warden at Brookline, his younger brothers were set up here as an auto mechanic and a clothing salesman. Daniel always was the smartest child."

The pastor was staring off into the middle distance, recalling these details from a long-forgotten place.

"The mechanic, Bill, had a wife who'd just had a baby boy when the asylum was closed. That would have been in, let's see, '72? Wasn't long after that before all the Crawfords left Camford, run out of town in shame."

"Why?"

"Oh, it was a regular witch hunt. Daniel was put on trial, of course, and the more details that came out during the case, the more people were calling for all the Crawfords to leave. Like they had bad blood or something."

"And what happened to—to Daniel?"

"Well, he tried to plead insanity there for a while. And he had a compelling case, too—some of the things he did in that dungeon, some of the reasons he gave . . . People were outraged, of course. But in the end it never came to a verdict. One of the other inmates got into his cell and killed him. Sounded like the locks on those cells weren't as tight as they could have been."

Dan was stunned. "Wow" was all he managed to say.

"Terrible thing," the pastor said. He still stood barring the entrance to the sanctuary, so that Dan started to get the feeling that the preacher wanted him to leave. "Anyway, I can tell you right now you're not going to find any of the Crawfords on our baptism registry. They were crossed off our records long before I became pastor here."

"I guess I can see why," Dan said, though he found it curious that the pastor already knew that information. "Well, I guess I'd better go, but do you mind if I ask you one more question first?"

"Not at all."

"It's about Dennis Heimline. The Sc-the *Sculptor*," Dan stammered. "I've heard some people say that he died the year Brookline shut down, but Mr. Weathers said that no one knows for sure what happened to him."

"I'm afraid Mr. Weathers is technically correct there. We all assume Dennis Heimline died, of course, given the nature of the things he must have endured at the asylum. But while all the other patients were eventually accounted for, Heimline's body was never found."

Dan shuddered. Then, with a mutter of thanks, he turned to leave.

"Oh, and Mr. Crawford?" the pastor said, catching Dan by the elbow. "I hope you won't blame Sal for any grief he caused you. I think you can see why he would've gotten upset talking about all this."

"I definitely can. Thank you for all your help, Mr. . . . ?"

"It's Bittle," the pastor said, and his eyes looked grim. "Ted Bittle."

✗ ✗ ✗ ✗ ✗ ✗

Dan left the church feeling more distraught than when he'd arrived. He'd gone there for *proof*, a confirmation, but all he had now were more possibilities. His grandfather had *possibly* been an auto mechanic. Warden Crawford, who was *possibly* his great-uncle, had died in prison, while the Sculptor was *possibly* still alive. And if Dan wasn't totally imagining the patient card Jordan had found in the basement, the Camford Baptist pastor was *possibly* related to another of Brookline's homicidal patients.

He was only too happy to leave the church behind.

But if it was raining before, it was absolutely pouring now. The gravel road outside the church was slushy and treacherous. Dan tried to point his flashlight ahead of him and run at the same time, but he kept twisting and slipping on loose rocks. He'd barely made it to the main path when he decided it was foolish trying to get all the way back in this weather. He ran off the side of the road to the dense protection of the forest. Two steps in, and already the deluge was reduced to a few scattered drops that found their way through the limbs overhead, which crowded together like a tangle of fingers. Now Dan just had to wait for a break in the downpour.

A branch snapped behind him, loud even over the sound of heavy rain.

Dan turned just in time to see a deer darting through the maze of trees not ten feet away. He let out a heavy sigh.

Just a deer, Dan. Calm down.

But when he aimed his flashlight at where the deer had been, Dan saw a glint in the darkness, like a reflection on steel. At first he thought it could be some kind of animal trap or a path marker . . . until he saw the rope tied around it, pulled taut and stretching into the shadows, and realized that it was a metal stake driven into the tree.

"Hello?" Dan called, imagining a hunter who'd been stranded in the rain. But that was ridiculous—who would be hunting this close to the school?

"Anyone there?"

Dan pulled out the pair of scissors from his pocket. They hardly made him feel any safer. Carefully, he stepped over fallen limbs and riots of underbrush. He reached the tree with the stake in it, then shined his flashlight down the length of the rope.

He still expected to find a net at the end, waiting to catch an unsuspecting animal.

Instead, he found a human hand.

"Oh my God, oh my God, oh my God," he jabbered, shaking uncontrollably as he tried to take in what he was seeing in the careening beam of his flashlight.

It was a man, his hands connected by ropes to two neighboring trees, pulled slightly behind him so that he was forced into a forward bow at the waist.

"Are you all right?" Dan called, though he was already sure of the answer.

He got up as close to the man as he dared. He was afraid to touch him, so sure that he would spring up and grab him or bite him like some zombie. But he forced two shivering fingers onto the man's neck. He waited for a pulse. Nothing.

"Oh my God, oh my God."

He moved to cut the ropes with his scissors, but then stopped himself. This was a crime scene, and he'd better not disturb it.

At this proximity, Dan could finally make out the details of the man's face. He recognized this man.

Sal Weathers.

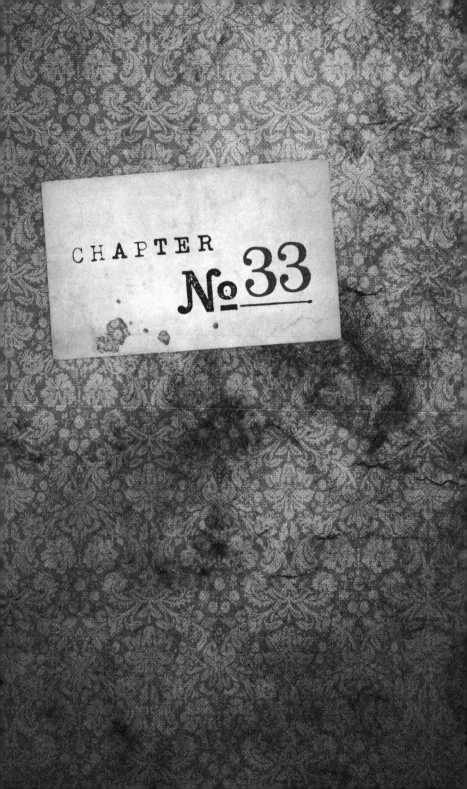

CHAPTER № 33

*D*an ran headlong through the rain, no longer caring that he was soaked to the bone. He needed to get back. He needed the safety of other people. He needed to tell the police what he'd found.

But they'll suspect you. You know they will.

Dan pulled up short, a final sprint away from the front doors of Brookline.

It was true. They would. They would think he did it.

Hadn't Mr. Bittle just told him that Sal Weathers was spreading news around town of his little visit? And wouldn't Officer Teague find it *more* than coincidental that once again Dan was the first at the scene of a crime? It hardly mattered that Dan hadn't blacked out or anything at all this time; the circumstantial evidence would be more than enough.

Play it cool, Crawford. No one knows where you were.

Oh God, in his panic, he'd dropped his scissors back in the forest. Should he go back and get them? No, too late.

He waited for his pulse to slow as much as it possibly could, barely even noticing the rain by now. With a last deep breath, he jogged through the front doors at exactly the pace any other student might run in from the rain.

Second floor. Third floor. 3808.

Dan opened the door to his room as calmly as he could, then slammed it closed when he realized Felix wasn't home. *Thank God.*

You're fine, you're fine, everything's going to be fine.

Dan dried himself with a towel, still shaking violently, then slapped his face with both hands, trying to think of what to do next.

Where did you go? What's your alibi? Will anyone think to ask Mr. Bittle if he saw you?

Mr. Bittle.

Relative of a murderer. Could he have been the copycat all this time? What was he doing at the church tonight with the doors locked anyway? Why had he wanted to keep Dan out of the sanctuary?

Oh God, Dan thought he was going to be sick.

A sudden pounding at the door nearly gave him a heart attack.

"Who is it?" he shouted, his voice cracking on the last word.

"It's me," Jordan said. "Open up."

With one final glance in the mirror, Dan fixed his hair and tried to look something like normal.

Out in the hall, Jordan was no better, a flustered ball of energy, scarf, and spectacles.

"Come quick," Jordan said breathily. "Abby's a total wreck."

Abby? A wreck? Of course. The phone call. Her father. Lucy.

"I take it the call didn't go as planned?" Dan said, following Jordan out into the hall.

"Not even a little bit. Hey, why are you all wet?"

Tell him you were in the shower.

"I was outside."

Why were you outside?

"I went to scrounge for food. I was still hungry after the pie."

Nice save, Dan.

"Bring an umbrella next time, doofus."

They found Abby sitting on her bed, knees tucked up to her chest. Dan noticed the portrait of the girl that had once hung over Abby's bed was gone.

"Hey, hey," Jordan said, rushing in and taking the spot beside her. He put one arm over her shoulders. She was shaking uncontrollably as a fresh wave of sobs hit her. "Calm down, Abs, and tell Dan what happened."

"I c-called him . . . I called him and . . . Dan, he was so mad! I've never heard him yell like that. He was yelling and yelling, and then he got so quiet, which was worse." She paused, out of breath, and then sniffled, her sobs slowing for the moment. "Maybe I got it all wrong." Abby peered up at him, brown eyes glossy with fresh tears. "Should I have just kept my mouth shut?"

"I don't know. I'm not sure, Abby, really. I don't know your dad."

Abby stopped crying just long enough to stare at him. Jordan gave him a look like he had lost it. *If only he knew.*

"All I know is that you had the best intentions, and you can't get mad at yourself for that."

"Exactly," Jordan chimed in. "Your dad will come around eventually."

"P-pops's refusing to talk about it again. Understandably, I guess. I mean, I *tried* to explain but he s-said I was sick. Delusional for even bringing it up . . ." Jordan pointed to the box of tissues on her desk and Dan retrieved them. "He doesn't understand! I didn't do it to be m-mean. It's his sister. . . . I thought he would be happy."

277

Abby took a tissue and started shredding it.

"You tried," Jordan said gently. "You tried and that's all that matters. He probably just needs some time to think it over."

"Jordan's right, it's— What the hell was that?" Dan had gone to sit on Abby's desk, but he stopped, hearing a rustling outside the door.

"Shh-hh." Dan pressed his finger to his lips.

A tiny square of paper appeared under the door.

"That's not possible," he babbled.

You were the one writing the notes. No one else. It was you all along. Who the hell is this?

Dan threw open the door, but he was a second too late. The corridor outside lay empty. He bent down and picked up the note, unfolding it with a familiar sick feeling in his stomach. At least the handwriting on this note wasn't the spidery script of the warden. Dan hadn't completely lost it.

"What does it say?" Jordan asked from the bed.

Dan read the note.

It's time for treatment. Come to the basement at midnight.

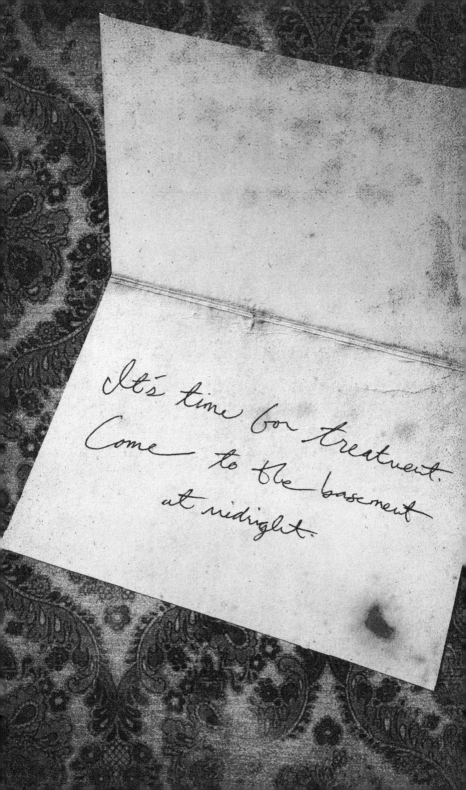

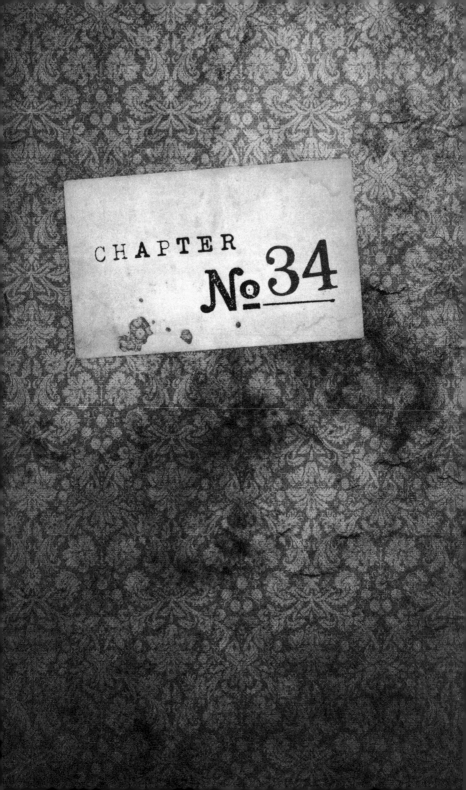

CHAPTER
№ 34

"*D*an, this is ridiculous," Abby whispered urgently. "Why are we going down to the basement if there's someone dangerous down here?"

She and Jordan were trailing him on his warpath to the old wing.

"You and Jordan don't have to come. In fact, you probably shouldn't. But I have to do this. I have to confront him."

"I, for one, am not going back down there," Jordan said. "And for the record, I think you're nuts for even considering it. Please . . . Can't we just go to the cops with this?"

"*No,*" Dan growled, scaring all three of them. "No. I can't. You have to let me go. I'm not asking you to join me."

"And I'm not letting you go alone," Abby said stubbornly. She shot Jordan a look, but he just put his arms up to say his hands were tied.

"Seriously, you guys, I love you both but I just can't do it. I wish you'd listen to reason and stay out here with me."

They'd reached the door to the warden's office. It was unlocked, just as Dan expected. Whoever had sent him the note was already down there.

"It's fine," Dan said, pulling open the door and taking one step inside. "This isn't your fight anyway, Jordan. It's mine."

Before following him inside, Abby darted after Jordan, giving him a squeeze and then a kick in the shin. This gesture seemed to sum up their trio nicely.

"I'll be seeing you soon, butthead," she whispered over her shoulder.

"You better," Jordan called back.

Dan tugged Abby along, anxious to confront whatever was coming. One way or another they would find out who had been terrorizing them, be it ghost or copycat or *what*. Reception was, of course, deserted, silent and cold.

They walked the now familiar path to the warden's office. Dan remembered the weird email he'd received during his date with Abby: "RE: Patient 361—question about Thursday's session." *For two more hours, it was Thursday night.*

"Dan?"

He looked up to find Abby staring at him, a tiny worried smile on her lips. He shouldn't have been involving her in this. She should've been upstairs in bed, safe and warm, away from whatever madness lurked down here. But he couldn't think of anyone he'd rather have at his side.

"Let's go," he said.

He shivered, convinced someone was just on their heels, breathing tendrils of hot air down his neck. Whenever he glanced behind there was no one there, yet he couldn't shake the feeling that they were being watched and followed.

Dan and Abby ducked behind the filing cabinet and through the gap in the wall. The darkness was heavy, impenetrable, but Dan tiptoed ahead, turning to make sure she made it safely through the passage. He squinted into the shadows. There was nothing unusual about this room either—the alphabetized cabinets were all in their correct places, and the familiar moldy chill blustered up from the stairwell to the right.

Abby put her foot on the first stair, looking braver than Dan felt.

"Was it always this dark?" Dan wondered.

"Yes," Abby replied wryly, tapping her cell phone against her head. "You just have to point your flashlight up instead of at the floor."

"That doesn't do much. . . ." Dan swung the beam of his light around to emphasize his point. "I still can't see a damn thing." Dan joined her on the stairwell, shining his light down into the bleak tunnel below. Abby grabbed his hand and they took one step at a time, stopping halfway to pause and listen. There was nothing to hear but the hushed sounds of their own breathing.

This was part of the killer's plan, he thought, as they turned the corner at the bottom of the stairs and continued into the long hallway of empty cells. The descent was its own torment. He could feel his body wanting to go faster, *rush*, adrenaline flooding his senses, but he knew they could be ambushed at any moment. Vigilance might be their one line of defense.

They moved back to back down the row of abandoned cells, each of them casting their glances in every direction. This way, they could make sure they weren't being followed and weren't going to stumble over any of the gurneys and debris littering their path.

Dan peered into each room as they passed, taking mental stock of what should be in each one. Near the end of the row he stopped, staring at a floor that was empty but shouldn't be. Not only did he distinctly remember an object of some sort, there was a spot in the dust where that object had been.

What is it? What's missing?

Dan held his breath, a fragment of a memory—a delicate song—returning. The music box was no longer where he'd left it. He didn't even see shards of porcelain. *Someone has been here.*

"Shit," he whispered.

"What?" Abby whirled to face him. "What's wrong?"

"Someone was here," he said. "Or someone *is*."

No sooner had he spoken the last word than he heard a shrieking metallic scrape overhead. They froze, and for a long moment Dan wondered if it was a pipe bursting in the ceiling or else . . . Abby snapped into action, sprinting back the way they'd come. He followed, realizing a second later what must be happening. It was the file cabinet—someone was trying to trap them inside.

Abby raced ahead, scrambling up the stairs as she took them two and three at a time. But they reached the top too late. The cabinet was already blocking their way out. Abby ran over and shoved herself against the cabinet, scrabbling for purchase with her fingernails. Dan could hear her gulping for air just above the deafening thunder of his own pulse.

Trapped. They were trapped, locked up in the dark of their final cell.

No, they couldn't be trapped. . . . Dan thought of Jordan out there, first hoping for a savior and then wondering darkly if Jordan was the one who had done this. Dan could hardly trust his own mind—it stood to reason that his "friends" were no better.

"Come on! Help me!" Abby grunted, giving another push with her shoulder.

"Who's out there? Stop being a coward and show yourself!" Dan shouted.

He moved to Abby's side, adding his own strength to hers, but the cabinet wouldn't budge. He beat his fists against the metal, shouting, "Let us out, let us out," until his voice went hoarse. He heard Abby suck down a shuddering breath before collapsing in tears against the wall.

She checked her cell phone.

"No reception," she said, wiping a tear out of her eyes. "Who would do this, Dan?"

"*Shh!* I hear something. . . ." They fell silent and listened. Behind the cabinet Dan distinctly heard the shuffling of footsteps. He thought he heard a click, maybe the soft tap of a woman's heel. But then nothing.

They listened as the footsteps moved away from the office and became faint. Abby pushed against the cabinet one more time, digging her legs into the ground, but it seemed to have been wedged into place from the other side.

Dan aimed a kick at the cabinet and then stumbled backward, grabbing for the wall to keep from falling over. "I can't believe it. . . . Why would he lead us down here just to trap us inside? Unless he has further plans, and he needed us out of the way. . . ."

"Who's 'he'?" Abby said. "You're really scaring me, Dan. Let's just give ourselves a second to catch our breath, and then we'll try to push it again together, okay?"

Dan nodded. She was right, panicking wouldn't help anything. They'd get out of here and they'd punish Dennis—or whoever was copying him—once and for all.

Then Dan heard a sound like the soft scrape of a shoe over wood. It was coming from the stairs behind them.

"What was—" But he didn't get to finish his question. A dark shape emerged, hurtling toward them.

He heard a hollow thud and Abby toppled into his arms. Dan's last thought before he fell was of her, of how pretty she looked just then, poised as if dancing, her lips parted and her dark braid coming undone.

Then he felt the blow on the back of his head.

CHAPTER
№ 35

*H*e came to under the light of a harsh white bulb. The filament twinkled and the old electricity was humming loudly, ready to cut out at any second. Dan groaned and tried to move.

He couldn't.

At first, he thought it was the pain in his head that was trapping him, but as consciousness and feeling returned, he could tell that there were straps buckled tightly over his chest, head, waist, and ankles.

He screamed, and the sound echoed back at him. The straps held him fast, and his struggles only increased the pain and the fear that were making him frantic. The most he could do was turn his head a fraction of an inch from one side to the other.

The operating amphitheater. That's where they were. The tables, the gurneys . . . That meant there was a tray of sharp surgical instruments mere inches from his skull.

"Let me out!" he shouted. "You can't do this to me!"

Dan twisted his neck the other way. Abby was strapped to her own table, and she had a gag in her mouth. A metal gurney was set out next to her. The white light reflected the stainless steel tray at her side, illuminating drills, scalpels, hooks—the horror show of tools needed to perform a lobotomy.

The overhead light flashed as if there'd been a power surge, forcing Dan to blink. When the electricity stabilized again, a shadow oozed from the dark perimeter of the amphitheater. Dan could just make it out in the blurry spots of his vision, but he couldn't see who it was. The man with the crowbar? Ted Bittle? *Jordan?* Dan was shaken enough to believe anything.

Then, in the light, the reality shocked him.

"Felix?" His voice was almost drowned out by the bouncing echoes of the chamber. "What the hell is going on? How did you get down here?"

"I never left," said Felix slowly.

"Untie us, you idiot! Get us out of here."

"Oh, you're not going anywhere, *Daniel Crawford*," Felix said with a snicker. As Felix came closer, Dan saw that he was barefoot and wild-eyed. He wore a white doctor's coat over a pair of boxer shorts.

"What do you think I should call my masterpiece? I was thinking: *Revenge.*"

His mouth twisted freakishly when he talked, moving too much over every word. And his voice didn't sound like Felix's; it was high and mocking, like a clown's. He walked strangely, too, lurching from side to side as if he were tied to puppet strings and being manipulated by someone high above.

"Felix, what are you talking about?" Dan said. This was *Felix*, quiet, unassuming *Felix*. Why the hell would Felix of all people want revenge?

But deep down, Dan knew that this wasn't Felix anymore. This was his roommate's body, but the man inside—the man wanting revenge—was someone else. Someone who didn't want revenge on Dan, but on Daniel Crawford. This was the Sculptor.

Felix slunk up to Dan's table and leaned over him. "You're all so easy to mold, fleshy clay fools," he sang.

His eyes were completely black. He moved his thumb almost tenderly down Dan's nose. "The first was too easy. I found him alone on the stairway, thinking he could watch over you all. But I was watching over *him*, and he didn't even see me coming. That one I called *Prelude*. The only tricky part was finding another fool to pin it on. That's where I needed Felix's help. A late-night biology lab to mix a little chloroform, and *poof*! We were ready for anything."

Dan thought he could see the real Felix fighting on the inside, trying to take back control. The lights in his eyes brightened and darkened, as if the power in his body was blinking on and off. He needed to give Felix enough time to win.

"So you killed Joe and framed that man in town," Dan said. "You only *pretended* to find Joe's body."

Felix touched Dan's nose again, making him sick to his core.

"The second statue was just for fun. For laughs. That one I called *Chaos*. Too bad the molding didn't stick."

"Yi." Dan remembered how he thought Yi had been posed, the legs too neatly arranged to be an accident.

"*No.*" Suddenly Felix was in his face, eye to eye, saliva dripping from his too-pink mouth onto Dan's chin. The giggly insanity had all run out, and now it was just rage. "*Chaos. Chaos.*"

Felix danced back away from him, making a full circle around Dan's table as he talked. "And then, for my *curtain call*, I had to take action before that horrible man ruined all our fun. He'd almost found us, Daniel Crawford—he knew what was happening. I called that sculpture *Precautionary Measures*."

Sal Weathers had almost found them. He knew what had been unleashed in Brookline.

"But now those fools are out of my way, and it's your turn, *your turn*." Felix was chuckling with glee. Then his eyes narrowed. "I've been waiting for you, waiting for so long. You will be my finest sculpture, my magnum opus."

Dan wondered when exactly the transformation had happened. Maybe it had started on day one—it was Felix who'd found the photos and planted the idea for Dan to see them himself. Maybe Dan had never known the real Felix at all.

But the fact that he'd been sleeping next to this *thing* for days, maybe weeks, gave him hope. He felt like Felix must still be in there somewhere—otherwise he would surely have killed him long ago.

"And that man with the crowbar? The one who attacked you?" Dan said, trying to buy Felix time, to make him talk.

"Oh, *him*," Felix said, as if the thought of the man bored him. "I let him in through the window with a false promise of drugs. When I couldn't deliver, he got a little—*angry*." Felix said this last word with a flutter of his fingers. "Of course, my real target was your friend, the mathematician. My plan was to meet him downstairs, then meet my alibi in the attic. I didn't count on him coming with a crowbar, or you waking up, not after I borrowed your phone. Not my finest hour, to be sure, but I did do a bang-up job messing with your mind. Just as you used to *mess with mine*." He hissed the last words into Dan's ear.

"You're crazy," Dan shouted, lashing out against the straps. Still too tight.

"Am I?" Felix seemed genuinely taken aback by the idea. He picked up a scalpel from the tray and stuck the blunt end in his mouth to chew on. Then he plucked it out again and flourished it. "Maybe I am. Hardly matters now. I'm finally going to get you back for all those *failed* experiments. Although I suppose one of them didn't fail, did it, Crawford? I mean, here we are!" Felix was on top of him again. "Does that make you happy? Or does it make you saaaaad?" With the sharp end of the scalpel, Felix lightly traced his own clown-faced grimace. It left behind a red curve, a thin scratch that was visible even after he'd taken the instrument away.

"But I'm not Daniel Crawford! I'm Dan, your roommate!" Dan shouted.

"Roommate?" Felix mused. "Yes, you and I, we were in the same room, *this* room. But we were never *mates*. Oh no." With this, Felix dipped the scalpel toward Dan's head until it was poised just above his eye.

And that's when the light cut out.

"No!" Felix shouted. His rapid footsteps echoed across the room, moving farther and farther away as he went toward the switches.

Dan breathed a sigh of relief, but it was short-lived. A hand clamped over his mouth, making it impossible to talk. Dan tried to shake it off, but it was no use.

"Shhh" came the voice in his ear. Even with that one sound he knew who was there to save them.

Jordan.

Dan stopped struggling. He felt the straps that were holding his head down fall away, then those around his chest, and finally those on his waist and ankles. He sat up quickly, massaging life back into his numb legs. Jordan's hand squeezed his shoulder in warning.

The light snapped back on with a loud, electric hum. Jordan was there, squinting, his glasses reflecting the sudden burst of light.

"I knew you two were useless without me," Jordan muttered, backing up close to Dan.

"Sneaky!" Felix shrieked from the switches near the door. He jumped the stairs leading down to the operating floor, bounding side to side like a deranged jackrabbit. "Fleshy, bendy, moldy, sculpty, sneaky *fools*!" His words ran together in a crazed slur, eyes wide and wild as he charged at them, scalpel held high.

"Move!" Dan shouted, jumping off the operating table. He pushed Jordan behind him and grabbed a gurney.

Felix descended on him, slashing in every direction. Dan kept the wheeled table between them, moving it to block wherever Felix moved.

Felix laughed, tossing the scalpel from hand to hand.

"I haven't had this much fun in *years*."

On the last word he lunged, flying across the table. Dan ducked, but Felix was stronger and quicker, and he grabbed Dan by the collar, throwing him to the floor. Dan clamped his hand around Felix's wrist to keep the scalpel from cutting his face. But Felix had at least twenty pounds of muscle on him, and the strength in Dan's arms was fading fast.

Felix pinned him down. The scalpel lowered inch by agonizing inch, until Dan could feel the sharp tip of it grazing his cheek.

No. You will not let him do this to you. You are better than he is.

With a strength he didn't know he had, Dan pushed back hard and sent Felix tumbling. The scalpel fell out of Felix's hand.

Dan rolled hard to one side and jumped to his feet. He loomed over Felix and Felix screamed, recoiling. Dan reached down, suddenly strong, so strong, and grabbed him by his coat. He hauled him up, throwing him onto the operating table. Dan roared from the effort, but then it was over and Felix was lying down, helpless.

"Strap him down!" Dan commanded. "Strap him down! We can't let him get free."

As Dan held Felix to the table, Jordan grabbed the straps and buckled them quickly. Chest first, then legs. Felix was struggling wildly, and it took two tries to get the head buckled in—finally Jordan had to cradle it in his hands while Dan tightened the strap. There were flecks of saliva and blood on Felix's lips, and his muscles were bulging and pulling against the restraints.

Soaked in sweat, firing on all cylinders, Dan reached down to pick up the scalpel.

The time for experiments and cures is over. You need to end this, Dan, once and for all.

"Dan, what you are doing with that?" Jordan asked, nervously eyeing the scalpel in Dan's hand. "He's not going anywhere now. Let's go and let the police handle this."

"No," Dan seethed. "No one else. Only *I* can finish this."

The scalpel lowered against Dan's will.

No, no, this isn't what I want, this isn't me. . . .

I am *you.*

The scalpel drew closer and closer to Felix.

No.

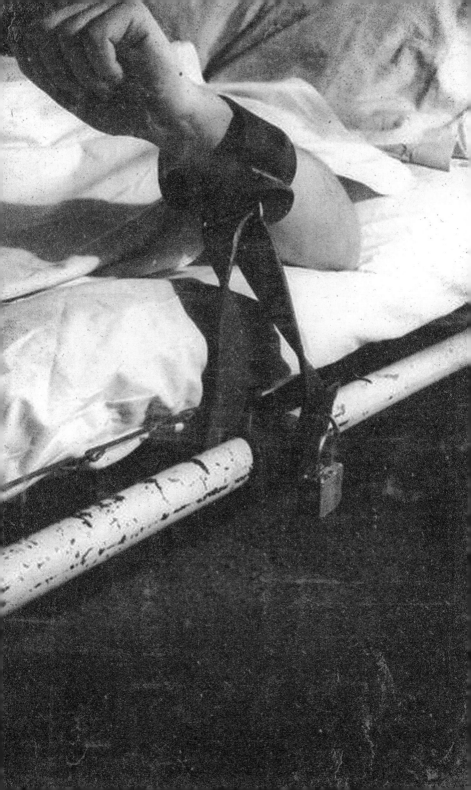

The vision descended on him hard and fast, ripping him out of his body and into another. It was another time, another decade, and he was Daniel Crawford, the warden, again.

The amphitheater was packed with observers. Everyone craned in their seats to witness his technique. Half of them believed his claims and half of them didn't, but they all wanted to know his secret procedure, just in case it worked.

And poor, broken Dennis, strapped to the gurney. At least, as a side effect of the preparatory operations, he had finally been cured of his rage.

Then came the screech of the intercom. That stupid new secretary, Julie. If this was anything less than dire, he'd have her head.

"The police! The police are on their way!"

The police? Coming here?

Somebody told.

And now his audience was fleeing in a frenzy. He seethed in anger at the pounding of their footsteps, and the voices rising around him like the tide of some obliterating sea. Those cowardly doctors tumbled over one another as they ran. . . . So the police were coming. How about that.

Dennis screamed, shocking Daniel out of his thoughts. Had he not given him a high enough dose of sedative? Did it matter? This was to be the final experiment, after all.

Cursing, Daniel hurried to finish—far sloppier than he would have liked—and then, throwing off his bloody gloves, he fled, the last to leave. The last but for Dennis. He switched off the lights.

The others were long gone when he reached his office. He lost precious time moving a cabinet over the door to the lower levels, his last hope to pretend that his practices were entirely aboveground. He took off his spectacles and jammed them onto the hook, residual blood smearing down the wall. Papers, photographs, all of it scattered. He hardly cared. This was a minor setback, he'd give them that, but his work would live on. His legacy. His life.

The door was flying open. The police were pouring in. And then there were cuffs and shackles, much like the ones holding Dennis down below.

Somebody told.

It was the girl, *he thought,* it had to be the girl. *She was every nurse's favorite, with her dancing, her smiling, her beautiful hair. . . . One of them must have gone soft, let her slip, and now it was all crashing down because of her, the snitch with the little scar on her head. She'd seen and understood too much.*

But his legacy had lived on, and now Warden Crawford was back where he belonged. In the amphitheater where Dennis had waited for him all these years.

Only one thing wasn't right. His vision wasn't quite perfect. . . . Everything was spinning.

"Dan? Dan?" Someone was calling his name.

He reeled and tumbled forward, finding the gurney and gripping it for balance. A pale, quivering face peered up at him. Dennis, or was it . . . Felix? Either way, he had the scalpel, it was right there in his hand, waiting to carve. . . .

Dan forced himself to focus, to look again. This wasn't him. He wasn't the warden, and would never be.

He dropped the scalpel. The clatter echoed through the amphitheater.

I'm not you. I will never be you.

"Fleshy, bendy, moldy fool, this isn't over," Felix whispered. "It's far from over."

Dan shoved the gurney away in fear and disgust, far, far out of his reach. It tumbled and fell over, and, strapped to the top, Felix groaned before going quiet.

"It's this place," Dan shouted. Jordan had gone to Abby,

forcing open her restraints and shaking her awake. "We have to get out of the asylum." He stumbled toward his friends. "We need to leave, all of us."

He reached the other gurney just as Abby was woozily climbing down. She flung herself into his arms, but Dan only gave her the quickest squeeze before pulling away. "We have to get out of here, it's Brookline. . . . Me and Felix . . . You have to help me get him far away from here."

"That's going to be tough. He's out cold." Jordan had sprinted back to the fallen gurney. He glanced up from where he knelt, glasses askew. "But if we all lift together I think we can carry him in the restraints."

Dan nodded, steeling himself as he returned to Jordan's side. "Then that's what we'll do."

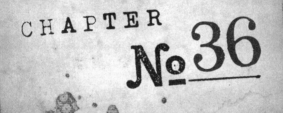

CHAPTER № 36

They were met halfway up the final staircase by Teague, flanked by two other officers. Sagging under the weight of Felix, Dan threw a hand up to shield his eyes from the blinding flashlights.

"Now you decide to show up," Jordan muttered, though the three of them were only too happy to relinquish the job of carrying Felix to three grown men; Dan's roommate had put on some serious muscle weight, and each moment they spent trying to haul him out of the basement was another chance for the warden to sink his hooks back into Dan.

"I couldn't find these yahoos anywhere in the building, so I called the station before following you two in," Jordan explained. "At least one of us was thinking straight."

"Anyone injured?" Teague asked, herding the kids up the stairs. When they reached the top and the alcove with the alphabetized cabinets, he oversaw the transfer of Felix to the other officers.

"Felix took a hit to the head," Dan answered. He watched as they lifted Felix between them and struggled to fit through the hole in the wall that led to the warden's public office. Curious, Dan thought. . . . If it hadn't been Jordan trapping them inside with the cabinet, who had it been?

Teague shot him a look, arching one brow.

"Yes, I'm the one who knocked him out," Dan continued, smoothing the hair back from his head; a terrible headache was brewing at the base of his skull. "I'll tell you everything, just . . ."

"We need to get out of here," Abby spoke up for him, appearing at his side and hooking her arm through his. "Please, just question us outside, or at the station. Wherever you want, but not here."

"Fine. But I'm keeping my eyes on you three."

Teague made good on that, corralling them right outside the door to Brookline. Mercifully, the rain had stopped. As soon as the deputies had loaded Felix onto a stretcher and then into an ambulance, they reappeared to help guard the kids. "So," Teague said, shining his flashlight in their eyes again.

"Cut it out," Jordan said, ducking his head. "We just found your killer, so could you please not—"

He wasn't given the chance to finish his sentence. Through the glare of Teague's flashlight and the police car lights, Dan saw a shadow speed across the grass.

"Teague!" he shouted. Something small and sharp had reflected off the whirring lights. The figure held a knife. "Watch out!"

But Teague wasn't the target. Dan had just enough time to guard his face with his forearms before the woman was throwing herself at him, screaming. Dan recognized her a half second before she was in his face. It was Sal Weathers's wife.

She screamed an ungodly scream.

Dan fell back, feeling the knife slash close enough to cut his sleeve. His friends and Teague joined the fray, trying to reel the woman back in without getting cut. Teague pulled out his gun and shouted, "Nobody move!"

"Wait! Don't hurt her!" Abby rushed over to the woman, throwing herself between her and Teague. Sal's wife went still for just a moment, but it was all the officers needed to grab her by the arms and drag her away across the grass.

She was screaming again, absolutely ballistic. "Wait!" Abby cried, following. "Did you see that?" she called to the boys over her shoulder. "Her forehead . . . Did you see it?"

She wasn't waiting for an answer, and both Dan and Jordan had to run to keep up.

"Did she cut you?" Jordan panted.

"No, but my shirt got it pretty bad."

One last spike of adrenaline carried Dan to where Sal's wife was kneeling in the damp lawn, the knife finally wrestled from her hands. Abby stood in front of her, slowly drawing an object from her pocket. A chipped piece of porcelain that sparkled under the blazing police lights.

He might have known Abby had been the one to take it. Of course she would have been making trips to the basement without him. Dan finally understood.

"Do you recognize this?" Abby asked the woman softly.

The woman's hair had gotten ruffled in the commotion, and now, with her bangs swept aside, the scar on her forehead was plainly visible. A scar just like the little girl in the photo. Abby spun the figurine, making it dance.

From where she knelt, Lucy reached for the ballerina. Abby let her take it, smiling sadly.

"You're Lucy, right? Lucy Valdez? My name is Abby Valdez. You had a brother . . . *have* a brother. My father. I know it's a lot to take in, but I think he would love to see you. And I want you to know that your dad, he . . . Well, he never forgave himself for sending you here."

Lucy cradled the chipped ballerina in her palms, holding it close to her chest.

Dan wondered if she'd found Sal's body in the woods, or if her rage came purely from the fact that she suspected he was the warden.

"Officer Teague," Dan called, and the policeman hustled over to him.

"Everything all right?"

"In the basement, before we knocked Felix out, he told me that he'd killed someone else. A man from town. He said he left the body in the woods near Camford Baptist."

"That's awfully specific," Teague said suspiciously. "Are you sure about that?"

"I'm just telling you what he said."

Dan knew he was going to have a hard time getting out of this mess. When Felix came to, he might not remember all the things he'd done. And then it might be his word against Dan's. Dan had a feeling he knew who Officer Teague liked less.

But now Teague just nodded and radioed in for someone on his team to check out the woods.

Jordan slid up next to Dan with a blanket wrapped around his shoulders. "She was right," he said. "Can you believe it?"

"I can. I should have believed her sooner."

Abby was kneeling in the grass near her aunt, watching her from a cautious distance.

"So what about Felix?" Jordan asked with a sigh. He stretched his arms in the blanket out like a cape, covering a yawn with the crook of his elbow. "Was he . . . Do you think he'll recover? Are they going to put him in jail?"

Dan shrugged. "It's up to the police, I guess. I don't think what happened was entirely his fault, but I have no idea how the law works in cases like these. I just hope he gets help, the right kind of help." He glanced over his shoulder at Brookline looming behind them. "Not the kind of help this place had to offer."

"And us?"

"They'll shut the program down," Dan said, certain, "and we'll go home."

"Awesome." Jordan kicked at the dirt. "I guess I always knew gay rumspringa would end and I'd have to leave Oz. Now I have to go back home and pretend to be straight for one more year. How *do* you stand it?"

"It's a terrible burden, let me tell you." They laughed, but Dan couldn't help but worry for Jordan. What would his parents do when they found out where Jordan had really gone for the summer? "You know . . . If you want—I mean, if your parents get too terrible—you could come stay with me. For a while, or, I don't know. I'm sure my parents would be cool with it."

Jordan fixed his glasses and snorted, and Dan was certain he was going to be turned down.

"Can your mom cook?"

"No, but my dad can."

"Sold." Jordan stuck out his hand and Dan took it.

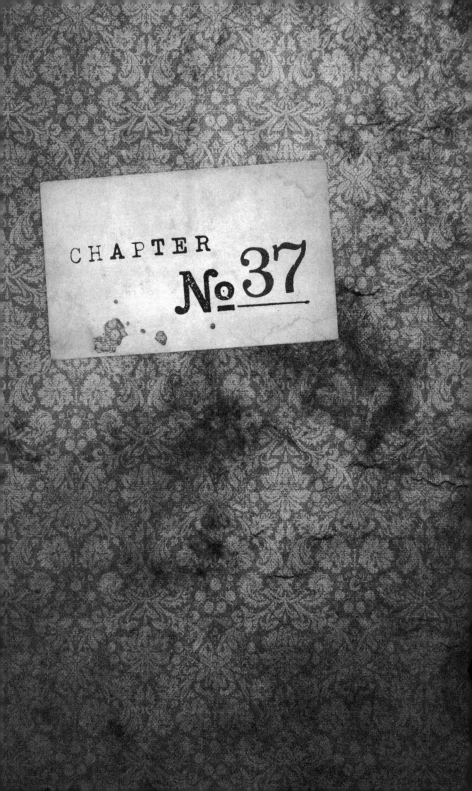

CHAPTER № 37

"I suppose they'll send someone for Felix's stuff," Dan was saying, shoving the last of his books into a suitcase. Sandy and Paul busied themselves with stacking the packed bags near the door. His side of the room was virtually empty now, but Felix's things remained untouched, a half-full Gatorade sitting on his desk.

"Poor kid," his mother said, joining Dan at the bed. He'd already stripped the mattress and balled up the sheets. He didn't let any of it put a hitch in his packing; even if he wasn't eager to say good-bye to his new friends, he wanted to be out of Brookline. Every second he stayed felt like a second too many.

"Knock, knock?"

All three of them turned to find Abby at the open door. She rocked shyly on her heels, waiting to come in.

"Oh, hey. I'm glad you stopped by," Dan said. A night's rest at the hotel in town had done them all good—Abby looked amazing in an off-the-shoulder tunic and rubbery leggings. Her combat boots were splattered with pink and yellow paint.

"We'll take these down to the car," his father offered, giving Dan a look that was anything but subtle.

Even so, Dan welcomed the privacy.

"Nice to meet you both," Abby said as his parents trooped by.

"You too, sweetie." His mom gave him a little wave of encouragement from the door, unseen by Abby.

The balled-up bedsheets joined his books. Dan had to lean hard on the suitcase to get it to close. "You all moved out?"

"Not quite. Things are packed but I'm still waiting for Pops. . . ."

Dan hauled the overstuffed suitcase from the bed to the floor. "He's coming to pick you up? Does that mean . . ."

Abby shook her head, her face suddenly sad.

"It turns out—" she said, and then stopped, choked up. "It turns out that she was married to a man in town, and he—and Felix—Felix *killed* him."

She burst into tears.

"Oh my God, Abby, how horrible," Dan said, wrapping his arms around her protectively. He hated that he'd gotten himself to a point where it was easier to lie and act surprised than tell the truth. He was sure she still had her secrets, too.

At last, Abby pulled away and wiped her eyes.

"I just feel like this whole summer was cursed," she said. "Like I made Aunt Lucy's life worse instead of better, and dragged you and Jordan into this whole mess."

"No, no, Abby, listen—this summer? This was not your mess. We all had our own stuff to work through, and I am so glad I met you and Jordan so we could work through it together. I mean, we're going to stay in touch, right? And what happened to your aunt is truly horrible, but she has you and your father, right? She's not alone, either."

"I guess you're right," Abby sniffled. "And yeah, we'll definitely stay in touch."

"Then see? At least the summer wasn't a total—" Something at the door made him stop. A silhouette appeared, the shadow falling across the open door a second before Professor Reyes appeared, dressed in her usual black. "Professor? Is something wrong?"

"Hm?" She hovered in the doorway, a huge, clinking set of skeleton keys looped over her wrist. "Oh, no, I only wanted to stop by and let you know that Felix Sheridan has been moved to West Hill General. They have an excellent psychiatric team there, and he'll get the care he so dearly needs and deserves. It's . . . such a shame about all of this, but I thought you might want to know what happened."

"Thank you," Dan said, nodding. "I just want him to be okay."

Professor Reyes nodded, her expression unreadable. "We all do." Then she seemed to remember something, starting and lifting the hand with the key ring. "And by the way, the old wing is locked up for good and a policeman has been posted until everyone is out of the dorm. No one will be seeing the lower levels until my seminar next year. Which, by the way, the offer is still open for you to join." With a quick, shallow smile, she was turning to go. "Don't worry, Dan. I'm sure this will just be a bad memory soon."

That was hardly comforting. The thing about memories was, you never could control when they came up again.

She closed the door softly as she left, and Dan stared at it for a long moment afterward. He kept picturing the keys in her hand and the door. . . . The door that seemed to hold in all of Brookline's secrets . . .

"Dan? Dan, what is it?"

He couldn't shake the feeling that the keys were important somehow. Felix had said the door to the old wing had been open the day they moved in—that that was how he got inside in the first place. If Professor Reyes possessed the keys, she would have been the one to leave the door unlocked that day. And she could easily have entered the ward whenever she wanted. Like to follow them. Like to trap them in with a cabinet.

"It's nothing," he said, shaking his head. "I'm just being paranoid. It's this place. . . . I'm not myself here." That was an understatement. "Want to follow me to my car?"

"Sure," Abby said, giving him a quick peck on the cheek. "I can't wait to be anywhere else."

Together, they each took one handle of the suitcase, lifting it and turning for the door. He wondered if he ought to give her one final kiss here, before they parted, or wait until he got down to the car. It seemed like such an important moment, he really didn't want to spoil it. Turning that thought over, he started out.

Definitely at the car, he decided, that was more romantic. He grinned and opened the door for her, dreading saying goodbye but happy to know they'd see each other again, when all this trauma with Lucy had blown over. They'd call, of course, and email, and she might even want to visit, especially if Jordan came to stay.

"Daydreaming?" she teased, bumping the suitcase against his thigh.

"Nah," Dan chuckled, beaming at her as they stepped out into the hall. "Okay, maybe a little . . ."

"Hey, what's that?"

"Hm?" He followed Abby's gaze to the floor, where a small piece of paper waited, half-trapped under his shoe. Dan moved his foot aside and squinted, his heart dropping to his toes as he read the chillingly familiar handwriting.

It was in black ink, centered, in confident, almost playful script.

I'll be seeing you real soon.
Daniel Crawford

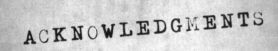

huge thanks first and foremost to my agent, the indomitable Kate McKean, for giving me the opportunity to work on this project. Thanks also to Andrew Harwell and the team at HarperCollins for making this book possible, and for his creativity, generosity, and guidance. To my family for being patient and supportive (Mom, Pops, Nick, Tristan, Julie, Gwen, and Dom). My gratitude, as always, to the professors who inspired me to reach (Fran, Steve, Rod, Chris, Lisa) and to my high school teachers for making my teenage years much happier than Dan's (Larry, Adrienne, Naomi).

My thanks and apologies to Beloit College for being the physical inspiration for New Hampshire College—thanks for the inspiring layout and apologies for being turned into a haunted campus.

And last but certainly not least, to the friends who propped me up and kicked my ass when I had bad days: to Kai (too much to name—company, support, dinner, and *Doctor Who*, giver of Appa and maker of monitor Plops), Taylor (aka My Least Favorite Son, support, friendship, laughter, patience, cat pictures, and gossip), Jeremy and Christi (lifesavers!), Anna and Nicholas (and their little ones), Maria, and Kimber (those mice belonged to you, m'dear, even if they apparently drowned).

The images in this book are custom photo illustrations
created by Faceout Studio and feature photographs from actual asylums.

79	Profile skull X-ray	Oliver Sved/Shutterstock.com
	Front skull X-ray	Vadim Kozlovsky/Shutterstock.com
	Profile neck X-ray	Igor Kovalchuk/Shutterstock.com
100	Spectacles on hook	Peter Zijlstra/Shutterstock.com
	Hook	igor gratzer/Shutterstock.com
	Blood stains	Stephanie Frey/Shutterstock.com
106	Nurses	Library of Congress, Prints & Photographs Division, HABS LC-DIG-npcc-33370
	Warden	Ysbrand Cosijn/Shutterstock.com
117	Journal paper	Mark Carrel/Shutterstock.com
	Finger scratch marks	D.J.McGee/Shutterstock.com
	Envelope	Faceout Studio
	Wood background	Photomim/Shutterstock.com
127	"Kill a hydra?"	Faceout Studio
	Notepaper	IgorGolovniov/Shutterstock.com
	Vintage background	Annmarie Young/Shutterstock.com
135	Tunnel	Tuomas Lehtinen/Shutterstock.com
	Footprints	Ispace/Shutterstock.com
147	Floor plans (top)	Library of Congress, Prints & Photographs Division, HABS NY,15-CATRES,1B—6
	Floor plan (bottom)	Library of Congress, Prints & Photographs Division, HABS NY,15-CATRES,1C—6
	Graph paper	pockygallery/Shutterstock.com
148	Man on cot	Jerry Cooke/Getty Images
153	Equation notes	Jiri Vaclavek/Shutterstock.com
	Additional illustration	Faceout Studio
	Legal pad	imging/Shutterstock.com
159	Abby's illustrations	Faceout Studio
169	"Insanity is relative"	Faceout Studio
	Vintage background	Alex Roman
171	Surgical tools	Rudolf Vlcek/Shutterstock.com
176	Ballerina	Cloudia Newland/Shutterstock.com
	Springs	Sergey Shlyaev/Shutterstock.com
	Music box	Richard Peterson/Shutterstock.com
	Tile wall	chalabala/Shutterstock.com

182	Amphitheater	Ken Fager
185	Scattered tools	Meg Settembro
201	"A flash of" writing	Faceout Studio
	Stack of papers	Valentin Agapov/Shutterstock.com
	Torn paper	STILLFX/Shutterstock.com
	Scattered papers	Valentin Agapov/Shutterstock.com
203	Girl on bed	Jerry Cooke/Getty Images
213	"In a mad world"	Faceout Studio
	Vintage background	Aleeka Stock
219	"Each victim" writing	Faceout Studio
227	Clipboard	pio3/Shutterstock.com
266	Church	Roberto A. Sanchez/Getty Images
273	Man in straitjacket	Jerry Cooke/Getty Images
279	"It's time"	Faceout Studio
	Folded paper	Picsfive/Shutterstock.com
	Vintage background	Mario7/Shutterstock.com
295	Patient strapped	Jerry Cooke/Getty Images
310	Keys	Dougal Waters/Getty Images
311	"I'll be seeing you"	Faceout Studio
	Vintage background	Graphic design/Shutterstock.com
	Chapter openers	Alex Roman
		pp. 6, 8, 13, 17, 29, 43, 49, 60, 69, 80, 89, 97, 109, 114, 121, 128, 141, 149, 162, 167, 172, 179, 186, 189, 198, 204, 210, 217, 228, 235, 248, 257, 264, 274, 280, 287, 299, 305, 312